BOOM ROAD

BOOM ROAD

Shawn Lawlor

GALLEON

Boom Road
© Shawn Lawlor 2024
All rights reserved.

First Galleon edition, second printing, 2026
ISBN 978-1-998122-07-3

Published by Galleon Books
Moncton, New Brunswick, Canada
www.galleonbooks.ca

Cover design by Andrew Lannan.

Boom Road is a work of fiction set in some actual places, but places aren't people, and all of the people in this book, especially Jackie O'Connor, and his dog Ruby, are the result of the vivid imagination of the author. Should you recognize a person or two, that is wonderful. Fiction's funny that way.

Library and Archives Canada Cataloguing in Publication

Title: Boom Road / Shawn Lawlor.
Names: Lawlor, Shawn, author.
Identifiers: Canadiana 20240370945 | ISBN 9781998122073 (softcover)
Subjects: LCGFT: Novels.
Classification: LCC PS8623.A923 B66 2024 | DDC C813/.6—dc23

To Mom

bow

noun

the forward end of a vessel or airship (Nautical, Aeronautics)

a weapon for shooting arrows, consisting of an arch of flexible wood, plastic, metal, et cetera, bent by a string, fastened at each end

I

*"How did you manage to hit a jeezless rock
at high tide in the channel?"*

MOST TIMES WHEN YOU SEE an unused pair of skates, they are lonely. Even in the dry August heat of the Miramichi Valley, hanging on the wall in a shed, they look cold and confined. In winter, they are often slung haphazardly on a beam in the basement or cast into the corner by the door. Skates find use when the river freezes over, it's hockey season, and the winter air is so dense your breath swirls with the steam from a cup of tea. Skates are prized when they are being used and deserted when not.

Jackie O'Connor kept his skates by the back door during the winter months, which ironically was the front door; or at least the door used to go in and out of the brick home he owned on Boom Road. Jackie's skates were always sharpened, ready to hit the ice.

Jackie used skates and many other forms of non-vehicular transportation because he had no driver's license, which perpetually irritated his wife, Gen. She had to cart him all over the country, and it used to drive her up the wall. She often needled him by saying it was the only place Jackie was capable of driving her. His friends always got a laugh out of that taunt. Jackie would storm out, cursing under his breath. He thought he'd get used to the jabs about not having a license over the years but it still bothered him, making him feel like a child. Cars were never something he cared much about. He appreciated them and the speed in which they took him from Point A to Point B but gasoline fumes always made him nauseous, the exhaust fumes frequently made him cough and cars regularly needed repairs. Jackie thought they were more trouble than they were worth.

He spent much of his life outside. Jackie could remember his father putting him on the river in '43 at only four years old with the first set of skates ever made; at least that is how they appeared to him: two dull pieces of steel attached to soft leather, worn down by Jackie's older brother Clifford. He often received Clifford's hand-me-downs. Annoying and dreadful presents.

His father Henry worked at Sutherland's Sawmill – the same location where Jackie was now employed and had been for the better part of two decades. Henry did not earn all that much, and what he did make mostly went to booze and tobacco for his squat tomato pipe. Jackie could still remember how his father smelled. More than 40 years later, the scent of an old red-and-black wool coat lingered, thick with smoke from the wood fire and pipe tobacco, along with traces of cheap whisky and beer etched into the fabric. The heavy odor had been strong in his mind since Jackie was a boy and, he figured, would be there his entire life. He recalled sitting on his father's lap, always feeling itchy nestled in the wool coat, and his father's coarse stubble like sandpaper against Jackie's skin. *The mind is a strange thing,* Jackie thought. One smell and you are back to being four years old in front of the fireplace.

What Henry did not spend on liquor was left over for Jackie's mother to purchase the staples at Birch's General Store. Birch's went out of business in the 1960s, but when Jackie was small, he and Clifford would often make the hike with their mother and help bring home groceries – flour, ham, potatoes, coffee, salt, pepper, and molasses if you could get it. His father used to tease Jackie that molasses was actually made of "mole asses." Jackie never ate the gooey substance again, though he learned it was a joke.

Henry was not a mean drunk but he handled alcohol as poorly as he handled finances. They often went hungry because of Henry's vices but they never went cold. Henry would often be seen stoking the wood stove. When Jackie got older, he realized his father was always cold because he ate too little and he drank too much. The alcohol thinned his blood, as well as his mind.

At the sawmill, Henry scrounged plenty of extra kindling to burn at home, getting his brother Francis to drive him at the end of the day with lots of scrub wood. A fire in their two-bedroom home roared nearly every day of the year. In July, people would walk by the O'Connor homestead on their way to work or church and gape at the tranquil columns of smoke crawling out of the chimney.

"Gotta take the chill off!" Henry would say on Dominion Day, using a heavy poker to rustle the pulsating red coals.

When the ice froze solid, Jackie skated up and down the river as his means of travel to work or to Dickenson's Convenience store or to Donny's for a game of crib. It was too great of a distance to town, so these days without Gen around he had to rely on the good graces of others driving in for food or the real liquor store. Otherwise, he could make his way to Mike Emery's for booze. In return for alcohol, Jackie often made deliveries for Mike. In the months when the Miramichi River was not iced over, he could walk or hitchhike but preferred to travel the river the way the natives of old did – by canoe.

Jackie valued his canoe even more than his skates, storing it up on a rafter in Donny McGivney's barn in winter and covered with a noisy blue tarp in his own backyard during summer. He'd owned the vessel for 21 years and it had served him well, both in professional bootleg runs for Mike or for pleasant trips on the river. He loved the canoe and had no idea why he stupidly lent it to Paddy Brewster at the end of last summer. Paddy crashed into a big rock, cracking the bottom. *No doubt he was stoned on one of them jazz smokes,* Jackie figured. He hated the smell of them and they made a person go insane. That's what Jackie had heard when he was young. Some things just stick with a person.

"How did you manage to hit a jeezless rock at high tide in the channel?" said Jackie, interrogating Paddy.

"Didn't see it," replied a sheepish young Paddy, hands stuffed in his jeans' pockets. He had an Edmonton Oiler's ball cap on. *Edmonton for God's sake,* thought Jackie. He may as well be rooting for some team from the States.

"You were stoned on one of them dope smokes, weren't ya?"

"No sir. No way. You told me not to while I was usin' yer boat and I wouldn't do that, Mr. O'Connor. I only smoke that stuff once in a while anyway."

"Yeah, yeah. You'll have to work it off or pay me to get it fixed."

"Yessir. Of course. Whatever ya need me to do. I can work, Mr. O'Connor. You know that, for sure. I pull my own weight at the sawmill."

"You can start by helping Donny McGivney fix his antenna and any other odd jobs he might have for ya over at his place. I lost a bet to him on when the river would run this year and told him I'd work it off. Anyway, go on and talk to Donny about that. Once you're finished helping him, I'll need your help with some liquor runs for Mike Emery."

Paddy's face turned a shade of white at the mention of Mike's name. 'Mean Mike' he was often called but he and Jackie had been friends since they were boys. Many people were apprehensive about Mike but Jackie knew different. It was all for show. Mike was a lot of talk and though he was a bootlegger with a wicked tongue, he knew it to be just that. They were buddies and it made him chuckle that Paddy was a trifle scared of Mike.

He shook his head in distaste as Paddy shuffled away. *He's a good young lad but his brain is gone from smoking weed. He'll have to learn there are consequences to actions.* Paddy's father was not exactly a model for parenthood. He'd had his troubles with the law, and everyone was well aware of the time he broke into all of those camps up the southwest part of the river, mostly looking for items he could pawn and make some quick cash. Jackie knew the boy's father was unkind to Paddy when he was small, as well. There were rumours that after Paddy's mother ran away, Carl Brewster was cruel to the boy, even making him sleep in the bathtub when he wet the bed, crying for his mother who was so desperate to flee the searing rage of her drunken husband that she left one morning without her children. Nevertheless, Paddy would have to learn you could not damage a man's means of transportation and not have to account for your behavior. As Jackie's own father would frequently preach to him, "A man's gotta be responsible for his actions."

Jackie O'Connor was such a man.

"Jesus, Donny, I never had front steps now
for more than twenty years!"

THE EPISODE JACKIE SPOKE OF – owing a gambling debt to Donny McGivney – was a fabrication. It was actually a way for Jackie to prevent Donny from suing him.

A person could find Jackie's brick home easily. It was not far off R.R. #1 and anyone walking by could look down the driveway and see in the big picture window where Gen used to sit every morning with coffee. There were few brick homes in the area and fewer still had a front door without steps.

One terribly cold night in January 1982, Donny McGivney, loaded off his arse, forgot Jackie did not have front steps. He had entered through the back door as he had done one thousand times, being that was the only entrance with a set of stairs to the home. The wood fire was strong and warmed the small home to a sweltering heat.

"Nothing heats like wood," Jackie's father was oft heard to say when he was small. Jackie had to agree that nothing heated a house or felt as comfortable as heat from a wood stove. Heating a home with wood is hard work; it needs to be split several times then delivered and piled. Kindling wood is also required in order to start a good fire. Wood is also dirty and dusty but truly, no form of heat tiptoes its way into your bones and warms the marrow inside as a wood fire.

After lengthy games of crib that involved a flat of beer between the two of them, Donny got up to leave and walked toward the front of the house. Jackie belched under his breath, regarding him with muddled eyes. Donny opened the door with purpose to walk home and crow to his wife Claire how he skunked Jackie in one game and won 3 out of 5. Confident that rock-hard wooden steps, made of golden, splendidly sanded bird's-eye maple would greet his old pair of steel-toed boots as he strode out of the house, Donny took a wondrously large goosestep into the void, smashing into the frozen earth.

Jackie heard the door flapping against the house in the strong gusts and the muffled moans from Donny. He ran to the front of the house, already tittering at Donny forgetting about the exit-to-nowhere. By the time he looked out and saw Donny lying on the snow, Jackie was laughing so hard he started to pee his pants.

It was a serious fall. Donny McGivney would have been better off falling into the shallow end of an empty pool. The front of Jackie's house was rough. He did not have a front lawn. Jackie had always figured a front lawn meant mowing. He felt looking after a lawn was an American idea or at the very least, Upper Canadian.

"Jesus, Donny. Alright?"

"Christ almighty…where's your steps? What happened to yer steps? I think me shoulder's broken," wailed Donny.

"I never had 'em! Where in Christ's name do ya think ya are?" Jackie spit his replies through bouts of chuckling.

"Ain't we at Boyd's?" said Donny, snatching his hunter orange ball cap off the snow, struggling to one knee with one good arm. "Jesus, Mary and Joseph. Never had the wind knocked outta me like that in some time. Where's your GD steps?!"

"I don't have no steps. Ya alright?"

"Alright? Alright? Where's your jeezless steps? How come ya never build front steps?

"How come you didn't remember?"

"How come I didn't…wha? A lad's gotta have front steps for crying out loud, Jackie!"

"Jesus, Donny, I never had front steps now for more than

twenty years!"

"Well…build the fuckin' things, will ya? Nearly died here! Quit laughin'!"

Donny spun and took a swing with his bad arm, forgetting it was his bad arm and that he was three and a half feet lower than Jackie. He hit the doorframe with his fist and fell over again, pain shuddering from his shoulder to his chewed cuticles. Jackie's amusement overtook him and he laughed so hard he committed a cardinal sin and dropped his beer.

"Quit it!" said Donny angrily. He was a wounded bear now, though his pride hurt more than his shoulder. "That's it. I'm suin' ya! Neglectful sonuvawhore!"

"Suin' me? What are you, some falutin' businessman out of Fredericton?" Jackie said, drying his eyes on his shirt.

"You're gettin' sued and yer gonna have to build them steps! I coulda been killt!"

"Yeah yeah, g'won home and sleep it off. You ain't suin' no one. I've seen yer truck."

"I'm suin'!" Donny furiously yelled. "I'm talking to Claire and I'm suing! You're gonna pay for my shoulder goddamnit! I'm callin' a lawyer! He'll know what to do to sue ya!"

"G'won home, Donny. G'won." Jackie was getting a mite irritated at Donny's legal threats. The house was the only property he owned outright.

Jackie *had* meant to build steps at the front when he and Gen bought the house all those years ago. As far as Jackie remembered, there were never steps at the front and Gen asked if he could build a set as soon as they moved in. Jackie promised to do so but then he realized he didn't care for people all that much and thought it looked less inviting from the road that way. It drove Gen crazy.

With one hand, Donny deftly pulled his pack of Player's Filter from the breast pocket of his black and red mackinaw, shuffled out a smoke, put it in his mouth and fished his lighter out of his pants. He cradled his face inside his mackinaw and lit the cigarette and began walking out Jackie's dooryard.

"Jesus, Jesus, Jesus. Expect a call from Claire! And my *lawyer*!"

"Is that my lighter? It is! That's my goddamned lighter, Donny!"

"S'not yours. S'mine!"

"It's mine! I just got it from the store three days ago! I remember buying a green one! Thief! I'm going to sue *you* for stealin'!"

Donny put his hood over his head, walking gingerly on the frozen driveway.

"I'm suing *you*!" yelled Jackie. "Hear me? I'm suing you for bein' an idiot! Go to hell, Donny McGivney!"

"Who uses the front door anyway?"

TWO DAYS LATER, JACKIE RECEIVED a visit in the late afternoon from Claire McGivney. Claire was Donny's wife, and she was also Jackie's first cousin. *At least she knew enough to come around to the back door,* Jackie thought as he put the kettle on. He was getting the sugar and milk out, placing a tea bag in each cup. The weather was cold with glacial January winds, and the sun was noticeably lower on the horizon. By the time the water had boiled, the light had disappeared. The sky went from dark violet to black in those few moments.

"Jackie, Donny's laid up pretty bad. I think he's serious when he says he wants to get a lawyer and sue ya. I've never seen him so ugly."

"Look, Claire..." Jackie put his hands up in exasperation. "I know I'm supposed to have steps there but I just never got to it and honest to Jesus, who uses the front door anyway? It's bad enough he sent you, my own cousin, to come fight his battles for him."

Claire dipped her tea bag and shook her head a little. "Now look, Jackie, cousins or not he's my husband, foolish drunk as he might be. He hasn't been able to go to work for two days and I think you'd better come up with a way to fix this. I appreciate you covering for him with Mr. Sutherland but Donny was some angry when he come home the other night."

"Alright, alright. Jesus, Claire. Lad is supposed to be responsible for his own actions. Whatever happened to a man taking it upon himself to know what door he's supposed to go in and out of?"

"You know darn well he knows what door!" Claire shouted while almost flinging her teabag. "He was just drunk!"

"Again, responsible for his own actions."

"Look, you know I worked as a secretary for the crown attorney's office. The home insurance company might come after ya. I ain't no lawyer but I know he's got a quarrel with you and he's on solid standing."

"More solid than his footing the other night," Jackie muttered, crushing out a dart. The kitchen window was open a crack to let in the fresh, winter air. Smoke from the rumpled cigarette wafted out, wandering into the black evening.

Claire cast her hands in the air.

"Okay Jackie, I'm just tellin' ya. He's not going to let this go and maybe he shouldn't. He hasn't been able to work and he's nowhere near his hours for UI. He's also drinking too much these days, even for him, in case you haven't noticed. I know I sure have."

"I said alright, Claire. I'll figure something out and come down to see ya's in a day or so."

Jackie already knew he would have Paddy go and work off his own debt to Donny McGivney but didn't feel like disclosing it at this moment. Sometimes, things worked themselves out. Jackie did not feel he owed Donny anything for being stupid. But sometimes, a man had to make compromises. In this case, Jackie surmised, it would keep things between him and Claire civil, and he'd also put that fog-brain Paddy to work for driving a crack in his canoe last year. Yes, Paddy desperately needed to learn some responsibility. It was going to cost to have his treasured canoe repaired. He had already made a deal with Mike

Emery to ramp up booze deliveries this year and he absolutely could not go back on the agreement. Jackie knew what Mike was capable of, if people refused to hold up their end of an agreement. Not that he personally felt Mike would do anything to *him* but no need to upset a friendship, especially with the main bootlegger in North Esk.

"What in hell is a 'morning person'?"

THE RIVER WAS FROZEN SOLID, well suited for Jackie on his two-and-a-half-mile skate to the sawmill. He quite enjoyed the morning exercise but less so in the evening. Gen used to call Jackie a "morning person." He loved his wife but was often mystified by what she was talking about.

"What in hell is a 'morning person'?" Jackie quizzed his wife one evening. "Don't we all have to get up?"

If you were not a so-called *morning person*, you were a *lazy person* as far as Jackie was concerned. He never voiced this to Gen, a self-described "nighthawk." It was true she definitely did most of her best work after supper. Often Gen would start a large project, either refinishing a chair in the shed or start baking a cake at 10:00 PM and not stop until the wee hours of the morning. Jackie would wake up at three o'clock in the morning, feeling the cool sheet on her side of the bed. He would roll out, placing his feet on the cold floor and creep down the stairs to peep at what she was doing during the witching hour. More than once, Jackie silently sat on the stairs with his chin resting in the palm of his hand, quietly observing her sip coffee at the kitchen table, or reading a book, or waiting for something delicious to finish baking.

This morning, skates removed and boots tied tightly, Jackie tramped onto the premises of Sutherland's Sawmilling LTD and made his way to the barn where, in addition to stalls for two workhorses, Mr. Sutherland kept a small breakroom. Mr. Sutherland was not a farmer; sawmilling was his business and he operated three in the area – one on Boom Road, one on the other side of the river in South Esk and another in Napan. His brother Bill managed that sawmill, due to the distance, but Mr. Sutherland made sure everyone knew *he* owned all three. He dealt face to face with the bigger companies on selling lumber, driving to Saint John or Fredericton a couple of times a month. He never took his wife, Mrs. Sutherland, with him on these overnight trips.

As far as the breakroom went, no one said anything to Mr. Sutherland about men being grouped with horses; most had grown up on farms and had livestock. In summer, the breakroom was too hot to stay in and in the winter, the heat coming from the old barrel stove would turn the belly a dangerous shade of orange.

Mr. Sutherland's dislike for communism and socialists was well-known on the river. Allegedly, back in the '51 when Jackie's father Henry was working at the mill, a man was reading the paper while heating his coffee. The man reading the paper simply remarked on Joe McCarthy's crusade to oust communism from the United States of America. The man casually stated that he thought it was a big waste of money and government resources. One could not extinguish an idea, the man commented to no one in particular in the break room.

Mr. Sutherland flew into such a rage that he snatched the newspaper from the man's hands, crumpled it into a ball and fired him on the spot, but not before tearing a strip off him. In telling Jackie this story, Henry also said the man was a bit slack on the job and was rumoured to vote CCF, so he may have already done himself in before the outburst. It was not uncommon for people in the area to be pro-union or be supporters of the NDP, but none of them worked for Mr. Sutherland.

ooooo

It was a frigid January morning, typical except for the fact the men were working a half day on the weekend. Mr. Sutherland had promised time and a half to every man who came to work and pushed through the order of lumber that was requested by Carhart's Construction in Taymouth. Mr. Sutherland *never* did this and Boyd Meeks had quipped he saw four horsemen coming over the horizon not long after Mr. Sutherland guaranteed the extra pay.

Shy of 9:00 AM, Jackie was hanging up his skates on a 12-inch spike. He looked out through the large bay doors and took a deep breath. The mill yard was humming with conversation – men chatting about the Bruins vs. Canadiens game on CBC the night before – while the clanging of metal echoed through the icy air. Then, without warning, the loudest noise Jackie had ever heard caused every man to stop and turn to one another and watch in awe as a large stock of lumber, about 30 yards away from the mill, toppled over and nearly crushed Boyd Meeks, who was taking inventory of the wood.

"Get out of 'er, Boyd!" yelled Jackie.

Boyd Meeks was small in stature – 4'9 – and he had to scramble from the lumber pile, dropping his clipboard as he hurried from the falling planks. The cold and still January air made the sound even louder. Jackie had been next to a freight train once in Newcastle as it blew by him and Donny. They were both nineteen and out drinking. It nearly deafened them, and the ringing in their ears lasted for hours. The sound that hammered and ricocheted that January morning was louder.

Mr. Sutherland appeared from behind his desk in the office to join the men in the work yard, having somehow twisted his ankle in the process. He reached out to steady himself and grabbed the closest thing next to him – Jackie. Jackie was unprepared for the 76-year-old Sutherland clutching onto him like he was drowning in the river and subsequently grabbed onto Donny, who grabbed the next man and so on, creating a domino effect of men falling over.

Jackie sprung up quickly and began to help Mr. Sutherland, still on the ground wiggling his foot around to make sure nothing was broken.

"Easy, young O'Connor," said Mr. Sutherland. "Gotta get to my knees first, then on one knee and then up. Hips are worse in the goddamn cold weather. Now, what in blazes was that God awful noise?"

"I don't know, sir," replied Jackie. "Sounded like a jet taking off!

"Never heard nothing like that in my life," said Donny.

Around the yard, lumber had toppled over and was now scattered haphazardly.

"Jesus Murphy," said Mr. Sutherland. "I'm going to call my brother in Napan and see if the wood is alright down there. You men, start picking that off the ground and get to stacking it again. And for God's sake, someone see to Boyd."

Jackie nodded, then reached into his wool coat pocket and took out his silver flask filled with whisky, walking briskly over to Boyd further into the lumberyard. Boyd's face was ashen.

"Alright Boyd?"

Boyd seemed not to hear him.

"Maybe that noise deafened 'em," said Donny.

"No. Lad is just in shock."

A few other men had gathered around to make sure Boyd was unharmed. Jackie crouched down in front of Boyd and pressed the flask in front of his nose, like smelling salts. Boyd looked up, nodded and took a long pull off the flask.

"What the hell happened? I think that was an earthquake."

"*Earthquake?* In New Brunswick? No, I wouldn't think so," said Jackie.

"Don't them normally happen in Japan or California?" said Donny.

Boyd continued. "It was an earthquake, for sure."

"Ya think?" a surprised Jackie said.

"I spent seven weeks with my cousin in San Francisco back in seventy-two, and we had one, and I've never seen nothin' shake the world like that before," recounted Boyd. "Books fell off the shelves and then the bookcase itself toppled over. Then the dishes were thrown out of the cupboards. I didn't know what in hell was going on when she and her dimwitted son dove under the table but I guess I was the stupid one. I just sat there at Sunday dinner thinking the world was ending. She pulled on my shirt and yelled to get under the table. Good thing I did too because it weren't five seconds later and the ceiling came crashin' down on the table. It was terrible."

"Jesus that sounds scary," said Paddy Brewster.

"No, I meant the dinner. It was a big feed of longhorn steak she'd gotten from that Chinatown they have there. Ruint the whole dinner."

All the men bowed their heads and shook them in dismay. Donny removed his hat.

Mr. Sutherland hobbled out of the office and into the yard, annoyed at the lack of work. The ankle slowed him but only a little.

"What's the hold up?"

"Well, Boyd is kinda shaken up. Didja find anything out?" asked Jackie.

"I ask the questions around here; but point of fact I did. After I spoke to my brother, I called Fredericton. Seems like we may have had ourselves an earthquake. No way to tell yet if there was any extensive damage or not, although if you lads don't get up and get that wood back in form soon, there'll be extensive damage to your paysheets. Get back to work! Christ almighty, the planet just proved it moves faster than you lads!"

The men looked on as Mr. Sutherland walked straight into the office to check on Scout, his prized German Shepherd. They could easily see through the window that Mrs. Sutherland was shaken but Mr. Sutherland did not go to her and offer any comfort.

∞∞∞∞∞

"That's what they call an after shook."

"Imagine. An earthquake!" Donny said for the seventh time, restacking the lumber that had tumbled to the ground.

"Donny," Jackie said. "If you don't stop saying we had an earthquake, yer gonna get a cuff in the ear."

Boyd came to Donny's defense. "It is something though, Jackie. You've gotta admit."

"Yes, it is and it was a shock. I'm just gettin' tired of listenin' to Donny tell us we had one."

As the sun climbed high in the sky nearing its peak, Donny and Jackie were lifting a big piece of spruce, muddied from the dirt. The ground savagely lurched. Much of the wood they had stacked moments ago fell over again and Jackie felt queasy. Between the earth violently moving and dodging thick pieces of lumber, he thought he might vomit. As before, the shaking lasted ten seconds and then all was calm.

"Jumpin' Christ! What was *that?*" Jackie asked no one in particular.

"That's what they call an *after shook,*" answered Donny.

"After *shock,* Donny," said Boyd Meeks. "I figured we'd be getting one of those for sure."

"You knowed we be gettin' one and you didn't say anything before?" said Donny, exasperated.

"Sorry boys. Kinda thought everyone knew about them aftershocks but that felt the same as before honestly. Didn't feel like much of an after anything. Felt like a full-on earthquake."

"Well Christ Almighty, are there more to come?"

"What do I look like? Nostra-fuckin-damus?" said Boyd.

Mr. Sutherland opened the door from the office and leaned out.

"Jumpin' Christ! What was that?"

"The after shooks," said Donny.

"After *shocks,* ya friggin' dope," said Jackie.

"Well shit, are there more to come?" asked Mr. Sutherland.

"Why don't you ask our Nostra-fuckin-damus over here?"

"Shut up, Jackie, ya arsehole."

Mr. Sutherland took in a cold breath of sawdust-filled air through his nose, scanning the mill yard. He massaged his chin for a moment and rubbed his face in exasperation.

"Alright, that's it. Start tidying up the yard. We're shutting down. I gotta get down to South Esk and Napan and check the other mills for damage there too and can't have anyone getting injured. Goddamn workers' compensation will have my hide. Can't afford to lose anyone right now."

The men were dumbstruck. The mill *never* shut down, even on a rare Saturday they were called into work. The exceptions were Christmas holidays, Easter services (Mr. Sutherland was a strict Roman Catholic) and other statutory holidays the New Brunswick government had instituted over the years. "Always coming after small businesses," Mr. Sutherland would be heard remarking when a non-religious holiday was upon them. He despised Labour Day most of all.

"Alright, alright," said Jackie. "We'll get it together here and neaten all this up. I'll let the other men know." Jackie had become a de facto foreman over the years and Mr. Sutherland often relied on him to oversee things, even if he didn't pay him more money. For his part, Jackie did not mind. He enjoyed the respect it garnered him from the other men and the occasion to confer with Mr. Sutherland on work-related matters.

As Mr. Sutherland got into his new, 1982 Ford F-150, Mrs. Sutherland left the office, locked the door and began yanking it as she always did to make sure it was shut tightly. Mrs. Sutherland could often be seen doing this for up to 30 seconds. She would push and haul on the door, ensuring its seal, even though Mr. Sutherland would never have a door in disrepair, let alone the one to his office.

"Christ Almighty, woman! Would you get over here so we can get to town before the second coming of Our Lord and Saviour?"

Mrs. Sutherland stopped pulling on the door, confident it

was locked and picked her path through the muddy mill yard. She reached the passenger side, then, readying herself with a 1-2-3 motion, jumped into the truck.

Jackie turned his head, then looked down to see Boyd Meeks next to him, his eyes still fixed on Mrs. Sutherland. Boyd's gaze had followed her the entire distance and unless Jackie was mistaken, he'd caught Mrs. Sutherland scanning over her glasses in Boyd's direction, too.

"Stop giving them lip or start fighting
back on yer own."

BOYD MEEKS, A STAPLE AT THE MILL for 20 years, having just escaped certain death, was now seated warily on a small stool by the north side of the sawmill. The stool was most often used by Boyd to reach tools that hung on the wall. Men frequently used it to sit on and smoke during breaks or have a cool drink in the summer, and Boyd relentlessly had to play detective and go looking for the stool each time he needed it.

Jackie and Boyd had been friends since they were children, despite Jackie being two years older. He had always been very protective of Boyd, due to age and stature. Even normal-sized, Jackie would have towered over Boyd, but Jackie was a big man, nearly 6'4".

Boyd's parents ostracized their son, and Boyd's mother had even once said to Jackie that she wished she'd had *him* for a son instead. To them, Boyd was an afterthought and they made him feel that way.

Jackie was once invited on a family trip to the Bras d'Or lakes in Cape Breton, just to keep Boyd company. The lakes are a sultry place in summer, and upon arriving, Boyd's parents rushed to greet their relatives. He looked over at his small friend who was fast asleep after the six-hour car ride and decided not to wake Boyd. He was hot and he jumped out of the car, running to the water. Boyd never got out of the car. It was Jackie, swimming near shore, who realized that after another 30 minutes in the sweltering vehicle, Boyd had still not emerged. He glanced to see where Boyd's parents were and spotted them having drinks with the rest of the family. Jackie sprinted back to the car, now a scorching steel vault, only to see Boyd slumped over, delirious and sweat pouring from his brow. A blast of dead heat whisked Jackie's face when he threw open the door. He hoisted his friend onto his shoulder like a bale of hay and took him to the water, gently laying him in the lake and scooping up water with his hands to pour on Boyd's heat-stroked head.

Boyd did not often face the same difficulties many small men did, since he had a large friend who fought on his behalf, and young Jackie was indeed known for fighting. In time, Boyd developed a lively mouth, knowing Jackie would always come to his rescue. By the time they become young men, Jackie grew tired of Boyd's frequent provocations.

"Fuck sakes, Boyd. I can't go around fighting every fucking dummy who makes fun of yer height! Stop giving them lip or start fighting back on yer own."

Boyd did exactly that and between his time working in the lumber yard and lifting weights at home, he became a formidable opponent for anyone who dared to make fun of his height. On one occasion at The Old Creek Pub in Nordin, a man, drunk on musty beer, began chiding Boyd about his height. Jackie and Donny sat at their table, saying nothing, knowing that ignoring such people was often the best way to deal with these situations. Donny was never much of a fighter, regardless.

"What are you going to do?" the drunk man said. "Come over and suck me off? You're about the right height!" The man continued, laughing and slapping the lacquered wooden table. Jackie, Boyd and Donny cracked some peanuts and turned their attention to the baseball game, the commentators rattling out statistics from the television in the corner of the room. The man, though, hurled further insults, his face becoming more sticky and red with every 8 oz. draught.

"Hey! Hey! Hey leprechaun! *Leprechaun!* I'm talking to

you. Who else would I be talking to? If I give ya two bucks will ya wrestle one of the hogs I saw on the way into this shithole town? A little leprechaun mud wrestlin', eh?" laughed the man. "Oh! Oh! Or maybe you can lead me to a pot o' gold? Take me to the end of the rainbow, ya little fucker! Gimme that gold!"

Jackie jumped out of his seat, the chair squawking as the legs rubbed against the humid tile. Boyd put his hand on his friend's large forearm.

"You just going to sit there and take shit from that idiot?"

"Sometimes ya gotta let it go," counseled Boyd. "Come on, you know I've been dealing with fuckin' dummies like that my whole life. Tired of it but I can't fight every idiot who makes fun of me. I'd be fighting every day of my life."

The bar patrons went about their business, drinking and bantering about tomorrow's weather and how awful the politicians were in Fredericton or Ottawa or the United States.

The rude man continued downing glass after glass and conversing with his friend. Jackie was engaged in conversation with a young woman. Donny was watching the ball game. Boyd quietly rose from his chair, thoughtfully weaving his way through patrons and tables. The rude man was still talking to his friend when Boyd, at the perfect height to strike someone sitting down, punched the man with all his power. Beer glasses toppled and clattered as the man's head hit the table before his body collapsed to the floor. A few heads turned and the conversation in the bar lowered. The rude man's friend got up to check on him and asked for some help from one of the servers. The staff at the pub made no effort to assist. Boyd had not even broken stride and sauntered to the restroom to relieve himself.

Still, Boyd dealt with all the challenges one faces in a world that prides itself on melting everyone into the same pot. On some evenings and weekends, Jackie and Boyd moonlighted by getting squirrels out of rafters, mice out of walls, all sorts of buildings where vermin and unwanted wildlife entered a home or business. They made the perfect pair for this pest-removal task. If the crevice was too small, Boyd could scamper and tackle vermin, while Jackie handled locations higher up. If a place was too difficult to get to, Jackie could always boost Boyd into an attic or crawl space.

They made plenty of extra money at their side business, particularly in the fall of the year when field mice and other animals sought shelter indoors. Bats were always the worst. Once, Boyd was on Jackie's shoulders, gingerly attempting to net a bat out of a home in Strathadam. The bat came to life, fluttered in the crawl space and bit Boyd on his scalp. He tried to turn away but caused Jackie to fall to the floor, Boyd on top of him.

"Fuck! That fucking flying rat bit me!"

Jackie was too busy laughing to be concerned.

"Fuck off! I might have rabies now."

"You don't got rabies, ya dope. You'll be fine."

A few days later, Boyd became confused over the smallest things. He could not decide whether he should use a fork, spoon or knife for a bowl of soup, alternating between utensils. He became quite agitated when a dinner plate he was using in the breakroom at the sawmill was wobbly and kept making a noise every time he touched it. Boyd got up and grabbed the plate, stepped outside of the breakroom and threw it into the adjacent lumberyard. The men at the mill chuckled. Later that day, Boyd grew a terrible fever and had to be rushed to the hospital by Donny. It turns out the bat *did* have rabies. It took almost a month to fully recover and following that incident, bats were no longer on the list of pests that Boyd and Jackie would remove from homes.

∞∞∞∞

Jackie kept an eye on interactions between Boyd and Mrs. Sutherland in the days following the earthquake. He did not see it as being nosy but was curious. After watching Boyd leave the office one day (a rare occurrence for any of the men), Jackie could see that Boyd's face was flushed a rosy red. When he approached him in the breakroom, Boyd was reaching for a glass of water.

"What are you up to?"

"What do you mean?" replied Boyd. "Getting a drink. It's hot."

"It's *January*, so it ain't that hot. You know what I mean," whispered Jackie. "What foolishness are you up to with Mrs. Sutherland?"

Boyd stood there, looking up at Jackie.

"Not your business, Jackie," he said tersely.

"Jesus, Boyd. She's sixty-four!"

"Keep yer voice down ya friggin' dummy. Look, it just kinda happened, okay?"

"Kinda happened?'What did you do? Fall into her while she was knitting a shawl?"

"It's not like that. You know Mr. Sutherland don't pay her no attention ever. And it's not like women are coming out of the woodwork to fancy a guy like me in these parts, ya know?"

"I know but you're looking for trouble if he catches either one of you. Or both of you."

"Don't you think I know that? Mind your own business, Jackie. It ain't like you to get involved and I'm telling you right now: *don't* get involved."

Jackie slowly nodded his head.

"Apologies, Boyd. It ain't my business. We've been friends a long time and I don't want anything happening to you. That's all."

"Well, yer concern is noted. You ain't gonna tell anyone, are you?"

"What am I? Some gossipin' blue hair? I didn't want to know in the first place but I can tell you this: if I took note, others will too at some point. Be careful."

"You know me," Boyd said. "Stealthy like a skunk."

The nickname Mean Mike was fitting.

IN THE SPRING OF 1982, the river did not run until late. The ice weakened with the strengthening sunlight as the seasons changed. The thin ice meant Jackie could no longer skate to work, but he had to wait until the ice cleared before he could use his canoe, cracked as it was from Paddy Brewster's accident the year before. He needed to get to work, travel to the store and, most importantly, fulfill his obligations to make deliveries for Mike in the warmer months. It was only a lag of a week or two at most and even though they were old friends, Jackie did not intend to cross Mike.

He had worked out an agreeable arrangement with Mike. Mike had what everyone called "bad legs" – clinically diagnosed by doctors in Saint John as muscular dystrophy. Since he was a child, he struggled to stand or walk and had been bullied a great deal from both children and adults alike. While he may have suffered, it did not stop Mike from being ambitious, and he finished at the top of his graduating class, despite missing many school days. On the days he was unable to attend, Jackie would bring his homework to Mike and pick it up the next morning.

The riverfront homestead was not much to speak of and it was on poor land. That kind of property was not considered wealthy, and many homes were decrepit due to erosion causing the homes to partly collapse or fall into the water. In fact, at Mike's, the southwest corner was on a post to keep it out of the water when the river ran high.

There was no one to fix things, either. When he was a toddler, Mike's father had died, kicked in the head by a skittish horse while working in the woods. His mother had to work long hours cleaning homes to support Mike and his siblings, leaving kids to raise kids. Mike was not forgotten, but he was not doted upon. When his siblings got older, they wanted to go out and do the usual things teenagers do. They did not want to be stuck at home with their crippled brother. By the time Mike was ten, he was home alone most days and evenings.

His illness struck when he was just eight, and before that Mike and Jackie were always playing outside, running around the woods throwing sticks and rocks at make-believe bad guys. After Mike became sick and his physical condition worsened, Jackie believed keeping his friend company was the very least he could do. He disguised the pity by bringing the schoolwork Mike had missed and any other errand he could figure out that would take him to his lonely pal.

Mike was renowned for his temper, garnering the nickname "Mean Mike." Some people saw that frailty and believed it was a joke, thinking the name was ironic. Jackie knew better.

When they were in their early teens, Mike produced a pistol one day like he was presenting a new baseball card. Jackie was a little startled. He was fine with guns, had grown up hunting with his father and brother but it caught him off guard when Mike produced a very old Colt M1911 from his jacket pocket.

"Watch this," Mike said, taking aim before Jackie understood what was happening.

Mike fired two bursts and shot a stray cat 20 feet from them. Jackie was dumbstruck. Mike blew the smoke from the mouth of the handgun and from that day forward the gun never left his side. Mike tended to want to shoot small animals: squirrels, stray cats, rats. Dogs as well. Jackie had also witnessed Mike threaten people who did not take his reputation seriously. Once, while still sitting in his chair, he stabbed a man in the calf because the man not only owed him money but also made a lighthearted joke at Mike's expense. The man was forced to pay Mike before being allowed to seek medical aid. Before he got out the door though, he received a beating from Kenny Somers.

Kenny Somers, Mike's henchman, was maybe the only man in the area who could match Mike's temper. If people had problems with Mike or his business, Kenny Somers was sent to collect for him. In those instances, Kenny Somers received financial compensation. Otherwise, he got paid in wine.

Not that Mike approved. "Bad on the nerves, wine is.

You should switch to something else someday," Mike would advise every time Kenny Somers came back from town. Kenny Somers would say nothing. He simply dropped off all the beer, rum and whisky and took his 12 bottles of Canadian Sherry.

There was a great deal of gossip that Mike and Kenny Somers had a romantic relationship, seeing that the grown men spent all their time together and neither were married. Mike had never dated anyone in his life and Kenny Somers was too hateful for anyone, man or woman, to ever love. There was a deep dark hole inside of each man; something void and agitated. Rumours about such things are bound to make their way into discussions, though Jackie himself had never witnessed anything and frankly did not care. However, he knew a lot of people in the area were righteous and religious enough to make someone else's business their business. Most people figured they were simply two very disagreeable men who could not find company in other people's presence for long periods of time, other than their own.

Jackie detested Kenny Somers. They only tolerated each other because of Mike. The two men had tangled with each other years ago at the local Royal Canadian Legion in Sunny Corner.

It was a warm Saturday evening in early August and Kenny Somers, for once, was not drunk, but Jackie had had a couple beers. One man gave the other a dirty look, as such things happen, and in an instant the two were outside, hats off, sleeves rolled up.

The rest of the crowd had followed to the Legion's potholed parking lot. There had been a recent shower and the air had the tinge of rain simmering on hot pavement. Boyd Meeks gripped his bottle of Alpine, Donny carried a glass of rum and coke and a dozen other spectators stood with cigarettes and Colt Old Ports. Mike Emery came down the ramp, a bottle of Schooner wedged between his legs. Even the longtime bartender Harvey put his towel down and meandered outside.

Kenny Somers was the only man in the area the same size as Jackie, though more heavyset. It was inevitable the two big men would tussle. The men watching formed a semi-circle and the chatter died down as the two titans squared off. Nothing happened for several seconds. They just stared at each other until Kenny Somers flew forward with a left hand to hold onto Jackie's shoulder, pinning him in place and landing a right haymaker squarely on Jackie's jaw, the sound similar to a hammer hitting a block of cheese. The blow knocked Jackie to his knees and, in the dirt, Jackie heard the "oofs" and "ahhs" from the crowd of men though they were muffled and vague, like he was underwater. Kenny Somers, confident the altercation was over, was walking away when he heard, "Where in fuck you think yer goin'?" He turned and saw Jackie standing upright, fists raised.

"Atta boy, Jackie!" shouted Boyd Meeks.

"Come on, Kenny Somers! Finish the lad off!" cried someone else.

Mike Emery took a swig of beer and remained neutral, eyes pale and exhausted.

Kenny Somers rolled back with a head of steam. They jostled, clutching at each other's shoulders. Kenny breathed beer and rotted meat from between his teeth, causing Jackie to swallow vomit. He shifted his weight, jabbing left and hooking right and before anyone realized it, Kenny Somers' nose was bleeding.

An enraged Kenny Somers rushed at Jackie, who rolled with the tackle and threw him to the ground. The two men were pounding away at each other, dirt spitting, rocks crunching, grunts flying, fists scraping. And like a hockey fight, they both got tired quickly. Harvey the bartender, who always acted as referee in such affairs, walked over.

"Okay!" he bellowed. "Good tilt, boys. That's enough. Beer for each of ya when ya come back inside."

All the men nodded and began chatting again as they made their way back inside the Legion. Mike turned his chair around and a man offered to push him up the ramp but was rewarded with a curse word and smack on the arm. Slowly and irritably, he made his way back up the ramp and into the Legion.

Boyd and Donny walked over to help Jackie to his feet. Nobody helped Kenny Somers.

ooooo

Mike's bootlegging plan involved Kenny Somers legally buying alcohol in various locations across Northumberland County, and even parts of Gloucester, Kent, Sunbury and Queens counties. Kenny Somers then brought the liquor to Mike. He was an industrious man who hired a few friends like Jackie to deliver the booze rather than have everyone come to him, which helped to keep the government and the RCMP from interfering. When booze was delivered right to their doorsteps and they did not have to travel, people appreciated it. Jackie liked it, too. Jackie, like Kenny and his cheap sherry, received payment in beer, and since folks were so pleased to have their liquor delivered right to them, they often offered Jackie a bottle of whatever they had ordered. On any given night, Jackie would get an extra two or three drinks, simply by doing his job.

As far as Jackie was concerned, unless you were able to skim in some way, the government would take every dollar from you.

"Shut yer mouth! All of yous. I'll cuff you in the ear."

POACHING SALMON was how Jackie got himself tangled up in a net of his own. It was June 21, the first full day of summer, and it began with a gorgeous morning shower followed quickly by humidity as the sun seared through lilac clouds. Jackie had woken up early as usual. The emptiness of his bed still left an ache, as if a limb had been hacked off.

Jackie wanted to seize the day or "Carpet Dee'em" as Donny was disposed to say. It was the longest day of the year and a Monday. Unlike many people, Jackie liked Mondays, thoroughly enjoying the promise of a new week. He liked getting up early and turning on CBC to listen to the news. On this day, the government was making more changes that did not require changing again: shifting the name of Dominion Day to Canada Day. He registered that the changes were made some time ago but quickly forgot about it. That's how the government does things to people, Jackie reckoned: they make changes but it takes so long to take effect, you forget about it until it's upon you. By that point, it's too late to do anything.

"Why in God's name do politicians continuously fix things that aren't broken? It must be because they can't do anything else," he said aloud. The only living thing listening was Ruby, his Irish Setter.

"They must think we're all stupid and don't know we live in Canada, so we have to name the day after it now," he said, slurping instant coffee before work. It made little difference what they called the first day of July but he hated all the changes. Leave the day as it is; it was as simple as that.

Jackie did not believe much in holidays. It was something on which he and Mr. Sutherland agreed. "Who would take off one of the longest days of the year just to sit around on their arse trying to appreciate everything around him?" he was prone to say as summer holidays approached. Jackie figured the best way he could appreciate his country was to mind his own business and work. He had no real sense of patriotism, save for what he learned in social studies about the Fenian invasion from Maine in the 1800s. Far from being a monarchist, he certainly did not care for Americans – Irish descendants or otherwise – raiding lands in New Brunswick.

After the news was complete, Jackie hopped out of bed. He dressed in his green pants and pale grey GWG work shirt (a light one; it was promising to be a scorcher). He walked downstairs and made enough coffee to last for the day, pouring what he would not drink at breakfast into his red thermos. As the coffee brewed, Jackie prepared his breakfast – three hard-boiled eggs (one of which he would take with him for break at 10:00 AM), white toast with homemade raspberry jam from his cousin Claire and a *junk* of cheese. He grabbed his lunch (packed the night before), petted Ruby on the head and the two of them trotted to the canoe, loaded up and began paddling to the sawmill. Ruby sat at the bow and surveyed the waters while Jackie sat stern, paddling along the unruffled morning river. It was peaceful at this time of day and Jackie wondered to himself why anyone would live anywhere else.

The weatherman's prediction that morning was correct: the summer solstice arrived with intensity. Even for late June, 84 degrees was warm, charring the skin with any length of exposure. It made for a hot work environment, that's all Jackie knew. The sawdust coming off the blades searing through the wood stuck to him as if he were basted in honey. By noon, when the sun reached its peak and the motionless air created a hum when the saws ceased for lunch, Jackie's skin, even his face, was covered in a fine coating of sawdust and small chips of wood. Though they had seen it before on hot days, it was worse today, and Paddy, Boyd and Donny started to laugh and were unable catch their breath, coughing because of the sawdust and chain-smoking.

"Shut yer mouth! All of yous. I'll cuff you in the ear," Jackie chided, a smirk on his face. He knew he looked ridiculous, but all the same, he was not about to tolerate much chirping from the likes of Donny McGivney, Boyd Meeks or Paddy Brewster.

By the time the blistering workday ended, the men had sweated out every last bit of water. To replace that moisture, they cracked a few beers. On hot days, when the men shuttered the noisy machines – the gears and levers oiled and lubricated for the following day, the floors swept and cleaned – they would find a nice block of wood or a stack of newly planed spruce and sit down for a chat and a cold beer. Mr. Sutherland was always gone by the time the workday had ended, departing briskly with Mrs. Sutherland.

When the beers were finished, Paddy Brewster gathered the bottles. Once a week, Paddy would hitch a ride to town and take the bottles to the new recycling depot in Newcastle. Paddy made the bare minimum at the mill, and most people knew that

Paddy also resorted to selling marijuana, alongside smoking it. While most men, Jackie included, did not care for this sort of behavior, they gave Paddy a free pass, since his father gave him nothing except anger and an empty stomach. Paddy had once questioned Jackie on the difference between selling weed and poaching salmon.

"But they're both illegal, ain't they?"

"I supposed they are but they're different *kinds* of illegal," said Jackie.

"What does that mean?"

"Salmon don't rot yer brain."

"Well, weed don't neither, Mr. O'Connor. You can't tell me booze and gamblin' and poachin' fish is good for someone and then turn around and say marijuana is bad."

"I can because the law says that."

"But you're bootleggin' and Mr. Donny McGivney is poachin' salmon, and that's all illegal too!"

"It is but it's just… different… and don't go broadcastin' I'm transportin' booze for Mike."

After all the tidying was finished and the beer bottles emptied, the men said their "good evenings" and parted ways. Jackie was walking downhill towards his canoe when Donny called out after him.

"What are you up to tonight?"

"Oh, you know me. Sittin' down to connive and conjure up with another way for you to sue me."

Donny put his hands on his hips. "Come on, Jackie. You're not still sore about that, are ya? Fuck sakes. I nearly broke my shoulder."

"Naw, naw just givin' you a hard time. What's on the go?"

Donny looked at the ground a moment, then back up. "Nothin'. Nothin' really. Just wonderin' if you'd want to help me with somethin'."

"What's that?" Jackie said, lighting a rollie he gently withdrew from his brown reusable cigarette case.

"Well, I've got nets to put out and…"

"Nope," Jackie said, taking a puff with one hand and waving his other dismissively. "Not real interested in getting arrested by the wardens."

"Aw come on, Jackie," Donny implored, taking a step down the hill. "Normally, Paddy would give me a hand but he said he's busy tonight. Gotta a lady down in Newcastle he's going to see, he says. I just need a hand putting them out tonight."

"Newcastle? Jesus how's he getting way down there with no car?"

"I asked the same thing. He says he bought a new truck."

"New truck? Where is it then? He didn't drive it to work and anyway, he don't have enough money to buy a truck. Sounds like Paddy is lying about something.

Donny adjusted his cap and took a drag from his cigarette.

"I can't help you regardless, Donny. Christ, it's the longest day of the year. Only you would try to poach salmon at night with only about six hours of darkness."

"But that's what makes sense about it. The wardens don't think anyone would be foolish enough to set nets for just a few hours."

"And they'd be right except you *are* foolish enough. I'm heading home. Expos are playing the Mets at seven-thirty and I have to make a run for Mike before then."

"What if I was to pay you for it?" Donny said, jutting his jaw out.

Jackie stopped. "What're you going to pay me with? Foolish thoughts?"

"No. Don't think so, anyway."

Jackie stared at Donny.

"Look, I can pay ya. I'll give ya a hundred bucks if ya help me out."

"Where in hell did you come up with a hundred dollars?"

"I'll tell ya tonight. Bring a few beers with ya."

Donny turned to walk away.

"Alright, fine." Jackie relented, more curious how Donny came up with one-hundred dollars than interested in helping him out. "One AM?"

"Yessir. That'll be good. See you then."

Donny trotted away and Jackie loaded his gear into his canoe. Ruby, who roamed between the shoreline and the mill throughout the day, was waiting for him. In all his years, he had never known nor heard of a dog this intelligent. One day if she suddenly began speaking to him, he would not be all that surprised. Ruby hopped in the canoe and Jackie grabbed his paddle from the rungs, hauled the vessel into the water and pushed off into the early evening sun. The light cast a wonderful dome over the river, encompassing Jackie and Ruby as they lazily paddled, taking in the radiance of summer's first day.

"Out, out, OUT, OUT, OUT"

THE 36-27 MONTREAL EXPOS were facing a division rival, the New York Mets, who were slightly above .500 at 34-31. Jackie had been an ardent fan of the Expos since they came into the league 15 years before and recently they had been promising to make a run for the National League pennant. His antenna only allowed him to get good reception on CBC. Fortunately, the Expos played many of their games on the national broadcaster.

On game days, Donny and Boyd were frequent guests in front of the television, though Donny claimed to have better reception for a variety of networks. In the last couple of years, Paddy would often drop in as well. On this night though, Jackie enjoyed a secluded evening with a few cold beers, watching baseball while the metal oscillating fan whisked the early smells of summer through the window.

The Expos were up 4-1 in the eighth and Jackie was finishing his fifth beer, feeling good about their chances of finishing off the Mets. Gary Carter stepped up to the plate. The Kid smacked a solo shot to left field and the crowd at colossal Shea Stadium booed. Jackie cackled in his tattered brown recliner. He raised his bottle, warmed by his hand and the heat of the evening, tipped it up in the air as Carter rounded third base, and downed the remaining amber elixir.

It was almost 10:30 PM. He'd promised Donny he would help tonight but now he *really* wished he had not made the commitment. There was no way he would make it all the way to 1:00 AM without catching a bit of shuteye. *And* he had to work in the morning, which meant Jackie was unlikely to get any sleep from the time they put the nets in the water to the time he would have to get ready to leave for the mill.

What in Christ's name was he thinking? Donny seemed a bit off, more than usual. Donny was daft, sure, but had long been a friend of Jackie's (minus the week or so they fought about Donny falling out the front door). There was something unhappy in the man's voice. The only time he had previously seen Donny like that was in 1971, when his father died at the rail line in Newcastle.

Mervin McGivney was 76 years old and still with CN at the time. He used to work the freights from Hamilton to Halifax, but during the tail end of his career, had taken a position at home, performing administrative work he loathed but intermittently assisting with passenger trains and unloading luggage. Mervin's supervisor pleaded with him to stop helping with the luggage – they had younger men to do that heavy lifting but to Mervin, a Scotch Presbyterian, *not* working was a foreign concept.

In 1971, Lester Allison moved home for good from South Porcupine, Ontario, after 25 years of working in the gold mines. When he did, he moved home by train and decided to bring every item he owned with him. One of those boxes contained an industrial vise that Lester inherited from work after it was deemed unsafe.

Mervin hopped up when the train came in, decided he could wrangle the large box by himself, not knowing what the crate contained. He grabbed the bottom and heaved but it was far heavier than he expected. Mervin was a stubborn man and latched onto the box with the determination of an Olympic weightlifter preparing for a clean and jerk. He gave it another big heave and collapsed seconds later, dead of a heart attack. It was later proposed by his doctor that perhaps 50 years of smoking and drinking *may* have contributed to Mervin's sudden heart failure, but the community would not hear it. No, it was Lester Allison's vise that killed old Mervin McGivney. For his part, Lester felt terrible about the death, but not responsible. Nonetheless, the vise remained inside the box at his new bungalow on Falconer Street. It lay on the basement floor for the remainder of his days, which unfortunately for Lester, was only five months later.

Lester was attempting to repair a hole in his roof. The large vise would have been perfect to hold the sheet metal but Lester refused to bring it out of the box. Without something to stabilize the piece of sheet metal steel, his hand slipped and the shears he was using dug deep into his arm, cutting his brachial artery.

He bled out in minutes.

Now responsible for two deaths in six months, many thought the vise was plagued with an evil spirit. This included Lester's wife, who gladly donated the vise to the vocational section of the community college. There it lay dormant until the board decided to clear out the old utility rooms, where the vise had been stored. It was discarded at a scrap metal factory in Chatham, having never once been used after Lester Allison packed it up and transported it from Ontario.

ooooo

Jackie's mind wandered sometimes and now he couldn't remember why he was thinking about what killed Mervin McGivney: a sure sign he needed to sleep. He was never able to nap in bed. He always associated the bed with "sleep" and the couch with "naps." He removed his ball cap, undid his belt buckle and the button on his trousers, unzipped halfway and lay down on his grey chesterfield. Jackie stuffed his hands in his pants pockets, hoping he would sleep a little.

Soon enough, he found himself sinking into the cushions on the couch, his mind traveling nomadically to all sorts of places, none of them unpleasant. The sportscasters nattered about which player from the Mets would have played better if they had switched to jockey shorts instead of briefs for freedom of movement and which Expos pitcher was always better when the humidity level was low in Shea Stadium, rather than when it was high at Three Rivers in Pittsburgh.

He was on a busy city street. Some people were walking by and it took him a few seconds to get his bearings. After turning his head a few times, he realized he was in Fredericton, though could not remember how he had gotten there. It mattered not. He was drinking a coffee after leaving Kelly's Diner on King Street. It was a warm morning and he was causally sitting on a bench, waiting for Gen to come out of the record store around the corner on Regent. Gen was an aficionado of Patsy Cline, Merle Haggard, Johnny Cash, John Prine. She had even started listening to some of the soft rock bands (or as Jackie called them, "wuss rock"). He knew when it was, now that he regarded the streetscape. It was 1976. They had taken a drive over first thing in the morning, packing up Gen's sedan and leaving Boom Road before first light. It was May. The weather was always a roll of the dice this time of year but as fate would have it, the sun shone brightly and it was promising to be one of those spring days the body hungers for after a long, dark winter.

One of Jackie's favourite pastimes was people watching. In a respectable way though, not in a queer way like some men did at the The Old Creek Pub in town, ogling all the women. He simply enjoyed watching people pass by him while he sat on the bench. He saw a man and his son walk by with a beautiful German Shepherd, its deep black and brown fur sheening in the morning light.

A bell jangled lightly. A woman clutched a paper bag, opening the door with her hips and stepping out of Carleton Bakery, carrying the breads and pastries toward her bright orange car. *What a strange colour for a car*, Jackie thought. Orange. *She must be from the north shore.*

He saw a man with what looked like a bath towel around his head and wondered why a man would do that and what a rush he must have been in to get out of the shower and run outside. Gen, now sitting beside him (though he could not remember her sitting down), tastefully educated him that the man was a practicing Sikh, the head covering called a dastar and they rarely took them off in public. Jackie was dumbstruck.

"You mean they keep it on all the time? That's gotta be hot. How could a man wear something on his head all day every day?"

"Jackie, you take your ball cap off to sleep and that's about it. I think you wear it in the shower."

"I take it off before I get in the tub, woman. Jesus, I'm not simple."

It was one of the many things Jackie loved about his wife – that she knew so much about everything but never judged him for being oblivious – unless it was baseball, sawmilling, politics, canoeing or the history of the river. He could ask her anything, and most likely she had an answer; and she was able to educate without making others feel small. She was kind and calm. He was always after her to go on *Front Page Challenge*. She knew more than Betty Kennedy or that useless Allan Fotheringham any day of the week, Jackie would openly profess to one and all.

They rose lazily from their bench, he with his coffee and her with her new LPs under her right arm, her purse hanging from the same shoulder. They began walking south on King Street, the morning sun cradling their stroll, opening up the city to them. Jackie felt warm but not hot.

His wonderful, gifted wife by his side, a nice spring day and a coffee in his grasp, Jackie turned to face Gen.

"It doesn't get any better than this," Jackie said.

Gen was talking about what records she found at the shop. Four, if he heard correctly. She was explaining which ones she had purchased, though he really did not hear her speaking.

It was not that he disliked listening to her. It was that he was completely enamored with her and was staring at the happiness that *was* her face, relaxing in the joy it brought him.

He heard a car door slam. A woman exited a red compact car and gave Jackie an unfavourable look. He felt like he knew this woman. Yes, she was definitely giving him an unkind look. *No, not unkind*, he thought. *Is that pity?*

The woman wore a bone-white blouse with a cameo at the neck and lace around the collar. She wore a long brown skirt, practically touching the ground and old-styled shoes – Victorian era, if Jackie guessed correctly. She was well dressed for the 1770s, not the 1970s. He thought he recognized her but could not quite place her. The identity flitted through his brain and Jackie tried to grasp the name, but blinked and it was gone.

"No. Not again," Jackie said. "Not her. Not again." Troubled, he reached for his wife's hand but all he grasped was emptiness. He turned to Gen but she was no longer by his side. Dread settled between his shoulders. He looked around, spinning in a circle, dizzying himself. The coffee he was holding splashed and scalded his hand.

He grunted and flung the drink to the side. His hand bubbled he could smell his flesh cooking. He felt like he was on top of a merry-go-round and could not get his bearings. Then he saw Gen, off in the distance, in a parking lot by the Lord Beaverbrook Hotel. He called out but no sound came, as much as he hollered. He yelled and yelled but all that came from his mouth was emptiness. He waved at her frantically, a survivor from a shipwreck, lost in the vastness of the sea, with the waves lapping against his lifeboat, hoping someone from a passing plane or boat would locate him.

Gen was not looking at him. The glow from her had dulled and the left side of her body was grotesque, as if every cell was gorged with bad water. Her treasured new records were now smashed on the asphalt. He blinked and he was on the ground next to her, clutching at her feet and doing his best to pick up the broken records. Jackie hurriedly tried to put them back together but the shards cut his hands, blood leaking out of his fingers. Gen touched him lightly on the shoulder but he did not want to look at her. Jackie craned his head upwards but it was not Gen at all. The ill-omened woman was there. Her teeth were perfect as she grinned at Jackie. Jackie reached out, blood crawling down his sinewy forearms. The woman, now more than 20 feet tall, stared at Jackie. Her gaze sunk into Jackie's bones and turned him to ice.

A powerful feeling wrapped around Jackie. It was both vacuous and explosive. He felt he might grind through his molars if he bit down with any more force.

Wake up!

Pull up!

Get up!

Wake up!

Jackie could hear himself. "Out, out, OUT, OUT, OUT," but he could not stir. He was imprisoned in the void, knowing he was in a hideous nightmare but unable to wake himself from the cavernous depths of sleep.

A slit of light.

A moment.

A slither of light again.

Awake.

Blurred vision.

Jackie hurled himself off the couch, drenched in sweat. Ruby came up to him and he grabbed her and held on, then rattled out a few sobs of despair. She sat there panting. Jackie drew in some deep, ragged breaths. Then he stopped and remembered Gen had told him to always breathe in through the nose and out through the mouth. He tried inhaling through his nostrils but the air burned and he quickly returned to hyper-ventilating. Jackie picked himself up off the floor and went to the washroom, stumbling along the way and bumping into the kitchen table.

He turned the tap on full and slurped water straight from the faucet. The water was cold and wonderful. He upended the old coffee mug with his toothbrush in it, rinsed it a few times under the water and began gulping from it. When he had finished drinking, he looked in the mirror. He saw an old man, one he did not recognize and he felt unfinished, unhappy; the only man on Earth. He took another long hard look in the mirror, his face ashen with whiskers, water and spit dripping from his cheeks. He leaned against the bathroom sink with both arms and looked hard in the mirror.

"Jesus Christ."

"You're the only smart one in these parts tonight."

JACKIE CLEANED HIMSELF UP and downed a cup of instant coffee. Drinking caffeine so late was not something he would normally do, but it dawned on him that it was actually early, since the clock had freshly passed midnight. He disliked the taste of freeze-dried coffee and detested the wateriness of it but he was not about to make a fresh pot this late (or early), simply to have it go bad by the time he went to work. Instant coffee would do for now.

He sat down at the kitchen table to tie his boots, flopped on his ball cap and put on a light coat. He would need the extra layer. Even during summer it was chilly on the water in the wee hours. He cautiously chose dark clothing – blue pants and matching shirt with a black coat and navy-blue hat.

It was only a mile and a half walk to Donny's place and Jackie had made the journey many times. He and Donny used to run the roads together as boys – bicycling up and down R.R. #1. As teenagers they did the same, walking from each other's homes after drinking with Boyd Meeks or playing cards with Mike Emery. A few years later, they would be walking all the way home from the taverns in town. Sometimes, a kind soul would pick them up in a car and drive them but that was rare. Few people had motor vehicles on their rural road and even fewer would stop to pick up young men, drunk on stale draught.

This behavior continued for Jackie and Donny until they both got married, though even after nuptials, they made their way to each other's houses to drink and play crib or watch a ball game. Jackie would walk or canoe. Donny would drive typically although on occasion he might end up walking if he thought he was too drunk to drive home.

Ruby stirred as Jackie made his way to the door. He stopped and crouched down, patting her lightly on the head. "Stay here, girl. You're the only smart one in these parts tonight." Ruby looked at Jackie lovingly but confused, given the strange hour of his departure. Now 10 years old, she was not as spry as she once was but Jackie had known no better dog.

He loved dogs. He did not hate cats and while they were very useful in catching rodents and clearly many people loved them, he felt no affection. He simply had a connection with dogs; a clairvoyant connection of sorts. In all his life, he was never attacked or threatened by one. When he encountered an angry dog, he could always soothe it without breathing a word. He was certain of one thing about dogs: they could indeed sense anxiety. Fear, Jackie knew, bred more fear, which bred anger. Dogs that are angry are just scared and are uncertain how to react. Jackie could always transform an angry hound into a tranquil puppy.

He knelt to pet Ruby and chuckled to himself. Only one thing made Ruby go into a frenzy. Porcupines. For some reason, she had to attack them. Jackie went to great lengths to keep the spikey rodents away from his yard, considering Ruby had to be taken to the veterinarian on a number of occasions to have quills removed from her snout. After the seventh time, Jackie quizzed the veterinarian.

"What in hell is wrong with this dog? I know she ain't stupid but this is gettin' expensive. It must be some painful, getting all them quills stuck in her nose and mouth. You'd think she'd learn." Ruby lay on the table under anesthesia. The vet was rubbing ointment on the groggy Irish Setter, never taking his eyes off her.

"Ever get drunk, Jackie?"

Jackie crooked his head.

"What does that have to do with…well yes, I suppose from time to time I've probably gone over, by a drink or two."

The doctor was still calmly and thoughtfully smearing balm on the Ruby's snout. "Ever get a *hangover* from being drunk?"

"What? Of course."

"Ever do it again?"

Jackie stared at the vet, pursed his lips and nodded.

∞∞∞∞

He finished petting Ruby. She sluggishly laid her head back down on the warm linoleum floor and was asleep before he closed the screen door.

Jackie took a cool, deep breath and looked up at the vibrant stars. It was a clear night and even at 12:35 AM, it looked as though the sun was not far off from rising. He started down his dooryard and made his way toward Donny's, his footsteps tapping along the empty, battered road.

*He listened, hearing the sizzle of his tobacco
and the cigarette paper.*

ON THIS STRETCH OF RURAL ROUTE #1, there was no light. Poles had been installed decades before along the road but not on the stretch where Jackie lived. He could not see more than three feet in front of him, and he felt a bit jittery in the blackness. He carried his flashlight, though did not turn it on, not wanting to attract any attention.

He knew where every bump in the road was, where every stream or brook flowed out from the woods, where every root from a big spruce or maple protruded from the earth, and if he chose to do it with a blindfold on, Jackie was certain he could make it to Donny's and back.

As a child, Jackie would close his eyes and try to find his way around the house. When he was six, Boyd told him about a boy from Douglastown he had heard of in school. The boy went out into a field to plant a bag of sunflower seeds. Flocks of birds – chickadees, American goldfinches, robins – the kind that look sweet, and sing nice songs on tree limbs, came swooping out of nowhere, descending on the boy and pecking his eyes out. The yarn gave Jackie nightmares for weeks, and after, he grew afraid of becoming blind and figured if he was going to lose his eyes, he should practice. He knew now that Boyd's story was bullshit, but occasionally Jackie would feel his way around the house. He was still concerned about being alone and blind.

Many people poached salmon and few were apprehended, but that was no reason to make it obvious. If Jackie was on his way to help Donny McGivney, it would be his luck the rangers would be out and looking for poachers. The flashlight was for emergencies only. The only thing currently lighting his way was the bright red coal off his cigarette.

He walked down the road, enveloped in black. The nightmare had made him jumpy. He felt like something was peering at him from just beyond the trees, though Jackie could barely tell where the tree line began.

Jackie stopped, listening closely. He heard absolutely nothing. He did not hear a single insect or rustling of one of the many nocturnal rodents in these woods.

He listened, hearing the sizzle of his tobacco and the cigarette paper. The chirping of spring peepers, always calming, had stopped. His heart rate slowed. Then he heard the familiar *thump* and breathed out a long sigh. From this part of the road, Jackie could look to his left and see clear across to the south side of the river. Jackie knew he was looking across deep black water at Shillelagh Hill. The stretch of road was notorious for having dangerous turns on either side before dipping into a steep gorge. His eyes had adjusted to the night, and he thought he saw a flicker of light on the shore below Shillelagh Hill. Something or someone passed and then was gone.

His father Henry had once spoken about a ghost along this part of the road. Not one for church-going or the paranormal, Henry told Jackie there were unsettled spirits in these waters. Henry was certain he had seen a *banshee* – a premonition of something to come – but few believed him. He was often drunk and even Jackie's mother poked fun at the notion of a ghost. Henry though was unshaken. He knew what he had seen.

Two weeks later, Jackie's grandmother died from a brain aneurysm. She lay down one afternoon for a nap and never woke up. While no one believed Henry saw anything beyond his mind playing tricks on him, Jackie wondered about it. Like his father, he did not follow any religion nor did he believe an almighty God overseeing their lives. He trusted his instincts. His father was often drunk but there was something convincing in his voice all those years ago.

Now, between his nightmare and his father's tale, Jackie felt twitchy in the shadows of the tall trees.

He looked around and still there was nothing. The rational side of his brain regained control. He knew that being both bleary eyed and tired, the mind plays tricks on a man walking by himself at this late hour. He rapidly blinked. The spring peepers returned with their cacophony of song and the surrounding forest regained its nightly orchestral hum.

Jackie continued walking to Donny's house, picking up the pace to try and get away from the cold grip around his spine.

*"Yer just jealous that I have better
TV reception than you."*

BY THE TIME HE REACHED THE MAILBOX at Donny's, Jackie had smoked two more cigarettes. He rounded the corner of the house and Donny was in the backyard behind the pale blue bungalow with white shutters. Even in the low light, it was clear the house was in dire need of maintenance. A fresh coat of paint was required, and one eavestrough was missing. The chimney was missing a number of bricks on top, looking like it might collapse in a heavy wind and the oil tank outside appeared as though it could be leaking. On the south side, an antenna nearly four times the height of the house stood, braced with a long stake in the ground, secured strongly by zip ties and yellow nylon rope. Jackie referred to the antenna as "NASA."

On clear nights, Donny claimed he could get reception for ball games as far away as Boston. Jackie had to admit, the antenna brought in good reception for Expos games, and even occasionally for that new team in Toronto. The long antenna had broken spokes at the top but it was too tall for Donny to climb and fix. Consequently, it was also too long for him to safely bring it down and repair. Donny went to great effort to keep it upright and that was enough for him.

Claire, however, did not appreciate the haggard look of the antenna but did not say much, since she could watch *The National* with Knowlton Nash without wavy lines or snow across his face, as well as crisply view her beloved Montreal Canadiens on Saturday nights and *Dallas* on Sundays.

Jackie strode towards Donny. The backyard extended all the way to the shore and Donny was untangling the nets, spreading them across the grass. Donny wore an old canvas mining cap with a lamp bracket on his head. If he was trying to poach salmon, he was doing it with a light on his forehead that could land a rocket from Cape Canaveral.

"Whatcha doing?" Jackie hissed.

"Wha?!" a spooked Donny said, shooting his gaze towards Jackie, immediately blinding him.

"Christ!" growled Jackie. "Jesus! Jesus! Jesus!" He had just spent the last twenty minutes walking in the dark to adjust his eyes. Now he was back at square one.

"Keep it down would ya. We're trying to *not* get noticed, remember?"

"Then take that stupid light off yer head, dummy. I can't see a goddamned thing."

Donny switched off the light, then lamented that *he* couldn't see anything now.

"*I* can see that you're a fuckin' idiot," Jackie said, exasperated. He shook his head and started gathering the nets.

"I wasn't planning on wearing the lamp out on the water. I'm not simple, ya know?" Donny quipped.

"I'm sorry to tell ya, Donny Boy, that yer the only lad who thinks that."

They rolled up the nets and loaded them into the old boat. Donny had constructed the boat himself when he was only 20, and through decent artisanship and careful maintenance the boat had endured. Initially he had only planned on it being a rowboat; something to paddle around in and fish occasionally. But he assembled the back to be flat in the event someday he could afford an outboard motor. When he and Claire were married in 1965, his father gave them a motor as a wedding gift. Claire did not think much of the gift, but Donny had tears in his eyes.

"Can we at least take the motor off so we don't wake up half of fucking North Esk?"

"What's got you so sour tonight?" said Donny.

"First of all, it's not *tonight,* it's *tomorrow.* Or today. Or whatever. And that's why I'm sour. Because it's one o'clock in the goddamned morning and I'm out here settin' nets with you rather than being asleep in my nice bed."

"Sorry, Jackie. I appreciate it though. My shoulder ain't been too good since I fell out yer door last winter."

"Now don't go bringing that up again. We're square on that. Paddy come down and worked off the debt," argued Jackie.

"I know he did. Just sayin' is all. You know that young lad smokes a lot of dope?"

"Everyone does."

"It's making him jumpy. When he was down here a few weeks back helping out with the new bathtub we put in, he was constantly having to go somewhere and said he had to make trips to town and such. Real nervous, these days."

"Yeah, well weed can sometimes do that, I hear. That's why I stay away from it."

A rustle in the woods, the cracking of branches. Jackie peered into the forest. A mass was emerging from the thick darkness.

"A bear!" he said.

"Quick! Play dead!"

"No! Get yer gun!"

Donny panicked "Play dead! Roll over! Roll dead and play over!"

"What are you a dog?" chuckled the bear.

Jackie clicked the button on his flashlight. Boyd was brushing some thickets out of his finely combed hair.

"Don't shoot! Don't shoot!" Boyd had his hands up in the air, laughing.

"Oh yeah. Forgot to tell you I asked Boyd to come, too."

Jackie flung the flashlight at Donny, the twirling light smacking him in his bad arm.

"Ow!"

"*You* forgot Boyd was coming, you tit. Not that you forgot to tell *me* Boyd was coming!" Jackie shouted.

"Are you boys trying to wake up half of fucking North Esk? Keep it down," Boyd hissed.

Donny rubbed his arm.

"Come on," said Jackie. "The faster we get these nets in the water the faster we can go home."

The air was cool at the water, and they loaded the nets into the boat, grabbing their paddles as they worked. They were not planning to go out far. The channel was roughly 70 yards from the shoreline at high tide. Jackie, Donny and just about everyone else knew where the channel lay. All of them had grown up next to the river and all of them knew the dangers of not respecting the water.

As children, they had heard about the Lynch brothers, ages 8 and 10, who got up early ran to the river on a July morning when the water was warm and the tide high. Most days throughout the summer the boys were swimming before their mother woke up, always returning for lunch. But by noon there was no sign of them. That evening, a massive search was held and people all the way from Trout Brook to Eel Ground searched from dusk until dawn for two days. People from the south side of the river brought their boats to search as well. Three days later, they found the youngest Lynch boy washed ashore, concealed in a large bed of eel grass only 300 feet from where they jumped in the river. The oldest boy was never found.

That story lingered in the back of Jackie's mind as they paddled out. There were no lit cigarettes or loud talking. They took great care to use J-strokes with their paddles in order to be quiet. Jackie, Donny and Boyd knew that sound carried over water very well. A soft splash could be heard across the river as if it was a foot away.

When they reached the channel, they began laying the nets out quietly and stringing them along, carefully setting the anchors so they also did not make a sound. Stealthily, they pushed themselves away from the immediate area of the green nets, only barely visible by the small white buoys attached to the lines.

Back closer to shore, the boat wafted on the calm dark water. Donny softly spoke.

"Thanks for helping me. Needed a hand tonight."

"What's on the go with you?" Jackie probed. "Yer face was so ashen at the mill, I thought you'd plowed your head into one of the stoves."

Boyd nodded in agreement.

Donny shuffled about for a couple of seconds, toeing at a faded ice cream container used to bail water, rocking listlessly on the floor of the boat. He grabbed at his smokes in the chest pocket of his red and blue plaid shirt and lit one up. The glow from the lighter (the green one he stole from Jackie, Jackie still reckoned) cast a brilliant orange flame.

"Donny!" Jackie whispered. "Put that out!"

"Fuck off for a minute, would ya, Jackie?"

Jackie and Boyd sat there, gob smacked. In all the years of knowing each other, they could not remember a time when Donny McGivney had ever spoken to anyone that way. Jackie held his tongue and sat quietly with his arms crossed in the dim light of the stars. Boyd lit up a cigarette.

Jackie looked at him.

"Don't make no difference now, does it?"

Donny sucked the cigarette back. Jackie raised an eyebrow when he threw the butt into the river. He quickly lit another. Jackie sighed heavily and lit one up, too.

"Look, there ain't no easy way to say this, so I'll just start: Claire is leaving me. I know she's yer cousin an' all but we've been friends about as long as you've been cousins and I needed to talk to someone about it. That's all."

Jackie sat there, contrite after having been told off by Donny. But at least he understood now. He sucked in a deep breath, and sighed. Boyd said nothing, flicking his ashes into the shadowy river.

"She tell you why?"

"Drinking, mostly. That and she says I'm not out of the house working enough, even though I go without so she can have lots to eat and a roof over her head."

"You never laid a hand on her, did ya?" Jackie knew the answer. Donny might have been a great many things but a violent man he certainly was not. His father Merlin was a hateful bastard and sometimes that runs in a family, or at least the environment continues from one generation to the next.

"No, Jackie. Never. Couldn't never hurt her. I know there are some lads around here who do terrible things like that but I wouldn't do that to Claire. Or any woman for that matter."

Jackie nodded. He also knew his cousin well enough to know she would not accept that type of behavior. Claire was the furthest thing from a shrinking violet.

"Had to ask."

"Yup for sure. I know. But now I don't know what to do because she's leaving me and I've pleaded with her to stay but she's made up her mind. She's been working these last ten months, selling something called VitaMax. It's some sort of food supplement and vitamins in pill form. Some weirdo New Age thing outta Vancouver or Halifax or somethin'."

"Food supplement? What the hell is that?" asked Boyd.

"It's like powder and shit or sometimes looks like a pill you'd give a horse just before gelding, it's so goddamned big. She got me taking it at the beginning of the year for a week or two but the pills were so jeezless large I almost choked to death and the powder, that's the protein stuff, tastes so fucking bad I threw up afterwards."

"Powder? What do you do with it? Snort it? Like that cocaine you see them doin' on *Dallas*?" asked Jackie.

"No no, just mix it in with water or milk or something and drink it. Supposed to make ya healthier and add vitamins to yer system or some shit. Stuff tastes like chalk dust."

"Sounds like nonsense to me. Kinda surprised Claire is into that sort of thing, but then again, she's been reading a lot of them books on self-help."

"Yeah. She even listens to tapes on self-help."

"Who knows what kinda junk that's putting into people's heads now. That's all that 'New Age' bullshit I keep hearing about," said Boyd.

"Well, she's been making her own money off of it and doing pretty well, I guess. Said her mind's made up and she's leaving."

"Are ya fighting for her, Donny? Like, do you want to stay together?" said Jackie.

"'Course I do. I must have asked her to stay *twice*."

Jackie shook his head. "Well, if you asked her twice, I don't know how much more ya can do."

Boyd grunted in agreement.

Donny was grief stricken. The men continued to light cigarettes, one off the other so they did not have to flick the lighter again. They sat in the stillness of the night.

Jackie broke the silence.

"I've been having nightmares."

Boyd looked up.

"Like, what do you mean?"

Jackie took a drag from his cigarette. "Remember all them ghost stories we heard as kids?"

"You mean like the Dungarvon Whooper or the Headless Nun at French Fort Cove?" asked Boyd.

"Yeah, like them. There's a ghost in my dreams. Been popping up the last few years."

"Dreams are just dreams. They don't mean anything," answered Boyd.

"I dunno. Sometimes this one feels different. It feels like she's telling me something."

"She?" piped in Donny.

"Having one of them wet dreams?" joked Boyd.

Jackie got annoyed. "If I had a wet dream at least it would be with a woman who ain't a quarter of a century older than me."

Boyd's face twisted with rage but he said nothing.

"What's that supposed to mean?" said Donny.

Boyd's expression changed from angry hornet to pleading beggar.

"Nothing. Anyway, the nightmare is weird. It's different. Feels like an omen."

"Like what they say in church?" asked Donny.

"That's 'Amen,'" corrected Boyd.

They fell silent again.

"Bring any fly dope with ya?" whispered Donny.

"Yeah right here. I put lots on before coming since I had to walk over so they ain't botherin' me much. Here."

Jackie passed the spray bottle over to Donny in the dark. He could hear Donny take the cap off, followed by the spraying of bug repellent.

"Ow!"

"What? What?"

"My eye! I sprayed the bug shit in my eye! Fuck!"

Jackie and Boyd chuckled and Donny was dipping his

hand in the river, drawing out handfuls of cold water to wash his eye. When he was finished, Jackie grabbed a clean handkerchief from his breast pocket and gave it to Donny.

"Obliged. Thanks."

Donny dabbed at his face, drying up the water. The night was quiet, except for the lapping of the river against the boat. The men sat peacefully in the discreetness of the wee hours.

"At least I won't have to split the winnings with her now," Donny finally said.

Jackie was gazing off in the distance, wondering if he was seeing lights from a boat or it was the gleam of the stars on the river. He did not quite hear Donny at first. He stopped staring at the horizon and turned to his friend.

"Winnings?" asked Boyd.

"Yeah. You know that new lottery thing they've got on the go? Lotto Six-Forty-Nine? New thing they started up."

"Yes Donny, we'd have to be livin' under a rock to not know about it," answered Jackie. "It's all everyone around here's been talkin' about."

"I got a ticket the other week and got it checked in town a couple days later. Kinda forgot about it until I went into my wallet to put five bucks of gas in the truck."

Donny stopped talking as if he had nothing else to say, toeing his paddle on the floor of the boat.

"*And?*" asked Boyd, a little too loudly.

"Oh, and I won. The lad at the store told me. Good chunk of change, too. Five hundred thousand."

Donny casually lit up another smoke, as if he had just said he won a ham from the grocery store.

Jackie turned to Boyd, sitting on a bucket with his mouth wide open. Jackie leaned in closer.

"You. Donny McGivney. Won a half million dollars? And they just give it to you? Do they tax you or somethin'? What's the catch?"

"Nothin', I guess. I just won the money. Honestly, I was on my way to tell Claire when she told me she was planning to leave me. So, I just kept my mouth shut about the lotto money after that."

"You mean to tell me you're almost a millionaire now and we're out here in the middle of the goddamn night settin' *fucking salmon traps?*"

"Shhhhhh. You're being too loud."

Jackie grabbed his paddle and stroked toward shore.

"Wha…what are ya doing? We gotta get the nets. Where ya goin'?"

"Kiss my arse, Donny. To hell with your nets. Jesus, Mary and Joseph."

With Jackie paddling in the bow, it was hard work to tow Donny who was sitting stern and in control. Boyd sat in the middle and opened a beer he pulled from his jacket pocket. Donny started paddling backwards, trying to swing the boat towards the nets, the two men creating their own whirlpool on the Miramichi River at 2:30 AM.

"Would you fuck off," Donny said.

"You fuck off!" replied Jackie.

"Both of ya's fuck off," said Boyd, tossing his empty bottle into the river.

"Out here in the jeezless middle of the night, poaching salmon when you're the next goddamn K.C. Irving collecting millions of dollars," hissed Jackie.

"Doesn't mean I don't need salmon."

Jackie dug his paddle deep and flung as much water as he could backwards, soaking Donny. Donny responded by reciprocating lavishly and suddenly both men were thrashing with their paddles, sending torrents of water onto each other, like boys playing in the river.

Boyd was caught in the middle, completely drenched.

"Would you two dummies smarten up!"

"Quit it!"

"Eat shit, ya rich bastard!"

The water fight continued for nearly a minute until all three were soaked, then the men stopped, blinded, three drenched deer caught in a spotlight.

"Fuck! It's the wardens!" said Jackie.

"Paddle! Paddle! Paddle!" said Boyd.

They drove their paddles into the river and clawed with all their might. Boyd didn't have a paddle. He dug his hands in the river, trying to propel them faster. They were not far from shore but they could hear the roar of the game warden's engine. It was hard to paddle, the boat having collected a lot of water from their fight.

"What about my nets?" asked Donny, furiously paddling.

"You want them, you're welcome to dive out of the boat and go get them, Your Royal fuckin' Highness!" answered Jackie.

They were propelling themselves faster now, running the boat ashore, just getting out of the light from the game warden's beam.

"Come on! Come on! Help me drag the boat up and hide it," exclaimed Donny.

"I'm doin' it, fuck wad! Do you think I want to get caught?"

The warden's boat was fast approaching but the men had done this before, although they were not this old the last time, nor were they as soaking wet. They pulled the boat in, flipping it over to dump the water out then dragged it up the hill as they climbed, sliding and slipping in the mud. The wardens stopped where the salmon nets were and started hauling them up from the water.

Panting, Jackie, Donny and Boyd sat on their haunches, hidden by the tree line, waiting to see if the rangers came closer. They sat on their haunches, desperately trying to control their ragged breathing.

"I gotta stop smokin'," said Donny.

"Quiet," Boyd wheezed.

They watched as the boat, well camouflaged in green and black, started up the engine again. The spotlight made a pass through the woods but the brush was thick and concealed them. The wardens slowly came closer to shore. They cut their engine. Jackie was breathing into his arm to hide his gasps. Donny was doing the same but inside his coat. Boyd had his toque over his mouth.

"We saw you out here! Don't come out poaching anymore. Next time, we'll do more than confiscate the nets! We'll come ashore and take you into custody! You hear?"

Donny sat up and looked as though he was about to tell them off when Jackie, a murderous look in his eye, socked him in the shoulder. The wardens fired up the engine, shone the beam a few more times from left to right and turned the boat around. The noise of the engine late at night echoed across the water.

Jackie sat on the ground, completely exhausted. He looked over at Donny rummaging through his coat pocket.

"Shit. My smokes are wet," said Donny.

Jackie stared at his friend. He shook his head, got up off the slick ground and started to climb the rest of the hill.

"I'll see ya at work then," said Donny.

Jackie did not look back.

"Shame about those nets," Donny said to Boyd.

Jackie was too tired and too wet to care. He climbed the rest of the hill and began walking home to get some sleep before work.

"Them cards were no good, anyway."

FOLLOWING THE EVENTS on the summer solstice, Jackie went home, slept a scant few hours and promptly rose at 4:58 AM to catch the news. He had a cup of coffee, immediately followed by a second cup.

Jackie prepared his lunch the night before, with the exception of pouring coffee in his thermos. He knew drinking this much coffee would give him gut rot by noon, but he needed something to sharpen his senses. It was going to be another sultry day. His shirt was stuck to his back before he left the house.

By 9:30, Donny had still not arrived at work. "No doubt

rich boy is taking a day off," Jackie grumbled to Boyd as they worked around the table saw.

"Fucking imagine," Boyd mumbled, a smoke in the crook of his mouth. "Just winning half a million dollars like that."

"Best to keep it quiet, all the same. Lot of people around here are hard up and if they knew Donny had that kinda money…"

"True. True."

At 10:00, Mrs. Sutherland called Donny's house. If there was one thing that Mr. Sutherland loathed (aside from communism) it was tardiness. After a number of rings, Donny answered the phone.

Mrs. Sutherland tiptoed out to the lumberyard from the office. She spoke loudly to Mr. Sutherland, her voice rising above the whirring of machines and clamoring of lumber. Jackie was within earshot, sweeping the floor beneath the large saw.

"I said, he sounds like he's quite sick! Says he's taking the day off to recuperate!"

"Did he sound like he was faking?" Mr. Sutherland queried his wife, looking her straight in the eye. Mrs. Sutherland was a tall woman at 5'10. Jackie wondered how the bedroom schematics worked for her and Boyd, then shook his head, trying desperately to erase the thought.

"No, not at all. He had quite the cough on him. Said it seemed to come on overnight."

"Well, where's Claire? What's he doing up if he's sick? She lookin' after him?"

"He said she wasn't there and he'd be fine. He just needed a day off and if he isn't any better tomorrow, he'd call to let us know."

Mr. Sutherland looked up at the burning, mid-morning sun.

"Maybe I ought to drive over and check on him. Losing a man without notice means we'll be short a set of hands for the whole goddamn day."

Jackie was still sour at his idiot friend but did not want him to get in trouble. He piped up.

"Mr. Sutherland, sorry to horn in on your conversation with Mrs. Sutherland, but I stopped in at Donny's last night and he weren't lookin' too good. Not coverin' for him or anything but if he's sick this morning, I'd say he's tellin' ya the truth."

Mr. Sutherland looked at Jackie. Then at Boyd, who was trying his best to work hard and not appear as though he was really looking at Mrs. Sutherland's long legs.

"Well, maybe you'll want to stop in tonight on the way home and check in on him," answered Mr. Sutherland. "If he's not lookin' too good, give me a call tonight would ya? That way I can have someone else come in tomorrow. Can't be having lads sittin' around at home if other men are off sick. There's too much to be done."

"For sure. For sure." Jackie nodded. "I'll stop in on my way home tonight."

Mr. and Mrs. Sutherland left and Jackie looked at Boyd, who was working away with a grin on his face. It was the look of a man in love or, at the very least, in lust.

Jackie took a deep breath. He and Boyd were working in the blistering sun while that useless rich boy Donny was playing hooky and probably diddling himself at home. He had meant it when he told Mr. Sutherland he would stop in at Donny's, but he intended to rag him out hard for making them go out in the middle of the night and nearly being arrested for no good reason. Now, Donny was playing a joke on them or at least felt entitled enough that he didn't have to show up for work. Jackie was furious. In a fit of anger, he grabbed a misshapen piece of cedar and threw it into the brush behind the sawmill.

∞∞∞

The hot workday grew to a close. Jackie was so exhausted he could barely keep his eyes open and he was not relishing the canoe ride home.

"Want me to come with?" Boyd called to Jackie as he was walking to his canoe.

"Naw, Boyd. Go home. Get some sleep. I'll give Donny a slap upside the head for both of us."

Ruby hopped in the canoe and Jackie dragged it into the river as harshly as he could without damaging the bottom. Plowing in, he violently dug his paddle into the water, each stroke a blow to Donny's thick skull. Though the workday had been heavy and the heat exhausting, his anger only propelled the canoe at top speed.

He entered through the back door when he arrived at Donny's house. He did not knock for he did not have to. His cousin lived here and he had been coming in and out of the McGivney house for close to half a century now.

He turned the mottled brass knob, opening the door which gave a loud creak. "Donny? You here?"

No answer. Jackie stood at the back door.

"I know yer in here, 'Wallace fuckin' McCain!'" Jackie chided. "Mr. Sutherland said if you don't show up to work tomorrow, don't bother coming in again!" A fib, sure, but it was worth it to rattle Donny.

A rustle came from the back of the house, then Donny walked out of his bedroom, dragging his feet as he moved. The brilliant evening sunlight flooding through the windows only served the contrast his terrible appearance. He started coughing hard. Much coarser than his usual smoker's cough. With each hacking fit, Jackie thought his ribs might crack, the vicious hacking sounding like boards breaking in half. It did not prevent Donny from lighting up a dart as he scuffled down the hallway.

"Y'alright?"

"Not too good today," wheezed Donny. He was not wearing his hat. It was in this moment Jackie knew for certain his friend was not faking.

"Got an awful chill after gettin' back last night, and I turned on the box fan to help dry me clothes out. Fell asleep almost right away."

"Where's Claire? She not home today at all?"

"She left this morning before I woke up. Said she wouldn't

be back until late. We're not exactly talkin' too much these days."

Jackie slowly nodded his head, hands on his hips.

"Well, ya better get some hot tea into ya or somethin'. Got any Aspirin or two-twenty-twos around?"

"Don't know," Donny wheezed out as he started a fierce bout of coughing. It racked him so badly he clutched the side of the stairs in the narrow hallway. Jackie backed up; he was a stout man and did not often fall ill but certainly had no interest in catching whatever bug Donny had.

"Jesus man, ya need to get back to bed. Go on. I'll make ya a strong cup of black tea and bring it to you."

Donny gathered himself together. He crushed the cigarette out with his thumb and middle finger, then wiped the spittle from his lips with the back of his hand.

"I'm alright. Probably go lay down on the chesterfield, though."

"Good enough, just go sit down and I'll bring ya some tea. Christ, ya look like Death himself."

Jackie set to work on making a cup of tea. He had spent many an hour in this kitchen, having beers with Donny or the four of them playing crib together at the battered Formica table. Games often involved men versus women. A fierce competition grew between Gen and Claire as a team against Jackie and Donny. In recent years, they would sometimes play board games instead of cards. Gen had purchased a new trivia game that was all the rage, invented by a couple of Canadians. Claire and Gen usually defeated Jackie and Donny handily.

Jackie stood looking at the table while the kettle boiled. Memories rushed back. One dreadfully cold Friday evening, Gen had driven the two of them over to play crib and have drinks. On that night, Gen and Claire skunked Jackie and Donny three times. At the end of the third skunking, Jackie was irate, the taunts incessantly piled on from his wife and cousin. Calmly, he gathered up the cards, neatening them into a pile while fuming on the inside. Gen and Claire were relishing their victory when Jackie stood up, grabbed the deck of cards, strode over the garbage can, pressed the pedal with his foot and threw the cards into the receptacle.

"There! Them cards weren't no good anyway!" He whisked away to the bathroom, the howling laughter from Gen, Claire and Donny following him down the hall.

Jackie turned his mind back to the rest of the room. Though he had been in their house often, he felt peculiar opening up another person's cupboard and see how differently they arranged their dishes, what dissimilar food they had behind the small doors. He felt it was an invasion of privacy. He found the box of King Cole, withdrew a teabag and then went hunting for a cup.

Homes have distinctive smells. Sometimes those were pleasant or familiar. Jackie could still smell his grandmother's house from when he was a boy: lavender and cloves. He was certain his own house had a smell. He assumed it was a mixture of wood fire, beer and dog but a person grows accustomed to their own smells. Donny and Claire's house smelled like fried bacon, fly dope and had an earthy tinge from the stone basement.

Jackie snatched a coffee mug from the cupboard, turning it in his hand to see "Hatfield '78". It was mostly white with some blue stripes on it and a New Brunswick flag. *Of course, Donny McGivney had a 'Disco Dick' mug,* Jackie thought. Not that he was particularly supportive of any politician but certainly not the man who had been ruining the province for the last dozen years. It looked like there would be another election in the fall of 1982. Jackie figured Hatfield would win. The Liberals were not looking good, even though their leader was from northern New Brunswick. At least that was closer than Carleton County and Jackie felt he would cast his vote for the man in the next election who probably knew the Miramichi better. Any time he encountered a Member of the Legislative Assembly or Member of Parliament, he turned the other way. More often than not, they wanted your vote or money but not your advice or concerns. He understood government was a requirement. Roads needed to be paved, schools needed to be constructed and people had the right to democratically elect the person they thought best to represent them in Fredericton or Ottawa. What he did not understand was how many unqualified people actually *got* elected.

The water burbled in the kettle. He opened the fridge and helped himself to a beer. Donny only had four bottles in there but Jackie figured if he was tending to him, the least Donny could do was let him have one. He used his jackknife to take the cap off, then regarded the kitchen, hot in the evening heat even without an oven on. The brown and yellow linoleum floor was peeling where it met the walls and floorboards. The cupboards had nicks and gashes. The walls badly required a coat of paint, and were covered in squashed mosquitoes from last summer, or perhaps two years ago. The ceiling had water damage and needed to be replaced. It was clear where Donny had let the eavestrough break outside.

Claire was right: Donny really had let the place go. He was thinking he should offer to help his friend make some repairs this summer when he recalled Donny had just won half a million dollars.

The kettle whistled, so Jackie removed it from the burner, turning off the heat and poured boiling water into the mug, allowing it to steep for five minutes, timing it on his Cardinal watch. Outside the kitchen window, the thermometer showed 84 degrees. Jackie sweated through his third shirt of the day simply making tea. He picked up the hot mug delicately and seized the sweaty beer bottle.

When he rounded the corner and entered the living room, Donny was shivering badly with a blanket covering him.

"Donny Boy, I think we need to get you to outpatients."

"No, no I'm good. I'm good. Just got a summer cold, is all. You know how they set right into the lungs. Let me have some of that tea."

Jackie set the mug on the coffee table, careful to use a coaster before placing it in front of Donny. He helped pull Donny to a sitting position. Donny gently grabbed the tea and took some sips, giving Jackie a reassuring nod.

"You lads didn't tell anyone I won the money, did ya?'

"Course not. What do you take us for?"

"Just with me and Claire splittin', I want to get that sorted before I collect the money."

"I never took my cousin to be some gold digger… unless you know something I don't."

"Never said that but a lot has changed in the last week. I don't want her to leave me but this is all confusin'."

Jackie shifted uncomfortably in his chair.

"Donny, you two have been together since we were kids. Don't you want her to stay? Maybe telling her isn't such a bad thing if that's a surefire way of making her stay with ya."

"Dunno. Did a lot of thinkin'. If she didn't want me when I was poor, maybe to hell with her."

Jackie sighed loudly, removing his ball cap to irritably claw his head.

"Yer puttin' me in an awkward spot, Donny. I can't be lyin' to her for too long."

"I know, I know. Look, I got an appointment with one of the lawyers in town tomorrow. I'm going to sort this out before it goes too far down the road."

"Jesus, Donny, in your condition you won't be able to get out of bed tomorrow let alone drive all the way to Newcastle and meet with that lad."

Donny fell into a coughing fit, one that rattled his chest so badly he clutched at it, ending with a gasp for air. He grabbed his handkerchief, red with white polka dots, and wiped his mouth and nose.

"I spoke to the lawyer on the phone about it this morning. He said he'd come to me, if necessary, he was so hungry for his payment on working the file or whatever they call it. I also spoke to the lotto people and they said I have a year so I can get things sorted out with me and Claire and collect it afterwards."

Jackie removed his ball cap again and brushed the sweat away with the back of his forearm.

"Sounds a little shady to me but it's your money and your

marriage. Just don't expect me to go around lyin' for ya for too long. Get this sorted and get yerself on your feet."

"That's the plan."

Donny took a hard look at Jackie.

"Is that one of my beers?"

Parts of those booms were still visible as deadheads in the water, splintered reminders of an era lost to the minds of television watchers and Walkman listeners.

WEDNESDAY PASSED like any other day except that Donny had not returned to work. Jackie had gotten up early and went to the mill, rowing home without stopping in at Donny's place. He spent the evening drinking beer on his back step, watching Ruby gleefully chase after crows and robins. As he downed his third Alpine, a fox appeared at the edge of the trees. Ruby murmured a low growl. Jackie rose from his seat and grabbed her collar to make certain she didn't take off after the crafty predator. The fox flirted with the idea of coming closer to snatch a robin but retreated sharply back to the forest behind his house.

On Thursday, Jackie rose from bed and paddled to the mill. Ruby sat in the front, sticking her nose in the water sporadically to see what lay below the murky depths of the river. Jackie would occasionally cast his gaze to the water but it often jarred his nerves to look into the dark river.

He walked into the mill yard to begin his workday, and quickly realized there was still no Donny. He had not checked on him since that Tuesday evening, avoiding Donny's house for two reasons: he did not want to catch a cold, and the gnawing knowledge that Donny had won half a million dollars and planned to keep it from his wife.

On Friday, a peeved Mr. Sutherland approached Jackie.

"Where's Donny at? He's not been here all week and every time Mrs. Sutherland calls, she doesn't get an answer. He alive or what?"

"He was the other day," Jackie said as he pulled a portion of cedar out of the planer. "Haven't been in since, Mr. Sutherland. I wouldn't want to catch what he has."

"Boyd? Paddy? You seen Donny?"

Boyd did not look up from his work. "No, sir. I haven't been down that way."

"I've been busy getting my new truck ready, Mr. Sutherland. But maybe I can take a drive down this evening after work," answered Paddy.

Mr. Sutherland appeared to not hear him and turned his attention back to Jackie.

"Ain't Claire your cousin? Where is she?"

"Seems she's got herself a job sellin' stuff door-to-door. First I heard of it was the other night."

"Door-to-door? Like vacuums? What's she sellin'? Make-up?"

"Vitamins."

"Vitamins?"

"Like in a pill or somethin'," Jackie said with a shrug.

"Vitamins? Just get a good feed of greens into ya, that's all the vitamins a lad needs, right? Not some pilled form of hippie garbage."

"Couldn't agree more, Mr. Sutherland."

"And she ain't around in the evenings?"

Jackie gently put down the piece of cedar he had in his hands and drug his dusty forearm across his brow.

"Well sir, if I gotta be honest, I don't think things are going too well between Donny and Claire. Don't want to gossip but sounds like she's leaving him."

Mr. Sutherland looked around to see if anyone was listening. "She's leaving *him*?" he asked with a cocked eyebrow. "What do you mean? Where's she going to go?"

Jackie shrugged. "I don't know, sir. Like I said, not my place and don't want to get involved in any of it. Don't think anyone's being harmed, so thought best to mind my business."

Mr. Sutherland lowered his head and nodded. "Just so.

Best to stay out of that racket, even if she is your cousin. Look, if you hear of him, you gotta tell him that if he's not here on Monday, I'm gonna have to lay him off. There are other lads around that need work. I'm not runnin' no fuckin' charity here. Runnin' a business." He slapped his neck angrily, squashing a mosquito.

Jackie nodded. "A lad's gotta be responsible for his actions."

Mr. Sutherland pressed his index finger against one nostril and blew a glob of snot from the other into the sawdust. "Good enough, then."

Mr. Sutherland walked away, leaving Jackie to his work with Boyd. Jackie sometimes hated being paired up with Boyd. He considered himself a hard worker and did not stop for much, other than for lunch or to use the restroom. Boyd was also a hard worker, but due to his height, Boyd had the ability to work much faster. For all of the difficulties that sometimes plagued Boyd, he was the hardest worker at the mill. Much of the work performed was done at table height or lower and Boyd could simply pick up lumber with ease and keep going, never having to bend over. This saved him both time and a good deal of pain in his back. Jackie, on the other hand, was well over six feet tall and ended most days with a sore lower back.

Mr. Sutherland had often stated if he had 10 Boyds, he would not need anyone else. When Jackie asked what would Mr. Sutherland do if those shorter men needed something high up and couldn't reach, Mr. Sutherland replied, "I'd just hang all the tools and everything down low." It was difficult to go against that line of thinking. Thankfully for Jackie and the other men, there was only one Boyd in the area.

Jackie did not stop at Donny's house on his way home, even though he did want to know if he was feeling any better. He had some deliveries to make for Mike and that was going to take him most of the evening. One person lived all the way down in Strathadam and wanted two quarts of Five Star Whisky.

One of Jackie's methods for transporting booze was to stash it on the old booms in the middle of the river on his way to work. Whatever supplies he picked up from Mike and had to deliver, he could take them out in the canoe in the morning, hide them amongst the shrubbery on the old booms and he would not have to go back on land to get whatever he needed to deliver that night. He made pit stops at the booms (there were only six that qualified as booms) – just pick up the alcohol and keep going. In the summer, nobody was on the water that early in the day when he stashed it and anyone driving by was too far away to observe what he was doing. In the winter, it was almost easier since he could store the liquor in the snow on the booms themselves as he skated by.

The old booms had not been in use since the late 1950s, when companies like Fraser's or Burchill's started trucking the logs down from the northwest or southwest branches of the Miramichi River. The booms, constructed out of wood and soil decades prior, were used to collect and direct logs harvested by men far upriver. Those logs were then transported and sent miles downriver, right in front of where Jackie grew up. He used to watch his uncle Francis work the booms. Jackie was young but could clearly recall standing on the riverbank, looking on with fascination as his uncle and the other lumberjacks steered the logs. The men would go from boom to boom, deftly leaping with acrobatic agility onto slippery logs, ensuring they aligned properly to be dispatched to the lumber companies in town. It was essential to direct the logs to their owner's respective booms, each log identified by its own patented timber mark. Fraser's, with their noticeable green boats, would use the same-coloured mark on their logs, while Burchill's would use blue to differentiate. It was a tried-and-true method that had worked for many years.

Mr. Sutherland's sawmill operation used these same logs, coming down river to the shores of his operation. It was part of the reason Mr. Sutherland's operation had been highly successful: he had no transportation costs getting the logs to his mill. All he needed was the tides and lots of water and as far as everyone was concerned, there would always be lots of deep water in the Miramichi River.

Even after heavy trucking started, the log drives and booms were still used into the 1960s, but in the early summer of 1961, there was an unforgiving rainstorm. The wind and water caused severe damage to the booms, or in some cases, washed them away completely. Combined with modern day transportation methods, log driving was abandoned and the booms left to rot in the middle of the river. Today, parts of those booms were visible as deadheads in the water, splintered reminders of an era lost to the minds of television watchers and Walkman listeners.

ooooo

Jackie had a good system in place to transport and deliver booze for Mike. He did not intend to miss deliveries because Donny was sick or having marriage troubles.

Jackie whistled sharply and Ruby came bounding towards him from the nearby forest.

"Good girl," he said, then threw her a piece of ham rind.

Ruby stood in place as Jackie pushed off with his paddle. He twisted the paddle until he course-corrected. He began paddling away from the mill and toward the second boom in from the north, 400 yards away. The sun beating strongly at his back, Jackie drove his oar into the water, propelling the canoe downriver.

"Have you been giving him tea?"

JACKIE AND CLAIRE had always been close as children and grew even closer after she and Donny got married. When they were small, they played together nearly every day, their fathers being brothers and working the booms on the river in front of Jackie's home. Claire was dropped off in the early morning and Francis would set out onto the river to collect and mark logs for Fraser's. Henry would go to the sawmill and Jackie's mother would watch over him and Claire for the day.

Jackie's mother would put the children outside and tell them to go play and not return until lunch. Their midday meal normally consisted of a slice of homemade brown bread slathered with butter and a drizzle of molasses, half of a Granny Smith apple, one *junk* of cheese and a glass of water. A cold glass of lemonade appeared in the summertime, if the children were lucky. After eating, they would run off again and not return until suppertime, when Francis would come off the water, typically have a beer with Jackie's father and pick up Claire, repeating the process the following day; and the day after that and the day after that.

Jackie had fond memories of playing with Claire by the brooks that ran on either side of his father's land. Springer's Brook ran on the southwest side of the property. It was large and not played in as much. Occasionally, though, Henry would whittle down some branches, tie some fishing line on them and attach a hook, so the children could try and catch the small trout that periodically swam the tributary.

They tended to play in the brook on the northwest side of the land, always referred to as "Little Brook." This stream was the playground of Jackie's childhood. They would run to Little Brook where he and Claire would spend hours in their own world under the partial shade of the spruce, pine and poplar trees, shims of sunlight slashing through the branches and leaves. They would take heaping gulps of water directly from the brook when they got thirsty, the water so cold it hurt their faces. Here they would play all the games imaginable: Cops and Robbers, Kick the Can, Red Rover. When they reached the age of 10, Claire wanted to play a new game: House. House was Jackie's least favourite game, since it made him feel queer to be married to his cousin, even if it was fictitious. He knew it was weird to be married to your cousin, unless you were from certain parts of the river. While Jackie and Claire played the married couple, Donny was cast as mailman, milkman or a variety of other roles, including police inspector should a murder have taken place at their make-believe home by the brook. Boyd was always cast as their son or in one case, the dog. That was the last time Boyd came to play with them at the brook.

On days when the weather was too hot, Henry and Francis would be relieved of work early. They would come to the homestead and open beers mid-afternoon, a pile of bottles collecting in a shaded spot by suppertime. Jackie's father would set up an old board with a loosely drawn target. Henry would bring out his bow and arrows and attempt to instruct the children on the finer points of using a bow. It was difficult in the beginning. The children lacked strength in their arms and hands but after a number of practices, Claire improved, hitting the target on occasion. Jackie also proved to be very proficient with a bow. It came to him naturally. Donny, less so. Boyd did not participate in archery but would sit with Francis, who taught him the finer points of whittling a stick.

∞∞∞

On Sunday night, Claire called Jackie.

"Donny's awful sick," Claire began.

"I know he is. Hasn't been to work all week. Mr. Sutherland's going to lay him off."

"It's worse than that, Jackie. I just came over to check on him. He's got a real bad cough. I think he has the croup."

"Have you been giving him tea?"

"I haven't been around. You know why. He told you we were separatin'. I've been away most days, trying to sell my products and giving Donny a little space to come to terms with things. I've been spending most nights at my mother's."

"You two can't work this all out, Claire?"

"Jackie, there's a lot to it all. And it ain't like you to get involved."

"I know, I know. Just asking."

"Anyways it's more serious than a cold now. I think we need to take Donny to the outpatients."

"I tried to get him to go on Tuesday but he wouldn't go. Want me to come with you?"

"D'ya mind? I don't think I can get him to the truck by myself."

"All good. I'll be over directly."

"I'll drive over and bring you here and then we'll head to the hospital. It'll be faster than waitin' for you."

"Good enough."

Claire hung up. The loneliness of the dial tone made Jackie shiver. He sighed theatrically, being put out of his quiet Sunday evening to go to the hospital. He had an exciting night planned of doing nothing. Now, he had to go to the damned outpatients with Claire and Donny.

He filled a bowl full of scraps and some dry food for Ruby, tied up his beaten brown boots and grabbed his summer mackinaw. It was a fine evening and he decided to wait for Claire outside.

He lit a cigarette as he waited in the dusk of early Summer. The situation with Donny sounded dire and Jackie was feeling a barb of regret for not having checked on him throughout the week.

"But where do they go? Out the window?"

JACKIE HEARD THE PHLEGMY MUFFLER from Donny's truck approaching a quarter of a mile away. He watched Claire pull into the dooryard, the tires crackling on the dry dirt. They sped back to Claire's house without uttering a word.

They laid a blanket down in the truck's open bed, so Donny could have some fresh air. Once they'd helped him into the back of the truck and set a blanket atop him, they set off for town.

Jackie left the rear window open so they could hear him if he needed anything. It was 7:07 PM, and it was still 82 degrees.

Claire drove the rutted highway quickly. This early in

the summer, the sun was high and the blue sky never ending. Jackie took in a deep breath, allowing all the fortunes of summer through his nose, the rich smell of thick leaves on poplar and maple trees, the scent of cow manure as they drove through Whitneyville, then the fresh smell of Little Millstream and the large brook that flowed into it. He drew out a cigarette from the pack and cupped his hands to light it. The windows were down all the way on both sides and the summer wind was blowing fiercely.

"There's no finer place, is there?" Jackie said, attempting to break the silence.

"It sure is pretty around here in summer," Claire said, a smile breaking through her worry.

"It's pretty all year. Ya just have to know how to find the beauty."

"Never looked too beautiful to me at thirteen below in January."

Jackie chuckled. "Well, you don't skate enough like I do. The river has plenty of prettiness when you're skating on it. The quiet when nobody else is on it in the middle of the winter is one of my favourite things."

Claire only nodded, then looked in the rear-view mirror to see if Donny was still back there.

"He ain't gonna float away. Lad weighs two hundred pounds, Claire."

"I know that. I'm just lookin' in on him, is all."

"He's gonna be okay. He's as sturdy as that old pine tree we can see from our place across the river."

"That one blew down last year."

"No, not the one down by Bryenton's. The one up from that a little."

Claire slightly acknowledged she knew which giant pine tree. There were several of them visible on the south side of the river from where they lived. Her mouth was twisted with concern.

Jackie could feel the worry pouring out of her skin. She

might have been able to defeat him at crib but she had no poker face. He quickly maneuvered to change the subject to anything but a sickly Donny in the bed of the truck.

"So, what're these drugs you're selling to folks?"

"They're not drugs, Jackie. They're supplements. They help you feel better. Did you know we only receive three out of the eight natural minerals and two out of the twelve natural sugars we should have each day from the food we eat? That's where the supplements come in. They fill that gap."

"Sounds to me like you should eat some more Swiss chard."

"It's not like that. Our food is so over-processed these days, the vitamins get taken right out."

"Not the ones that come out of my vegetable garden."

"Well no, that's different. I mean the ones we see at the SuperValu or wherever."

"I don't have nothing to worry about then because the only thing I buy from there is Crosby's Molasses or them doughnuts from down Sussex way that they don't carry at the convenience store up home."

Claire pushed the button for car lighter. "Even still, you should try some of the vitamins and powders. If you feel good, maybe these'll make you feel even better. Vitamins get taken out of everything."

"Where do they go?"

"Where does what go?"

"The vitamins."

"The processing takes 'em out."

"But where do they go? Out the window?"

"Look, don't be cute." The button popped and she put a cigarette in her mouth before removing the lighter. The red-hot metal lit the cigarette immediately and smoke puffed from her lips.

"I have scientific proof this works. Literature that explains it. I've only just started and I have a lot to learn but I know after six months of taking them, I've never had more energy in my life. I'll even give you a jar of the protein powder for free to start with."

"You know something? Gimme a jar and I'll let you know if I start swimming the channel next week."

Claire rolled her eyes.

"Don't be such a shit. Just because something is new, doesn't mean it's bad, ya know?"

"Yeah yeah. Good enough. I'm just not one for taking things that ain't good for me."

Jackie crushed his cigarette out in the overflowing ashtray. It would be dangerous to throw it out the window when the weather was this dry.

∞∞∞

They pulled the battered truck next to the door at the hospital outpatients, the burning red lights of EMERGENCY hurting Jackie's eyes. A walk from the parking lot would have been too much for Donny, so when Claire threw the gear shift into park and applied the brake, Jackie was already out of the truck and lowering the tailgate.

"You get him up. I'm runnin' in to get a wheelchair," said Claire.

Jackie hoisted himself up on the bed and started to move Donny.

"Okay Donny, we're gonna get you into the doctor's and they'll fix you up," Jackie whispered to his friend. He was not truly concerned until he hopped on the truck's bed. Donny's breathing was much more labored than when they'd left Boom Road and he was feverish, his face the colour of deep clay.

Claire returned with two orderlies and a nurse. As they whisked Donny away, Claire and Jackie stood there, abandoned by the staff. Jackie took out a smoke and lit it.

"Well, we may as well find ourselves a seat inside. Looks like we could be here for a spell," said Jackie.

Claire did not seem to hear him. She hugged herself and

stared vacantly at the Emergency doors. A looming darkness fell on them as the hot sun mercifully disappeared behind a row of pines.

"He'll be alright, Claire. Donny's a stout lad and he's in the best place possible."

"I hope you're right."

"You'll see. They'll have Donny in one of those embarrsin' no ass 'Johnny shirts' in no time and we'll be laughin' 'bout it later."

Claire took no notice of the joke. She looked absently around the nearly empty parking lot.

"Let's have a seat. I'll get ya some coffee from the cafeteria," Jackie offered.

"Tea please, if they have it."

"Tea it be, then."

"Friend of the family."

LONG AFTER JACKIE AND CLAIRE finished their second cups of coffee and tea respectively, Jackie was close to completing a crossword puzzle he had found in yesterday's newspaper. Most of the books in the waiting room were abandoned by previous poor souls left to stew in the sitting area, wondering how bad the break in the arm was for their son, if their husband's heart attack was serious, or if their mother was going to die of emphysema. Jackie had picked through the books and found mostly Louis L'Amour or Harlequin novels. A couple were from someone named Stephen King and Jackie thought he would get nightmares simply from reading the summary on the jacket.

A plethora of magazines littered the room – *National Geographic*, *MacLean's*, *Newsweek*. Someone had previously attempted the crossword he was working on. Jackie had already decided that person was a fool for starting it with a pen rather than a pencil.

The waiting room was nearly empty but for a few

unfortunate souls. A young man appeared to have a leg or ankle injury. He was reading an old copy of *MacLean's*, which had a photo of John Crosbie on the cover, from when he was Joe Clark's Minister of Finance. Jackie thought at the time there may not have been a more ridiculous choice than John Crosbie to run the finances of the country but Clark had at least selected someone from Atlantic Canada, which hardly ever happened for that post. Crosbie wasn't in the post long enough to even screw up. Joe Clark had miscalculated on a vote and his whip, Bill Kempling, could not even sort out how many MPs they had in the House of Commons. Kempling's ineptness allowed the NDP and Liberals to defeat them. *What a bunch of clowns*, Jackie thought.

Gazing around the room, Jackie's eyes stopped on a woman directly across from them. She snored at full volume, her head slack against the back of the chair and her mouth wide open, making a noise similar to Donny's muffler. Jackie wanted to walk over to the triage station, grab some gauze and stuff it down her throat. He decided against it and kept shifting loudly in his chair, coughing and clearing his throat with great theatrics and intermittently stamping his feet. The woman snored away.

Close to midnight, a doctor approached. He wore light green pants with a similar V-neck shirt but a traditional doctor's white coat over top, and stethoscope around his neck. The breast pocket of his smock carried a red pen and a black pen, along with a frayed notebook, bits of paper hanging out around the rings. Jackie took one glance at him thought he looked like he climbed right out of a TV show. The doctor was striking, with sandy brown hair and enough stubble on his face that practically gave him a beard. A person could draw a straight line with the doctor's jaw. The clinician's green eyes beamed from his face, although Jackie did not see kindness in the way he was looking. He saw only judgment.

Claire had nodded off, head resting awkwardly back in the uncomfortable, heavy blue hospital chair. Jackie nudged her on the elbow once, then a little harder, and put down his puzzle when she stirred. They both rose to their feet when the doctor reached them.

"Are you Mr. McGivney's wife?"

Claire blinked. "Yes, I am. Technically," she said self-consciously."

The doctor offered a strange look to Jackie. "And you are?"

"Friend of the family."

"Well ma'am, are you comfortable with him hearing this, too?" The doctor jerked his thumb at Jackie.

"Young lad, I'm staying right where I am."

"He can stay. He's my cousin."

Claire and Jackie sat down and the doctor dragged a loose chair over to them. The snoring woman had been woken by the discussion and moved away to a back corner. *Good riddance, you manatee,* thought Jackie.

"Mrs. McGivney, I'm Doctor Piers." He paused, looked at his notes and then raised his eyes. "Your husband is very ill. He has pneumonia and the state of his condition is quite prolonged. He certainly should have been to the hospital or at least seen by a physician a number of days ago. Was nobody with him during this time?"

Claire looked down, embarrassed. "We both tried to get him to see a doctor earlier this week but he wouldn't go."

"She was away working and I thought he just had a bad cold," said Jackie. Claire shifted nervously in her seat.

"When can he come home?" asked Claire.

"I don't think you understand what I'm saying."

Jackie interrupted. "Then just say it! No need to pussy-foot about. Christ almighty." He was surprised by the amount of worry in his own voice. The whole situation was surreal. The painful fluorescent lights, the smell of disinfectant, the chatter from nurses and doctors who didn't seem to care if people were sick. Laughter echoed in the distance from the triage station.

"Ma'am, your husband has been intubated."

"What's that mean?"

"It means he can no longer breathe on his own."

Claire let out a gasp.

"I'm sorry to tell you this but his condition is beyond treatment. It's a miracle he's lasted as long has he did. We're not expecting him to regain consciousness."

Claire and Jackie stared at the doctor.

"What?" replied Claire. "Isn't there anything you can do? There must be *something* you can do?"

She was on her feet now. Jackie removed his ball cap.

"Can't ya give him some medication or something?" a panicked Jackie asked.

"I'm afraid the inflammation is very pronounced and he required urgent medical assistance days ago. I assume Mr. McGivney smoked, as well?"

Claire absently nodded her head. Jackie stood up and began pacing, his hat in his hand. He scratched his head harshly, agitatedly.

"That would have contributed to his current state. I am sorry to be the bearer of this news but you may want to call your priest or minister. I apologize for being so blunt but he may not last much longer."

Jackie sat down, his head hanging low. Claire stared distractedly at the floor.

Doctor Piers lowered his head to fall within Claire's vision. "We've done all we can to make sure he's as comfortable as he can be. Would you like to see him?" he asked.

Claire nodded. She held Jackie's arm and they followed the doctor down the pea-green hallway. Jackie wanted to run toward Donny, and to run away from all of this. It felt as though none of it was happening, but only real life could be this painful.

"Where's his underwear?"

DONNY'S HEART GAVE OUT AT 1:17 AM, June 28, 1982. Father Alcide LeBlanc attended to Last Rights. Their normal priest from St. Agatha's Roman Catholic Parish, Father Arthur McKay, could not be reached. The late hour proved to be a problem when contacting the old clergyman. He was 73 and known to drink a considerable amount of rum most evenings. They had called three times from one of the hospital's pay phones, spending a dime each time, since Red Bank was considered out of the area code to dial from Chatham. Jackie disliked spending so much money on calls but Claire had made it clear she wanted Father McKay. Alas, not even an ear-splitting telephone call on a hard black rotary phone could wake him. Father LeBlanc was the pastor on-call for the hospital and Claire decided that *a* priest was better than *no* priest.

Claire cried when the young nurse affirmed that Donny had indeed died. Father LeBlanc blessed the room solemnly and said the Lord's Prayer, Hail Mary, Glory Be to the Father and the Apostle's Creed. Jackie removed his hat and stood solemnly until the priest from Baie St. Anne offered his condolences to Claire by holding her hand and patting it a few times. When he left, Jackie felt his legs go weak. He sat down on a chair with coarse and frayed pink fabric, the metal frame badly chipped. Jackie sat there, across from his old friend. The narrow blue lines from the bedding traced across Donny's toes. The reduced neon lighting buzzed a melancholy din. The room was a very comfortable temperature.

Only a week ago, he had been dousing Jackie in the canoe. *Oh shit*, Jackie thought, the realization hitting him. Donny had caught pneumonia that very night, later going home to fall asleep in front of the big fan. It was too much for him.

He teared up then began sobbing, the first time in years.

Jackie continued to sit while Claire stood over Donny and wept, stroking his forehead, smoothing back his thick strawberry blonde hair. A nurse quietly ducked her head in a few short minutes after. Claire did not notice but Jackie looked up and stared at her. It was not a harsh look but one of bereavement, a plea in his eyes that said, "Please give us a few more minutes." The nurse nodded and silently moved out of view.

Jackie did not know how to proceed. It did not feel right

to leave Donny alone in the room. *Who will look after him?* Jackie gave Claire a few more minutes before standing up and touching her gently on the forearm, signaling it was time for them to go. Jackie walked over to the Donny's body. He gave Donny a couple of pats on the arm, the mottling of his skin already turning the flesh a blueish hue, then shambled out of the room to allow Claire a final goodbye.

A moment later, she joined him in the blinding light of the hallway, a plastic grocery bag in tow.

They ambled to the truck with Donny's belongings. Jackie had offered to take the bag but Claire clutched it close to her breast.

When they got to the truck, Claire lowered the tailgate and dumped the bag out, spreading the items across the metal bed. The clattering of Donny's belongings echoed against the dead of night in the void parking lot.

They regarded the pieces of Donny that remained. All he had on him when he was admitted was his blue and black plaid shirt with pearl snap buttons, his green John Deere cap, grey pants with a worn leather belt and black socks along with his old sneakers. In his pants pocket were his jackknife, a lighter (Jackie was sure it was his), and $2.73 that had been loose in his front right pocket and his wallet.

"Hold 'er. Where's his underwear?" asked Jackie.

"He never wore them much."

"Wha?"

"Said it was always too hot, too uncomfortable to wear them. They bunched up."

"Wha? For how long?"

"For how long, what?"

"For how long *hasn't* he been wearin' any underwear?"

"All his life, far as I know."

"Wait. Bunched up? Why didn't he wear briefs? Why am I having this conversation? Jesus!"

"He didn't like how clingy the briefs were, neither."

Jackie shook his head. "You think you know a lad and

then you find out he weren't even wearin' no goddamn underwear when he was sittin' next to you your whole life? The man's been commando the whole time!"

Claire let a giggle slip.

Jackie turned to her with surprise and then chuckled.

In seconds, they were both howling with laughter in the empty parking lot, unable to stop themselves. At one point, Claire could not catch her breath and Jackie thought he might pee his pants. It was the kind of laughter where there is barely a sound, occasional wheezes and squeaks.

They regained their composure, wiping their eyes, settling into the hardship of reality. Claire withdrew a tissue and began crying once more. Jackie put his arm around her, silent tears skittering down his cheeks. Claire scooped up the belongings, putting the change and bills in her purse, along with the jackknife. Jackie grabbed the lighter.

Claire started the ignition and they began driving through Chatham toward home. Jackie lit a smoke, absently watching the dark scenery go by. Two miles into the drive, Claire pulled over.

"What's going on?"

"I can't drive. I don't feel well."

Jackie opened the passenger door, casting shadows as he walked around in front of the headlights and opened the driver side door. He gently moved Claire over to the passenger side and he got behind the wheel.

"I didn't think you could drive?" she said.

"Of course I can. I just hate it. I'm too cantankerous to do so unless it's necessary."

Claire put her forehead to the window and abstractedly looked at the interwoven coniferous and deciduous trees passing by in the dark.

Jackie was afraid to drive fast, given his own precarious emotional state and the fact he had not driven a car in years. At 25 miles per hour they crawled to Boom Road, where they both stayed at Claire's house. She could not bear to spend the night alone and Jackie was too tired to go any further. They entered the house without words. Claire immediately retired to the bedroom. Jackie grabbed a beer from the fridge and sat on the tan wingback chair in the living room. It was Donny's chair, the groove of his ass cemented in the seat cushion.

Claire must have left the television on. Flickering images of fighter jets, the RCMP musical ride, a hockey game between the Leafs and Canadiens and several other symbols of national pride fluttered by while an instrumental version of "O Canada" blared in the background. The SMPTE colour bars followed, filling the room with nothingness. Jackie felt hollow and alone. He took down the beer in three gulps, grabbed a throw pillow off the couch, crawled onto the floor and tumbled into dreamless sleep.

ooooo

AT 9:00 AM, Jackie woke on the floor of Donny and Claire's house. He was covered in sweat. Unnerved, he phoned the office and received a terse greeting from Mrs. Sutherland, but she quickly changed her tone when Jackie told her what had happened.

"That's tantamount to communism."

JACKIE SHOWED UP FOR WORK early the following day, given that he had taken Monday off. All of the men, including Mr. Sutherland, shook Jackie's hand and offered commiserations. Everyone at the mill, Boyd Meeks, Paddy Brewster, Mr. Sutherland and the rest, all knew and liked Donny but they were all well aware of the close friendship he and Jackie had. Even Boyd did not have the same bond Jackie and Donny.

The day slogged on. Jackie got perturbed by the intermittent condolences. Men would occasionally come to him and say they were sorry, interrupting his work. It was not that Donny did not deserve the tributes but Jackie was racked with guilt and wished he could step into a time machine and go back eight days.

At lunchtime, the men stopped to eat; as usual, the radio prattled in the break room. No one ever turned off the radio, it seemed. Perpetual Canadian white noise.

There were no daily newspapers in the area. When the hour struck 12:15, obituaries were read aloud by a commentator from the local radio station, CFAN. If another earthquake were to hit for those five to seven minutes when the deaths were announced, not a single person along the Miramichi River would notice. The day was warm as the men paused in advance of the obituaries. They could only hear the disc jockey rambling and the hum of grasshoppers.

"Maher's Funeral Home announces the passing of Mr. William Donald "Donny" McGivney of Boom Road. Son of the late Mervin and Alice McGivney. Survived by his wife Claire McGivney (nee O'Connor). Visitation will be held on June 29th from 2-4 and 7-9. Mass of Christian burial to take place at St. Agatha's Roman Catholic Church in Red Bank on June 30th at 11:00 AM, with Father Arthur McKay presiding. As per the wishes of the family, expressions of sympathy can be made to St. Agatha's Roman Catholic Church, the Knights of Columbus Hall in Sunny Corner or the Miramichi Salmon Alliance. I repeat…"

In each instance, a second reading of the same death was necessary due to people often not catching the entirety of the obituary the first time. Their exclamations of "No! Not so-and-so!" made for a great deal of discussion and residents missed the finer details of when and where the recently deceased would be laid to rest. On the rare occasion there were no deaths to report, it put most listeners into a state of indignation.

At the end of the obituaries (there were two other deaths, both from Newcastle way and nobody at the mill knew them), Boyd turned the volume down on the radio. Mr. Sutherland had joined them in the break room. Jackie was quite certain it was the first time in 22 years he had seen him fraternize with the men in this manner.

"I guess I'll have to shut the mill down for a couple of hours, since all his pall bearers work here. Christ almighty."

The break room remained silent. The clicking of grasshoppers beyond the mill yard was the only sound.

"Well, she sure sounds like it's gonna be a big funeral, anyway," said Paddy Brewster, peeling a Granny Smith. Jackie had witnessed Paddy use the same knife to pick his fingernails five minutes ago and took note he neglected to clean the blade between activities.

"What makes you say that?" said Boyd.

"Wha?"

"What makes you think it'll be a big turnout at the funeral?"

"You just heard the guy on the radio: *massive* Christian burial."

Jackie just stared at Paddy for a second before speaking.

"Are you that jeezless stupid or are you stoned again?"

"Huh?"

"It's *mass of* Christian burial, Paddy. Not massive," said Boyd.

"But don't ya expect a lot of people to go? Wouldn't that be massive anyway?"

"How the fuck should I know how many people are coming?" exclaimed Jackie. "I suppose three hundred people could show or it might be three people. I don't have tabs on how many people plan to attend a funeral the day before Dominion Day!"

"It's Canada Day now, Jackie," piped in Boyd.

"I don't care if it's 'Diddly-Damn-Go-Fuck-Yerself Day', Boyd!"

Jackie took one last drag off his cigarette, ran it under some water before throwing it in the trash can and storming away.

"Well, what does 'mass of' mean?" asked Paddy to nobody in particular.

Boyd, ignoring Paddy, spoke to Mr. Sutherland. "Mr.

Sutherland, not to tell ya what to do sir but you might want to consider giving Jackie the rest of the week off."

"Paid?"

"I think it would be a good gesture."

"I'll have to think about that. No charity here. That's tantamount to communism."

"I'm not askin'. I'm tellin'. Sit down."

JACKIE WAS PACKING UP HIS GEAR at the end of the day when Boyd, Paddy and a few other men pulled up blocks of wood and chairs and formed a semi-circle in the mill yard. Boyd was unable to locate his step stool and settled for a stump made of spruce. They all opened a few beers. Jackie made for an exit.

"Where ya goin'?" asked Boyd.

"Home."

"Come on, Jackie. We were all Donny's friends, too. I was with you last week, remember? Sit down and have a drink. We haven't had the chance to send him off."

"We're sending him off at the funeral. That's what funerals are for."

"In our own way. You know what I mean. Sit down."

"Not in the mood. Need to get home and feed Ruby. And I have to make some deliveries for Mike this evenin'."

"I'm not askin'. I'm tellin'. Sit down," pressed Boyd.

Jackie sighed and turned his head to Boyd. He did not have the energy to argue and if Boyd Meeks asked you for something, it was important. Boyd rarely asked anyone for anything except for the occasional drive. Jackie hung his head, setting his bag and lunch box on the hot dirt. He could tell he was not getting out of here without at least one beer. In fact, he wanted nothing *more* than a cold beer but he was dreading the talk that would inevitably come with the social beer. He relented, walking over to the shed and dragging a rough pine bench over to the makeshift half-circle. Jackie sat and Paddy reached down into the bottom of the communal cooler. It was old and was not well insulated but the beer never had time to get warm. Paddy handed a bottle to Jackie, wiping the water on his sleeve. Jackie opened it with his teeth. He took his first sip and instantly relaxed.

"So, who's all pall bearin'?" asked Boyd.

"Me, you, Paddy, Clive Estey, Fred Menzies who went fishin' with Donny all the time on the Renous River and Claire's cousin on the other side, Bobby Gilks."

"Who's doin' the readin's and whatnot?"

"I don't know, Boyd. I only told Claire I'd help out with the pallbearers and whatever other way I could. I'm sure we'll find all that out in the program."

Boyd grunted. He was already cracking his second beer.

"Well, I didn't know him as long as the rest of ya's but Mr. McGivney treated me awful well. Never had a bad thing to say about anyone," said Paddy.

The men all nodded. Jackie took another swig of beer. It was already getting warm.

"Except for that time we smoked weed together with Mrs. McGivney," Paddy added with a small chuckle. Then he took a drink as if he had not said anything strange.

"You smoked dope with Donny and Claire?" said a perturbed Jackie.

"Keep yer voices down," said one of the men.

"Mr. Sutherland's gone. It's alright," replied Boyd. He had a grin on his face. "You got Donny and Claire stoned?"

"So, not to be tellin' tales but one night after work here, he asked me if I could get him a joint. He and Mrs. McGivney wanted to try it."

"What happened?" said Boyd. Jackie was doing his best to listen without looking like he was hanging off Paddy's every word.

"Well, weed is a peculiar thing. Most people smoke it and the effect makes them laugh or hungry or sleepy. Or all three."

"That sums up a day in the life of Paddy Brewster, right there," added Jackie.

"But once in awhile it don't sit too well with someone. Sometimes they got too much on their mind or they can't settle into it. Or it just doesn't agree with them. Like liquor – sometimes it don't sit right with people. Seemed like one or all of them things were happening to Mr. McGivney. He got all wigged out. Started hyperventilating and everything after just a few minutes. Spent most of the night on the floor in front of the box fan trying to get himself composed. He cursed and swore a lot, too. That was peculiar."

Boyd started snickering. Most of the men had a laugh on their lips. Jackie sat stoic.

"How did Claire do?"

"Oh, the very best. She had a great laugh. Tears come streamin' down her face a bunch of times just watching Archie Bunker's Place or whatever it's called. Then she cooked up a big feed of leftovers and we ate it. Mr. McGivney was all good after that but he turned an awful shade of grey there for a while when he was on the floor. It was like he was in another dimension and we couldn't reach him."

The men shared a few laughs. Jackie even managed a smirk. A couple of men told their own stories of smoking marijuana. Jackie asked Paddy for another beer.

Boyd began to speak. "Jackie, remember the time when we were teenagers and Donny thought he could float better than everyone because he was a little fatter and jumped off Somers's Bridge? And then he didn't come up because he had those ball bearings in his pockets from work and forgot to take them out before jumping in? David had to dive in after him. Thought he was gonna drown, for sure...."

Though everyone else chuckled, Jackie nodded solemnly, then stood up abruptly. "Look boys, I know we all need to do this a little but I can't right now. I just don't have it in me to sit around and play 'Remember when'. I have to go. We'll see ya's tomorrow." He set the beer on the bench, half empty.

Jackie walked away from the group, hearing the fizzing sound of further beers opening. He strode toward the river to get in his canoe, to the fading sounds of the men walking down memory lane. It was a road he did not want to go down.

"Oh, remember when Donny got scratched by that tomcat that always hung around the mill and then he got so mad he…." Jackie did not hear the rest but knew the story. He was there. He was not prepared to talk about Donny and most definitely did not want to be locked in an emotional prison of nostalgia. He needed to check on Claire before going home.

If she was not permitted to make
sandwiches anymore, she was going to
damage the event in some capacity…

THE DAY OF THE FUNERAL was comparable to the days that proceeded the ceremony. The air was dry and the temperature had risen quickly in the morning. Jackie laid his hand on the roof of the hearse, stinging his calloused palm. Attendees funnelled into the church in the mid-morning sun as he adjusted the cursed black sock creeping down his leg.

Mercifully, the church had oscillating fans to cool the congregation. Jackie had been a pallbearer at a third of funerals for St. Agatha's Roman Catholic Church over the last 20 years. He never darkened a church door for services but when carriage was required to a final resting place, Jackie often got the call.

The service moved along without mishaps, which spooked Jackie. At least one thing went wrong at nearly every funeral he had attended. At his mother's funeral seven years prior, Father Creamer presided and tripped on his vestments, falling flat on his face.

The same could be said for funerals he attended at other places of worship: Pentecost, United Pentecost, Baptist, Calvary Baptist, Presbyterian, United, Anglican, Roman Catholic. It made little difference to him, only that the presiding reverend did their job well and perform the ceremony with dignity. Most did, but on occasion there was a blunder, sometimes from within the dutiful flock. A friend passed away suddenly from a brain aneurysm two years ago. More than three-quarters at the reception succumbed to food poisoning, thanks to Mrs. Sutherland's roast beef sandwiches. She was not allowed to make food for community events after this incident.

Jackie expected Paddy Brewster to be stoned and drop his end of the casket on the stairs, followed by Donny rolling out of the coffin, tumbling onto the road. Thankfully, Paddy did not smoke weed before the service and while the homily by Father McKay was appallingly long for a summer's day, the remainder of the funeral went well. The community heard accounts of how great a person Donny was (true but he could be terribly stupid, Jackie said to himself), how much devotion he had to the church (Jackie knew that was a fib), how he loved Claire (very true) and how he was now with his family in heaven, alongside all the angels and saints and God and Jesus and every other departed soul who had been good enough throughout their lives to be allowed into paradise, depending on who you talked to, what they believed or how much money they gave.

Jackie was the senior pallbearer and he sat at the end of the pew, closest to the casket. Across the aisle sat Claire, her mother, some of her cousins and a handful of close friends. She was quite stoic throughout the funeral, Jackie observed. He knew all the crying had been taken out of her in the days prior and she reserved all her strength for today. His cousin was not one to make a display at a funeral. Her mother however was inconsolable, bellowing croaking sobs more than once. A good number of people could be heard offering up the odd sniffle, the rustling of pockets for handkerchiefs and cough drops. Jackie, seated in the front, had no idea who. It is forbidden to turn around during church ceremonies unless directed. Periodically, he could hear the irreplaceable blare of a snotty nose into tissue. He had to restrain himself from chuckling. He knew it was juvenile but once you attend as many services as he had, you start to find humour in almost anything. Someone behind him sounded like a foghorn.

Nonetheless, sending off his old friend fashioned a lump of sadness in his stomach. He was anxious, too, about the secret Donny had kept. Jackie assumed his cousin was still unaware of the lottery winnings or she would not have fretted over the impending funeral costs. He wanted to tell Claire but also wanted to respect Donny's wishes. *Does the secret all go out the window now that he's dead and she's worried sick about money?* He did not know the legality around the matter and it was turning his stomach sour.

When the ceremony finally ended, Jackie led the pall-bearers in the procession to take Donny to the cemetery. Claire and the rest of the grieving family followed slowly as they made their way down the aisle, the choir singing "How Great Thou Art." Jackie could distinctly hear Mrs. Sutherland singing off-key. If she was not permitted to make sandwiches anymore, she was going to damage the event in some capacity. Jackie caught Boyd stealing glances at their employer's wife.

The beautiful summer weather was a cruel kindness. In their hearts, it felt like it should be raining sideways, the wind chilling them to the bone. Instead, most attendees removed their jackets or fanned themselves with the funeral pamphlet, Donny's face waving back and forth.

Father McKay gave his blessings, interwoven with the cries and tears of the family as the crank lowered the coffin into the earth. Paddy dug out a tissue from the inside pocket of his navy-blue blazer and dabbed his eyes. Mike Emery and Kenny Somers were there as well, though did not seem to be shedding any tears. It looked as though they attended only out of community expectations. Throughout the wakes and all the other proceedings, Mike had barely made an appearance. Jackie had spoken to him shortly after Donny had passed, saying he needed a few days and would not be able to make deliveries. Mike showed his displeasure with hanging up the phone after saying, "The world don't stop turning because one man dies ya know, Jackie."

Jackie was a little surprised at this reaction, but he chalked it up to the summer heat and Mike being perhaps in more pain than usual from his affliction.

He turned his attention away from Mike and the lump-head Kenny Somers. Jackie focused on the burial. It was so hot the inside of the freshly excavated grave had already turned to sand.

That's how we all end up, Jackie thought. *Sand.*

"Shhhh!"

THE RECEPTION THAT FOLLOWED in the church hall was pleasant. The funeral actually *was* a massive Christian burial as Paddy Brewster had mistakenly prophesized, with more than 300 in attendance. Jackie could see the exhaustion on Claire's face. With Donny's parents already passed, she was the only one present to receive condolences, though her mother took turns standing with her at the wake, simply so there was another person in the line. There is a limit to how many times one can hear 'Sorry for your loss,' and 'Thinking of you.'

The Catholic Women's League always took care of the fare at the hall, and when it was wrapping up, they gave Claire the leftover sandwiches, finger foods, squares and other desserts. Claire told them to take the fare for themselves – people had been dropping off heaps of food at her home for days.

The reception was winding down, and with it the clattering of Corelle dishes and laughter though the hall as more and more attendees departed. Jackie always noted how relieved people tend to be at the reception following the rigid ceremony of a funeral.

More cigarettes were lit up outside than inside. The doors on the flanks of the church hall were open to provide a draft in the building. New linoleum flooring had been laid, and the walls painted last year. The ceiling even had new tiles and fluorescent lights. *One thing the church always has money for is itself,* Jackie thought as he gazed around the room. Above an upright Boston piano that weighed 1000 pounds was a photo of Reverend Kevin Matchett. He was the priest at St. Agatha's for 15 years but died due to complications from diabetes in 1960. He was so well liked that when the diocese in Saint John tried to move him out of St. Agatha's to another church, the council and many parishioners wrote the bishop and pleaded to have him stay. Their campaign worked and Fr. Matchett remained until his passing, which was sad but not unexpected at 79 years old. He could play the piano so well, he held concerts in the church hall. In memoriam, the parish council had a photograph of him blown up and erected in the hall, its edges yellow with time, cracking at the corners.

Jackie had enough of this day and was certain Claire felt the same. She was surrounded by four people he did not recognize, but he could see the tension in her face as she struggled to be nice. When he finally caught her eye, he gave a quick uptick of his chin, the unwritten signal they should leave straightaway. She nodded, smiled wearily and quickly wrapped up the four-way conversation.

They exited the church hall together, shuffling toward the truck, saying thank you to those who remained. Claire had left the windows down a touch, though that effort did little to keep the heat out of the cab.

"Thank Jesus that's over with," said Claire as she undid the top button of her blouse. It was black with a hint of green throughout and a clasp around the neck. Her long black skirt was equally smothering. The stifling heat forced Jackie to remove his coat and tie long ago. Once a funeral is over, men can dispose of much of their clothing whereas women must endure the asphyxiating envelope of fashion. Jackie lit a smoke, inhaled deeply and hopped in the passenger side of the truck. They hurriedly rolled the windows down to let the heat out.

He wiped his brow with a handkerchief; the dirt from the dune-like parking lot clung to his face and turned the white cotton fabric to russet. Claire fished in her handbag, retrieved the keys and stuck the truck key in the ignition. Fiery air like the snort of a dragon breathed out of the vents.

"Ow! Goddammit!" Claire yelled.

"What? What?"

"The steering wheel is hot!"

"Jesus."

Father McKay had been passing by at that moment, walking toward the manse. He gave them a rueful look from 20 yards away.

"To Hell that guy," Jackie said through the smoke in his mouth.

"Shhhh!"

"G'way. I'm sure Jesus don't mind too much. We'd have been struck down by now, if so."

Claire let out a chuckle. She drove with one hand, switching between the right and left intermittently until the breeze cooled off the steering wheel enough. Neither of them uttered a word on the drive back to Boom Road.

Claire turned softly into Jackie's driveway, the crunch of tires on hot dirt resonating.

"You sure yer all good? You don't want me to come over or anything?" Jackie asked. "We could have a beer."

"Naw, I'm alright. Just need to sit, although a beer sounds like a good idea. Think there's a couple in the fridge."

"Well, if there isn't, let me know and I'll bring some over to you."

"I will. Listen, thanks for everything. It was a good funeral, wasn't it?"

"Yup. I've attended lots. It was as good as you're going to find. Better than most, honestly."

Claire nodded approvingly.

"Good enough then. You need anything, you give me a ring," said Jackie.

"Good enough. Talk to you later."

Jackie slammed the door. Claire backed out of the dooryard and was soon on her way home, a hand waving out the window. He knew too well the hollowness that awaited her in the empty house. Jackie offered up a half wave and turned to his own home, looking at the door with no stairs, thinking how only six months ago Donny had absentmindedly tumbled out. He snickered and crushed his smoke hard with his shoe into the dry earth. He looked up and saw Ruby eagerly waiting in the window, tail wagging.

*"Hey, I'm told by the believers that
miracles can happen."*

CLAIRE AND JACKIE WERE DRIVING into town for the reading of the last will and testament, as per Donny's wishes. Jackie was unnerved. He knew Donny's reluctance to tell Claire about the lottery winnings. The last thing he needed was to be ensnarled in a family dispute over money. He made enough to live on from the mill and his deliveries for Mike kept him in booze. He did not want or need financial aid from Donny, particularly after he had died so suddenly. Who knew what kind of debt he had put Claire in before his death, let alone the cost of the funeral and everything that went with that process.

The drive to town was soundless on the gloomy summer morning, the sky a deep indigo with a smatterings of white. A heavy thunderstorm was on the horizon and not too far off by Jackie's estimation. A bloated grey and purple cloud sat above them, waiting to burst. The wind had picked up and every breath Jackie took was filled with electricity.

"It's not for me to question why Donny wanted you there," said Claire finally, restless with the silence. Jackie could tell she was confused about why he was invited. Not only confused but irritated.

"Look, Claire. You and Donny were on the outs. He confided something to me that you're going to find out today and I just want you to know I never meant for any of this to happen."

"Were ya's gay or somethin'? Christ, is that it?"

"What? What? No. No! It's nothin' like that! Jesus

Murphy! What made ya think that?"

"I read about it in the *Daily Gleaner*. It happened last year. This woman was married forty years and had no idea her husband had a male companion the whole time. They even had three grown kids together. Imagine!"

"Who had three grown kids? The man and woman or the man and man?"

Claire took her eyes off the road, peering at Jackie over her sunglasses.

"Hey, I'm told by the believers that miracles can happen."

"The man and woman, Jackie. Jesus."

"Well, it ain't that! Jesus, Claire."

"Whatever it is, I'm sure it will work out alright."

Jackie remained quiet. He was not so sure it *would* work out all right.

"It's past 9 o'clock. The day is half gone!"

THEY SAT IMPATIENTLY in the waiting room at the lawyer's office. Jackie read the sign on the door, propped open with a brass paperweight in the shape of a rabbit.

Stenciled in gold on the frosted window read *J. Walter Mayhew, Barrister & Solicitor.*

"GD crook" is what should be written there, Jackie thought.

The bleeping telephone annoyed Jackie. It had a strange sound for an alert. It reminded him of one of those ray guns on that outer space show from a couple of years ago, Buck Rogers. He thought the telephone resembled an operation board at a nuclear power plant: big with all kinds of switches and lights and push button numbers on it. Jackie figured the phone was for show. There was only one lawyer here and one secretary.

The young assistant picked up the phone, nodded a few times in affirmation, made a note with her pen in the simple brown planner laid out on her desk, promptly hung up and look towards Jackie and Claire.

"Mr. Mayhew is ready for you, Mrs. McGivney and Mr. O'Connor."

"Finally. The fancy lawyer is ready to see us now. Let's jump up and down with joy."

"Hush, Jackie! We've only been waitin' five minutes."

Unfazed, the assistant smiled thinly and guided them down an antique hallway. The lawyer's office was on Pleasant Street in what was once the Corey Mansion. It was converted into several offices and J. Walter Mayhew's resided on the second floor. The boards creaked as they clunked down the narrow, softly lit hall. Jackie could smell the old maple in the walls and it reminded him of being inside a church, which only added to his uneasiness. The shadows of the hallway were exacerbated by the poor lighting fixtures sticking out from the wall. Jackie felt like he was in 1892, not 1982.

The assistant and Claire rounded the corner into the lawyer's personal office, Jackie trailing a few steps in back of them. He was alone in the hallway when heard rustling behind him. He whipped his head around, gasping when he saw the ghost from his dream walking across the hall, passing through the walls. He blinked. The ghost was gone. Jackie swallowed, not knowing if he'd actually seen her.

"Please come in and sit down," J. Walter Mayhew said from inside his office. Jackie took a deep breath and entered the office. Claire gave him a strange look.

J. Walter Mayhew did not rise from his chair to greet them. What struck Jackie about this man was that he was enormous. Certainly overweight but Mayhew must have been at least 6'6. It unsettled Jackie. He rarely encountered someone larger than himself.

Jackie wondered if he had ever seen a human being this size before and pondered how the man made it to the bathroom each day or how the floorboards did not crack underneath him. Jackie once had to help his father wrestle a cow off the road – it had escaped from a nearby dairy farm. He considered this man to be the same size. He looked J. Walter Mayhew up and down and reckoned if he had to wrestle him, he could take him down, as well. Mayhew was wearing a grey and black herringbone suit, a cream-coloured shirt with pocket square to match and a red tie with a silver tie tack. Jackie wondered where he purchased such a suit. It had to be custom made to fit the man.

Claire and Jackie both took the chairs on the other side of the big lawyer's very expensive and very expansive English Cherry desk.

"Mrs. McGivney, let me start by offering my condolences."

Claire, Jackie saw, almost vomited right there. On the drive over she'd already said she'd had more than enough condolences to politely choke down over the last week.

She let out a quiet word of gratitude and cleared her throat. "May we get right down to business, please? My cousin here has to get to work and I have more matters to attend to at home. I'm running a business now."

"Why of course, ma'am, and might I add, good for you! It's wonderful to see so many of *the ladies* out earning a little pocket money of their own. What a time to be alive, eh?"

Claire smiled at the backhanded compliment and took a deep breath.

"Now, it was the wishes of Mr. McGivney to have you both here for the reading of the will, so I'm pleased we could find a time to attend to this matter right away. It's best in my experience to have these concerns taken care of in an expedited manner."

Just get on with it, jumbo, Jackie said to himself. It was almost 9:00 AM. The day was half gone.

"I have to tell you that Mr. McGivney opted to do something rather novel: a video recording of his will. It's something I've seen conducted on a recent conference in Boston. We recorded it when he was here last week."

"Last week? But…how did he know he was going to die?" exclaimed Claire.

"Yes ma'am. To answer that question, your husband had actually contacted me prior to his illness. He did seem to have a bad cold while he was here initially but I have to say I did not think him gravely ill. Such a shame. I am sorry about his sudden death, but his contacting me was quite fortuitous. If he did not have a will in place, it would have made for a lengthy and difficult procedure following his death."

"So, he's just gonna pop up on the TV?" said Jackie.

"Yes! I don't mean to sound excited but it *is* rather unique and the first I've done." Giddy, Mayhew leaned over and picked up the phone receiver with his meaty paws. His beard matched his body: full and thick. It was black but had white and grey strands throughout. The man should have been a stevedore, not a lawyer Jackie thought; or else he would make a great addition to the mill if he knew what he was doing. Jackie guessed J. Walter Mayhew would not know what he was doing around a sawmill.

"Janine? Can you bring in the television and Betamax, please?"

"Is this legal?" asked Claire.

"Of course. It's been done in lots of places and the provincial government changed the legislation two years ago to permit it. A sign of the times. I have a transcribed copy as well to give to you for your records, once the recording has finished."

"Is it like a movie reel or something?" queried Jackie.

"No, not at all. I recently purchased the audio and visual equipment. There are new personal recording devices that allow you to watch movies or even record last wills and testaments, like we're about to see from Mr. McGivney. There are two major companies that make the machines: VCR and Betamax, the latter of which we have here. It seems to be the best of the two and promises to overtake VCR. Just an inside tip there, if you're so inclined to invest."

Jackie and Claire looked at each other, then back to the attorney. His feet were dancing, toes jumping like jack rabbits. He was chewing on a toothpick that had turned mostly to pulp. His stomach churned. He didn't know what rattled him more, the ghost sighting or the pending conversation about lottery winnings. *Who knew what that fool Donny did?*

Janine entered, rolling in a stand about waist high with a small television that looked like it had a box attached to the bottom. She uncoiled a long cord, using the outlet on the side of the wall to plug it in, then pressed a button and the screen came to life from the centre to the outer edges. She withdrew a black object from a white sleeve that looked like a giant 8-track and inserted it into the device. It made all sorts of clacking noises. Jackie could hear the gears rolling and spinning.

On the screen before them, in his usual cap and plaid shirt attire, appeared a somewhat healthier Donny McGivney. The setting was clearly the office where they currently sat: the bookcases were lined with leather-bound legal texts and you could even see the photo of Mayhew and Premier Richard Hatfield in the background, shaking hands and smiling.

Claire let out a wobbly breath, filled with both joy and sorrow. Jackie, agitated at the sight of his recently deceased friend, shuffled in his chair. He wondered if he might actually shit his pants in this lawyer's office.

When Donny spoke, it was eerie. He read from a yellow legal pad.

"Hello. I, William Donald McGivney, of sound mind and body, do solemnly swear that on this date, June 23rd, 1982, affirm this is my last will and testament. To my wife, Claire, I leave you the sum of $250,000 to do with as you please. I knew you was going to leave me and we had our differences. I'm sorry I wasn't a better husband to ya and I love you."

Claire sat with her mouth open and looked over at Jackie, whose feet were a little less jumpy, knowing that Claire at least got half of the lotto winnings. He did not want to look at her when the lawyer pronounced Jackie would get the other half.

"Wh…how? How did Donny have so much money? We were broke! Worse than broke."

Mayhew pressed a button on the box below the display and the video paused with some wavy white lines across the middle of the screen. Jackie thought the frozen image of Donny with his mouth agape and one eye half-closed was pretty close to how he looked when he was alive, too.

"Ma'am, your husband had recently won the lottery," said Mayhew. "I gather from your reaction he did not tell you?"

Claire slowly shook her head.

"The lottery? You mean that six-forty-nine thing everyone's been goin' on about? How come he didn't tell me? Is this what you were talkin' about, Jackie?"

Jackie was lighting a cigarette, trying to act surprised at the pronouncement of all the money. His hat was nearly off his head so he could get some air. He nervously nodded at Claire. He did not want a rift to form between them. Money does strange and powerful things to people.

"Shall I continue?" asked Mayhew.

Claire nodded slowly.

"To my good buddy, Jackie O'Connor, I leave the sum of $100,000 to do whatever you want with it. Thanks for bein' a good lad and buy yerself a new canoe because that stoner Paddy Brewster damaged yours. He says he got it fixed and I know it works well enough but you know it'll never be the same. Maybe treat yourself finally buy that bow and arrow set you've been talking about since your dad died. And I've got one more piece of advice for you old friend: forgive yourself."

Mayhew pressed the button again to pause the recording.

Jackie took his first deep breath since he got up that morning. *Goddamn you Donny McGivney fer giving me all that money,* Jackie thought. *Goddamn you.*

Claire said nothing but nodded to the lawyer Mayhew to continue.

"To Sutherland's Sawmill LTD, I leave $50,000 to install a proper breakroom for the men that work there. What remains should go towards any safety gear they need there since that cheap sonavawhore Mr. Sutherland won't buy none."

Jackie and Claire smiled. Mayhew remained stoic.

"I'm leaving $50,000 to St. Agatha's Roman Catholic church to pay for mine and Claire's funerals and headstones and for the parish council to use the remaining funds to fix up the graves of my parents

and any other family members buried there. Anything remaining can go to fixing up the gravesites of any other plot that needs repair.

"$20,000 I leave to the Miramichi Salmon Association. I stolt enough salmon from the river over the years. Very least I can do is give ya's back some money."

Jackie shook his head. *Jesus, Jesus, Jesus that lad was simple.*

"With the remaining $22,000 I am buying stock in Claire's company VitaMax of which she will be the sole owner of said stock. All my other possessions, except my jackknife, go to Claire. My jackknife goes to Jackie. Along with my truck. Claire, you can buy a new one with all the money I give ya."

Jackie sat there with his hand covering the left side of his face. *Leave it to Donny McGivney to bequeath a truck to someone who does not drive a vehicle. Jesus, Jesus, Jesus.*

"Claire, when I won the 6/49 I was on my way to tell ya but you said you was gonna leave me, so I wasn't sure what to do. I got all confused. Anyway, once I got sick I knew it wasn't good so figured I'd better be careful. I thought I could go over my will again in the future if I get better. If I don't, well I guess I'm dead and you're watchin' this on the video thing. I've got all the money taken care of, so there shouldn't be any arguin'. I'm giving this goddamn lawyer $8,000 to deal with the estate and all the doings here to look after it all, so Claire you don't have to worry about nothin'. There. Is that it?"

Donny was looking to his right, presumably off-screen at Mayhew and Janine. He coughed fiercely and took a sip of water from a glass that was next to him. He removed his cap and wiped the perspiration from his forehead with his sleeve. He turned back to the screen, looking directly at Claire and Jackie.

"Okay, guess that's it. Some hot in here, isn't it?"

The screen faded to black. A numbness filled the office.

"Wasn't that exhilarating?" said a jubilant Mayhew, jumping from his chair, shaking the floor beneath. Jackie held on to the arms of his seat and almost went for the window. "Technology really is something else, eh? Of course, Mrs. McGivney as next of kin, you receive a copy of this tape in addition to the transcribed version I mentioned earlier. We'll keep a copy here for our records."

Claire wondered what she would do with the tape since she had no personal home video device. "And that's it?" she said, bewildered. Her day went from being worried how she was going to afford her next power bill to confusion and wonder.

"From a legal standpoint, yes. I've drafted all the necessary documents. Once you sign, then Mr. O'Connor signs and then we go in order for the remainder of the recipients listed in the video. I'll need your signatures but have the cheques for you both today. I strongly recommend you take them to your bank for safe depositing. That is quite a lot of money! I know it does not begin to fill the void of your loss but Mr. McGivney was very responsible in all of these proceedings – with my guidance, of course."

Jackie looked over at Claire, relieved that she received the biggest portion of the inheritance but still concerned she might take offense to him receiving any.

"Can I give mine to her?" he asked Mayhew. "I don't want none of this money."

"After you sign the cheque, the money is yours Mr. O'Connor, so you are free to do with it what you will."

Jackie got up from his chair and walked toward the desk.

"Well then give me a goddamn pen, then. It's past nine. The day is half gone!" Jackie said.

Jackie bowed his head, crossing his arms.

Jackie distrusted cheques, especially big ones. So much money in one small piece of paper. He preferred hard cash but understood $100,000 was too much money to have on hand at an office. It made no difference to him, anyhow. He would be giving the money back to its rightful recipient soon.

"Come on then," urged Jackie as they left Mayhew's office. "Let's get to the bank so I can hand you over the money your fool husband left me. I'd like to get back to the sawmill by noon.

I can at least get half a day's work in. Mr. Sutherland's been so goddamn cranky lately, he's liable to fire me."

"Jackie, that money was given to you by Donny. *From beyond the grave.* I ain't taking it."

Her comment *from beyond the grave* made Jackie shudder.

"First of all, he didn't give me the money from beyond the grave. He was well above ground when he made that foolish choice. And anyway, I don't even have a bank account! I keep all my money at home in a safe place. I don't need this money!"

"Why are you so bothered right now?"

"Because I don't want all this money. I don't *need* all this money. He should have given my portion to you. I'm fine. I just want life to continue on. Havin' all this money is going to just complicate my life. I can feel it. I get premonitions, or whatever. Money always complicates life when you have too much of it. Also, you can take that damn old truck back, too."

Claire put her purse on the hood of the truck, digging for her cigarettes. She offered one to Jackie. He took it and lit both of their smokes. Claire blew a puff of blue smoke in the air.

"No, Jackie. That's your money. You're going to have to step into the twentieth century and get a bank account. Poor Donny left me a quarter of a million dollars. I don't need more than that. Cripes our combined debt is only about $45,000, and that includes the remaining mortgage on the house. I'll be fine and he gave *you* that money, so you'd better keep it or else he'll come back an' haunt ya," quipped Claire.

Jackie thought of the ghost he'd seen again in the hallway of the lawyer's office. He refocused his attention on his cousin.

"What's got you in such a good mood all of a sudden? Donny's still dead, ya know."

"I know. Look, I'm not in a good mood. I'm shattered, honestly. We were parting ways and he still found it in his heart to give me all that money. He thought he didn't deserve me but it's the other way around, for sure. I know that now. I know he loved me. He just didn't always have the means or the drive I wanted so desperately for him to have. And I was too hard on him. I feel so guilty about all the times I judged him. I mean, it was true at the time what I said about him not workin' enough but it weren't about him not loving me. I just wanted us to do better and I didn't see him wanting to grow or change."

Jackie tapped ash from his cigarette. He leaned against the grill of the old Ford.

"Look, I won't ever get over it," Claire continued. "But I feel a little closure I guess because he did all this and really meant it. It's not because I suddenly have a lot of money. It's because he loved me enough to give it to me, even though I was splittin' up with him. I'd give all that money back one thousand times over if it meant we could... I don't know... decorate our front yard for Christmas together once more."

Jackie bowed his head, crossing his arms.

"Right, right. And you're not sore I didn't tell you? I mean, I wasn't trying to betray you but he told me and I didn't know what to do. Said he was going to take care of it all right away. I guess he did."

"No, I'm good. He had to confide in someone and didn't think that was me at the time and for good reason. You and he were friends all yer lives. I'm okay and I'm happy he left you something."

"*Something?* What the Hell am I going to spend a $100,000 on?"

"I'd start with a new canoe, like he said. Get a new everything. New skates, new paddle. Get right outfitted for all your needs."

Jackie mulled it over in his head. He did need a few new things. A brand-new canoe might be just what the doctor ordered. He had long wanted a bow. He knew he'd never replace the one owned by his father but still, he could find a nice one.

"Maybe get yerself a shave, too."

ooooo

Claire took Jackie to her bank and helped him set up an account. He hated all banks and decided if Claire relied on this one, it would do well enough. He deposited $98,000.00 and kept $2000 for himself. He planned to use the cash to purchase a new collar for Ruby, a new colour television, a new Chesterfield and a new reclining chair and eventually a new canoe when he could make his way to Fredericton again.

Jackie and Claire exited the bank and hopped in the truck, driving to Boom Road. Jackie was almost giddy but not because he was suddenly wealthy. He was chortling at the thought of Mr. Sutherland's face when he would discover that Donny had paid for an expensive breakroom for the workers.

Jackie cackled and lit a cigarette. It was past noon now and he knew he would not make it back to work for the rest of the day. He would have to make that up to Mr. Sutherland in the future.

ooooo

Claire had a small smile on her face as she drove them north-west through the late morning sunlight. The storm that threatened earlier never came. On one hand, she could not believe her fortune but wished she had never spoken about leaving Donny – not because of the money but because he gave it to her in the end, despite the fact she intended to part ways. She wondered what would have happened if Donny had lived. She took a deep breath at the thought and rested her head on her hand, her elbow bent against the window on the door, driving the truck with her dominant hand. A hint of ease, despite her guilt over Donny, began to seep in, regardless. She had her new business of selling multivitamins and protein. She really believed it would take off at some point. She would put the money to good use; of that she was certain. She knew she had time now and that many of her financial worries were behind her. Claire told herself that she planned to leave him, but in her heart she did not know if she would have followed through. Even if she had, she would have spent the rest of her life checking in on him. They had known each other all their lives. They were as much friends as they were husband and wife.

"Think I'll stop off at Mike's and grab a few beers on the way home and I'll hoof it the rest of the way," Jackie said.

"You know, you could just kick me out of this truck now since it's yours," Claire replied wryly.

"Don't remind me. Friggin' Donny. He had to be a good lad even after he's gone."

Claire smiled at Jackie. She turned her eyes toward the road and kept driving.

ooooo

Jackie took a long drag off his cigarette and blew the smoke out the window, rolled all the way down to catch a breeze. He removed his hat and stuck his head out the window, looking at the pavement speeding by. The whipping wind lashing his skin felt good. Money wasn't everything but it was a help.

"What are you doing, ya fool? Get in here!'"

Jackie fell back into the seat grinning.

Claire laughed brightly. A genuine laugh that had not escaped her lips in months.

He looked at the bright sun. His depression lifted for a minute and all felt right in the world. Jackie started to think about how he might use his new truck, even though he didn't have a license. His next thought was how he had no problem driving Claire back from the hospital a week ago.

He became melancholy and the smile drifted away. There had been too much going on between Donny's sudden death and the racket over the money. He hadn't realized it until now. Last week was the first time he had driven since the time Aunt Abigail came to visit.

THE TIME AUNT ABIGAIL CAME TO VISIT

"Have I told you about my bowels?"

THE ROTARY PHONE CLATTERED at 8:44 AM. Gen jumped from her chair, her nerves frazzled. Still in her robe, she was enjoying a coffee at the kitchen table, on what was promising to be a rainy morning shortly after Victoria Day. She had even poured in a little extra cream and sugar that morning because it was a Tuesday and she felt she needed it. The coffee was made earlier by Jackie.

"How does that man get up so early each morning?" she said aloud holding her mug that read HALIFAX in red letters. There was a cartoonish drawing of the clock tower from Citadel Hill, a Nova Scotia Flag next to it and a man playing the bagpipes on the bottom.

The phone jangled a second time. The ringing brought Gen back to her kitchen. She looked at the north wall, the white paint now festooned with a large brown arc stretching six feet. She looked at her empty coffee cup.

The receiver clamoured a third time.

"Shit, shit, shit, shit, shit, shit, shit!" Gen tramped toward the phone, now clattering for a fourth time. She would have to attend to the mess later. *One does not miss a phone call,* her mother's frequent mantra echoed in the back of her mind. It could be a call about a job to make some money under the table, information on someone who had recently passed away or a call for a doctor's appointment. She wished once again they had bought an answering machine. For now, she took a deep breath and regained her composure. Midway through the fifth ring, she picked up.

"Hello?"

"Oh, it's you!" Abigail said. Her aunt always acted surprised when someone picked up the phone, even though *she* initiated the call. It never ceased to amuse Gen. She and Jackie would frequently go back and forth, imitating Aunt Abigail making a call and being astonished the person she was trying to reach actually picked up the receiver. It sent Jackie into stitches every time.

"Oh Jackie, its you! How wild to call you at your house and actually reach you there!"

"Good morning, Abigail, how are you?" Gen was holding the phone in the crook of her neck and right shoulder, attempting to dab some of the coffee from her bathrobe with her left hand.

"Fine, fine. Raining a little."

"Yes, I was just getting a coffee," Gen lamented, now able to see the full extent of the coffee on the walls and curtains. *Jackie is going to have a good laugh at that one*, Gen thought.

"Nothing like a cup of coffee in the morning, not that I would know. I drink tea. Do you know I drink tea? Haven't had coffee in thirty-four years. Last time was when I was in Toronto for a probation conference. You know that, right? Don't ever bring me coffee. Gets my nerves up. Your mother drinks coffee. Don't know how she does it. It's why she can't sleep at night."

Abigail was Gen's mother's sister, currently staying a short drive away in Whitneyville. Gen would often task Jackie with going to her mother's home and performing all the odd jobs often required by a son-in-law – insulating the bottom part of the house before winter since the house had no basement, shoveling the driveway in the snowy months and mowing the lawn in the summer – a task Gen knew he particularly hated. Gen saw her mother most days, although since Abigail had come from Saint John to stay for the last few weeks, she saw less of her mother and kept away on purpose. Abigail was older than Gen's mother and had recently retired, with little to do other than harass family members.

"Yeah, I know you only drink tea." It was quite literally one of the first things Abigail told people about herself; that and that she was the first female parole officer in New Brunswick. The latter was a huge accomplishment. Everyone knew it and

Abigail was quick to remind those same people on a regular basis.

"Are you going to town later? I need some items at the pharmacologists. Take me to town."

"Yup, I'm heading in. I have to get to the grocery store and run a few errands. Jackie wanted me to get him a level at the hardware store, too. I might be a while, just so you know."

Gen was hoping her aunt would give her a list of items to get at the drug store and not take the trip to Newcastle. It was going to be a warm day and her car had no air conditioning, but most importantly she enjoyed the time driving by herself. She loved the freedom, throwing on her sunglasses and letting the warmth hit her face, the radio playing as loud as she wanted, the touch of the wind on her arm as it hung lazily out the window. Jackie told Gen he had only seen men put their arms out the window. Gen told Jackie that if he drove once in a blue moon, he could stick his arm out the driver's side all he wanted, but until then, he could stick his opinion someplace else.

"Good. Can you pick me up?"

Gen covered the receiver and let out a deep sigh, hanging her head dramatically. She reached for the decanter to pour another cup of coffee.

"Are you there?"

"Yes, I'm here," Gen said as she leaned against the cupboard, already exhausted. The decanter clattered as she placed it back on the burner.

"I don't get out much these days. It would be nice to take a drive. The bus ride up here was lovely, last week. Have you ever taken the bus? I really only need to go to the drug store. And the grocery store but you said you were already going there. Oh, and that new bookstore everyone has been talking about. Maybe we could stop there? Have you heard they sell food? Sounds queer to me."

Gen had heard of the new bookstore that opened a couple of weeks ago. Everyone was talking about it. A man from Vancouver had relocated to Miramichi. Gen loved her hometown, but for the life of her could not imagine someone moving from a big city on the other side of the country to this little place. Apparently, he sold coffee, tea and some small foods like squares and scotch cakes *inside* the bookstore. The cafe even had a couple of tables for people to sit down, supposedly. Gen did not know who had the time to sit in a coffee shop and read books. She figured a business like that would not last very long. All those tables take up space for more books to be sold. Was that not the point of a bookstore? Regardless, she did read voraciously and a bookstore was her favourite place on the planet, aside from a record store. She certainly knew why Abigail wanted to go to the bookstore. Abigail secretly read romance novels and then burned them afterwards in the wood stove so no one would ever know. Everyone knew this about Abigail and the best part was that Abigail thought nobody was aware.

"Of course, I'll pick you up. I'm just going to finish my coffee and then grab a shower. Can I pick you up around 10:30?"

"Yes, yes that's fine. That's about an hour and a half. My bowels aren't moving well these days, so I'll have to go to the bathroom now and wait. Have I told you about my bowels?"

"Yes, yup. You have." Gen desperately wanted this call to end. She took a slurp of coffee.

"They're not moving. Have to eat an awful lot of prunes. And orange juice. Taking too much acetaminophen. That's what backs me up. They're not moving well. Orange juice hurts my stomach. Don't drink too much orange juice. Bad for your teeth."

"Mmmhmm."

"Good then. 10:30."

"Okay, bye Abigail."

Abigail hung up without a farewell.

Gen did her best not to get agitated. It did not help any situation. Abigail had always been very kind to Gen, even if that kindness meant you were expected to drop everything and help Abigail when she demanded. There were always strings attached to her aunt's generosity. Gen did not mind helping her, though. Gen rarely said no to helping anyone.

She took a deep breath and was refilling her mug when the phone rang again. She did not jump this time but she needed to hurry. She kept thinking, as she strode back to the phone, *Please do not let it be Maude*, her old friend from high school. It could sometimes take up to fifteen minutes before Gen could get a word in edgewise.

Anyone but Maude. Please don't let it be Maude. Anyone but Maude, please don't let it be Maude she prayed as the phone clanged for the third time. She finally answered midway through the fourth ring.

"Hello?" she answered hesitantly.

"Gen!"

Maude. *Fuck.* Gen shut her eyes.

"I just finished writing you a letter! Here, let me read it to you."

Gen grimaced. She deftly reached under the kitchen sink, where there was a pony of Royal Reserve tucked on a small shelf, hidden from view. Little remained in the small bottle, so she emptied its contents into the coffee and stirred it with her index finger. She was going to need every ounce of booze to endure this one-sided conversation with Maude.

"You mean the slut?"

SHE TURNED INTO THE DOORYARD at her mother's house at 10:37 AM. Gen was late. She knew Abigail would give her grief. Aunt Abigail believed in two things: the Roman Catholic Church and being unreservedly punctual. Gen felt the two were not mutually exclusive.

She watched as her aunt slowly exited the side door. She was wearing pants as white as snow, a comfortable looking navy-blue top, white sandals and a visor suitable for tennis. Her hair had been the same as long as Gen could remember: a very unflattering bouffant style with short fringe bangs, reminiscent of Mamie Eisenhower. Abigail held her anvil-shaped purse in the crook of her arm. When she made it to Gen's car, she fumbled with the door handle for 10 seconds. Gen undid her seatbelt and reached over to open it from the inside.

"Where's Mom?" asked Gen.

"She's not coming. She's fooling with that herb garden of hers in the back yard. Looks like there's marijuana in there. Dope. Weed."

Abigail took time getting into the car.

"What took you so long?"

"I got delayed," answered Gen. "A friend called right after I hung up with you and talked my ear off."

"Which friend?"

"Maude Richardson. She lives in Fredericton now."

"Who was she? Before she was married."

"She was a Jardine."

"Maude Jardine? You mean the slut?"

"She wasn't a slut."

"She tramped up and down the roads here like she was some whore. You did well to stay away from her and all her whoring. That whore."

Gen sighed. "Why do you think she's such a whore?"

"Didn't she get pregnant out of wedlock? No wonder, showing off with those whorish skirts."

"She did but she was eighteen and they got married before the baby was born."

"Bah. Doesn't matter. What took you so long to open the door for me? You know my rheumatism means I can't grip things well."

Gen almost said, *"Does that include your grip on reality?"* but thought better of it.

"I had to undo my seatbelt."

"You *wear* one of those things? Goddamn nuisance," said Abigail, placing her purse on the floor, searching for Chiclets. "Your car is too close to the ground. It's hard for me to get into."

"Well, they're in the car for a reason. Same reason why they put childproof caps on medication now."

"Goddamn nuisance, too," complained Abigail. "I can't get into them neither. I need the man who lives next door to come over and help me open them all the time."

You need a man in your life for lots of reasons, thought Gen, but again, held her tongue. Her aunt was married once a long time ago but it ended in divorce. Neither Abigail nor her own mother spoke of this often. Only once had her mother said something. Gen recalled that Abigail's ex-husband committed adultery and his existence should never be mentioned to Abigail.

"His name is David," Abigail continued. "The man next door. Nice man. Well groomed. Lives with his friend Gerry. They seem very close. It's good that he has such a close friend living with him."

Gen did not bother asking if her very Catholic aunt might have a problem with two men living together. It would never cross her mind they could be in a relationship. For her part, Gen could not care any less. *Who honestly cared what people did in private as long as it was not hurting anyone else?* Gen knew the answer to that question: her aunt. If Abigail realized her male neighbours *might* be in a relationship, the result would be calling the police and the archbishop. A letter to the Vatican would also be written to absolve herself of the sin of living next door.

"I heard seatbelts are going to be mandatory someday," said Gen, steering the subject back to something less controversial. "The government is going to start fining people if they stop you and you're not wearing one. I figure I should get used to it now. Might actually save my life, too."

Abigail snorted. "I'd like to see them try that on me. Can't wear one because of my gall bladder. Presses against me too much. And my bowels. They don't move. They don't move very well."

Gen glanced over at Abigail.

"Bowels."

Gen restrained herself from chiming in on the fact her aunt had her gall bladder removed five years ago and the scar had healed easily in a month.

"That's the government for you," continued Abigail. "Always trying to control you. Well, they don't control this lady."

If Gen continued biting her tongue, she'd soon cut it in half. She couldn't take it anymore.

"You remember you were employed by government for thirty-five years and that's where your pension comes from, right?"

"That's different. That's owed to me. That's not controlling me. That's my money. I earned it. You don't deserve a damned thing in this life unless you've worked for it."

Gen could not disagree with that fact. She did believe in working hard and was not a fan of freeloaders. Abigail was certainly a hard worker. It was difficult to be patient with someone so narrow-minded but at the same time, Abigail had always been very kind to her and her sisters. With no children of her own, Abigail doted upon them as children and still did as adults.

Gen fastened her seatbelt and threw the car into reverse. She started backing out of the driveway and had to abruptly stop where the dirt met the chipseal. A truck went by at high speed.

"Christ almighty!" said Abigail. "That's them goddamn drug addicts driving the roads! Filthy dope heads. Where's the police when you need them? Nowhere. Where are they when you don't need them? Pulling you over for not wearing your seatbelt. Bastards."

"Who? The drug addicts or the police?"

"Both. Bastards."

Gen backed out onto R.R. #1 and drove to town. The light rain from the morning had stopped. The sour smell of the drying pavement in the spring heat flooded the air, filling Gen with a good feeling. It was turning into a beautiful day. Gen rolled her window down further and took in a deep breath of late spring.

"You're going too fast."

"I'm going 40. That's the speed limit."

Abigail began rolling up her window.

"What are you doing?"

"I'm cold."

"It's beautiful."

"The wind will get me. Draft gets into my neck. I won't be able to turn my head for a week. Happens to me."

"But the air is warm!"

"I can still catch a draft. Then I'll get sick. Pneumonia. Then I'll die. I've seen it happen."

"Who did you know died because warm air was blowing on them?"

"Doesn't matter. It can happen. You want me to die?"

If I pull the car into the ditch and it rolls, I wonder if it would just kill her or both of us? Best not to. I can't afford a new car right now.

"Now be careful with all that."

GEN TURNED HER CAR into one of the dozen diagonal parking spots on Henry Street in front of the pharmacy. After a mere twenty minutes since picking up her aunt, Abigail's chatter had begun to grind on Gen's agreeable demeanor.

"Why do they have all the parking spots at an angle? Who designed this place? And the spots are too narrow. How am I supposed to get out without hitting the car next to me with your heavy door?"

"I don't know, Abigail. Just open it slowly. I'll go run a couple of errands while you're in getting your medication."

"Don't go too far. I won't be long. Only be about ten minutes."

Gen knew this to be categorically false. Her aunt was extremely slow and would be asking the pharmacist every question imaginable about the same heart medication she had been taking for 20 years. Not to mention how slow she literally moved. Gen guessed she had at minimum thirty minutes before her aunt was finished.

"Fine. Fine. I'll just be here around the town square."

"There's too much pollen on your car. You should get that husband of yours to wash it. It's the least he can do since he can't drive a vehicle. Never heard of such a thing. A man who can't drive a car."

Gen sighed. "He can drive. He chooses not to."

Abigail ignored the reply and got out of the car, making her way to the drug store with laboured, painstaking effort. Gen waited until the pharmacy's glass door closed before leaving, backing the Plymouth out and then driving around the town square towards Pleasant Street.

There were only a couple of cars parked at the liquor store and she did not recognize any of them. She barely used this store and would go in at various times to different stores, so she would not be tagged as a regular. She knew how small this town was and how people talked. It was nobody's concern but that was just the kind of business everyone put their noses into: someone else's.

Gen knew she was drinking too much. She knew because she was hiding it. She did not acquire alcohol from Jackie, who made bootlegged deliveries for Mike Emery. She would have drinks with her husband and back in their twenties and early thirties, she definitely did her fair share of partying with friends. Jackie was always able to maintain discipline with alcohol, though. Of course, there were times he was so drunk he could not keep his balance, but Jackie would never go down the road of drinking too frequently in successive days. Gen figured it had to do with the fact his father Henry was a sloppy drunk, from what she heard. Henry had died before Gen had the chance to meet him. When Jackie was 19, Henry peacefully drifted away while napping on the summer couch on their front porch. She often hoped for a similar death. She wasn't itching to leave anytime soon but thought it was a good way to die.

Somewhere along the way and without any signs, Gen needed a drink at 8:30 AM to take the edge off and move forward with her day. She knew it was an issue but she had rules:

she never drank and then drove the car without at least a few hours passing by or did anything foolish that might endanger herself or someone else. Her discipline allowed her to maneuver life as what a psychiatrist on television once proclaimed as a "functioning alcoholic." Gen actually liked the term and felt that while she had a bit of a problem with drinking, she knew she had the self-control to keep it in check.

She walked into the Newcastle outlet on Pleasant Street, weaving her way to the gin section, casually picking up three pints and carrying them to the cash.

"Going to be a warm one today, eh?" said Jim; his white nametag gleamed against his maroon polo shirt with white trim on the collar and sleeves. She took him to be about 10 years older than her. It was difficult to tell with some men. Many of them aged so well, Jim could have been almost 20 years her senior. He was balding but not excessively, a blotch of harsh psoriasis on the front of his scalp.

"Yup," answered Gen.

"Will that be all, little miss?"

"Yes, that's all. Thanks."

"I don't need to see some ID now, do I?" quipped Jim, a sly grin on his face. Gen knew she did not look anywhere near 19 years old. She feigned a smile.

"No, no. I've been legal for a while now." She desperately wanted to extrapolate herself from this interaction. She was not impressed when men attempted any level of flirting, nor did she want to be seen at the liquor store at 11:00 AM. *Why do men think women are here for them to gawk at and hit on?*

"Young lady like you, I gotta check," said Jim. Jim thought he was funny. Gen stared through Jim. *Fuck off with your 'witty banter', Jim,* she thought. *Just. Fuck. Off.* Gen stared straight at him.

"Not in a talkative mood, eh? Strange for a woman."

Another critical comment from a pathetic man.

"That will be eighteen dollars," Jim's tone was now an aggravated one. Gen smiled inside.

She reached into her purse, pulling out her wallet. Jim's patronizing tone aside, she really did not have much time to double back and pick up her aunt, then go to the grocery store, as well as the hardware store. She withdrew a twenty-dollar bill from her clutch and handed it to Jim. He rang in the exchange and when the drawer opened, he took out two one-dollar bills and gave them to her directly. It was clear he was now irritated that she did not take to his overtures. Gen was as friendly as anyone, but Jim was looking at her in a strange way. It made her uncomfortable and she did not have to put up with it. She knew that sometimes her manner put people off and could care less about it. While she was filing the bills into her wallet, he put the three pints of gin into a paper bag.

"There ya go. Now be careful with all that."

"Thanks."

She snatched the paper bag from the counter and immediately walked out of the air-conditioned store into the heat of the late morning.

A total of two people witnessed Gen entering and leaving the liquor store. Idiot Jim at the checkout and another man who was walking by the store as Gen was leaving. Gen took notice of him but he did not even turn his head to acknowledge her. A small sense of relief.

She took out her keys and unlocked the trunk, placing the bottles underneath the flap that covered the spare tire. She slammed the trunk and got in the car. She was happy she had remembered to leave the windows down a little to let the air in. The car's dark blue vinyl interior was cooking in the late morning sun as it sat upon the blacktop.

Gen did not burden herself with worry about drinking too much. She had a problem. Life was full of problems. You simply overcame them or managed them; for the time being, she decided to manage this problem.

She had heard from people who attended Al-Anon that the first step was admitting you had a problem. Gen admitted to herself she had a problem. She chose to deal with it in her own way without compromising the safety and well-being of her loved ones, keeping it hidden. The alcohol was stashed around the house – the toilet tank, the small ledge underneath the kitchen sink, the inside pocket of an old winter coat at the back of the closet. People kept secrets, even from those you care about the most.

"Can you imagine?"

GEN DID NOT PLAN on being an alcoholic. The disease embedded itself unknowingly to the host, like a tick. She did not plan on much of what had happened in her life and where she was today.

In 1956 when she was 10 years old, she took a shine to field hockey. It was the number one sport at the Roman Catholic all-girl's school she attended in Newcastle – St. Agnes Academy for Girls and Young Women.

She did moderately well in scholastics but better in sports. Gen not only liked field hockey, she excelled at it. The sport is grueling and is as rough as ice hockey, sometimes even more so. There was no protective equipment; in fairness, even the boys did not have much in the way of defensive gear for playing on the ice but there was absolutely nothing for the girls at St. Agnes. The nuns needed a sport for girls to play that was energetic enough it would provide good physical activity but not be too mannish. Field hockey struck the right balance, according to the diocese, ruled by men who did not have children of their own. At the young age of 10, Gen inquired with tongue in cheek to Sister Catherine Kelly about why girls could only play field hockey.

"Why should old men tell young girls what sports they should play?"

Sister Catherine nearly fell over in shock. The question alone earned Gen six demerit points and a week in the kitchen after lunch, scouring the pots and pans, her fingers becoming raw and purple from the S.O.S. pads.

By the time she reached seventh grade, her prowess for

playing field hockey was starting to make a positive impact on her education. It gave her focus and a sense of pride. She started doing better in school. During games, her parents stood at the sidelines, cheering her on as she finessed her way through the opposition, scoring goal after goal. Her father in particular would jump up and down, shouting and applauding. He made a real show of it, to Gen's mother's embarrassment.

There was no future as a professional field hockey player, so gradually her confidence in participating in something she enjoyed was whittled down by her teachers. *A lady must be reasonable when considering one's future,* Sister Catherine would say. Genevieve should focus on accounting or home economics in order to be a good secretary at a local business or homemaker to a husband someday; or even nursing if she did well in sciences and wanted to "reach for the stars."

Gen had nothing against women who wanted to do those types of jobs or live that kind of life, but it was not for her. She wanted something bigger. What that something was, she had not quite figured out at sixteen. She just knew that she was destined for something bigger than her small town had to offer. She wanted to sing, like Carly Simon. She wanted to paint or sculpt, things like the art she saw when they visited the Beaverbrook Art Gallery on a school trip to Fredericton. Most of all, she wanted to run for elected office – something she was laughed at for mentioning once to Sister Catherine. She got a similar reaction when she raised the topic with her mother.

"Why can't women get elected? Seems to me the best thing to do would be to elect more women."

"Now Genevieve, let this go," her mother said. "You have to be realistic. There just aren't very many women politicians. Those who are have had long careers or are already well established in those political parties. It's a nasty business, not always for the faint of heart. We have to stay home and look after the children. Can you imagine? How could you raise kids and run a home while being in Fredericton all the time?"

"What if I wanted to be Mayor of Newcastle?" Gen

questioned. "That way I'm not traveling all the way to Fredericton."

"Genevieve, stop. That's enough of that kind of talk."

"But…why?"

"You have to think about how difficult all of that would be. You should focus on what is really possible, dear. Not some far-off dream that you can't achieve."

"But…you and Dad always said I could do anything."

"Well, anything within *reason*, dear. We mean a husband and maybe some children with a job as an aid. Or a nurse. Yes, a nurse! You'd make a wonderful nurse. You'd have to get those grades up in math and science, though."

"What if I don't want to have children?" Gen asked.

"What? What if you don't want…?" answered her mother. She marched over to her oldest daughter and slapped her hard across the face. Gen welled up immediately. Stunned by what had happened, she was only capable of standing in shock, holding her left cheek.

"We'll speak to your father about this when he gets home tonight! And don't you mention this to your grandmother! It will kill her."

Her mother blessed herself.

Her father was equally displeased at the thought of no children, although Gen could see in his face he did not approve of her mother striking her. She heard them arguing about it that night but knew she was in for it. Looking in the bathroom mirror as she could hear her parents' raised voices down the hall, the redness of her cheek had turned coral. The physical sting was gone but the emotional fragments remained. A mirror cannot be unbroken. She vowed to never speak to her mother again about her life plans.

Her father came to her room later that night. She was going to be grounded for a week. Her parents also told Sister Catherine about Gen's headstrong ways. Gen hated them for ratting her out to the church. Sister Catherine assured Gen's parents that many girls go through "stages" and to trust in God.

The church would smooth out all the rough edges and they need not worry.

No screams, no cries. Only pain.

IT WAS NOT THE FIRST TIME she considered the concept of *What if I'm not even here? Wouldn't that be easier?* There had been other occasions, the niggling worm entered through the base of her skull, slithering its way into her mood. It occasionally made her feel off for a day or two. She knew she would burn in hell, her family would be riddled with shame. As much as she tried to extinguish the thought before it took root, it crept up on her from the void.

She lay in bed, the covers drawn tight and the thick, cotton curtains closed most of the way; a slash of sunlight cutting through. She could not get up. She felt no reason to eat.

The first day she told her mother she was unwell. Her mother permitted this one day, feeling Gen's forehead. It was not warm in the slightest way. She told her daughter to rest and she would phone the school to tell them her daughter was ill.

The second day was like the first, except Gen *wanted* to stay home. Once engaged in school, and excited about seeing friends, she now started to loathe the idea.

What's the point if I'm only going to end up handing some man his slippers and cleaning up baby shit the rest of my life?

Her mother allowed one more day. When Gen's father returned home, he paid it no mind. He waved his hand dismissively and decreed that "Women's issues should be left to women," before striding to the living room and rolling the dial on the black-and-white television to catch the evening news. The dulled voice of the broadcaster permeated through Gen's bedroom walls.

Days went by. The clock on the wall ticked so loudly, she forced herself up to remove the plug and quickly returned to her sanctuary. Gen rose to use the washroom and little else. Her mother brought her soup that went cold and milk that turned sour.

"We don't waste food in this house, Genevieve." Gen drank water and watched the food become a still-life painting. The milk smelled. Her mother left it in on the nightstand for several days until it curdled.

Friday rolled around. Her father was at her bedside. *When did he get here? Have I been asleep?* He was speaking to her but she could barely hear him. She was in a cave, tucked far in an echo chamber. Gen turned away from him, rolling herself up in dense blankets, comforted by not living. Life became too difficult. Her bed was impenetrable. If she stayed here, the world could go on without her.

Gen remained in bed, the emptiness of her body unforgiving. Her mind cloudy with nothing. She listened to the cheerful screams of her younger sisters playing outside in the warm spring weather.

Friends called or stopped by. Doctors came. After three weeks of not attending school, Reverend Mother Colford, the school's top officiate, visited the house. Gen had quickly taken the chance to get up, cracking her door faintly to hear the conversation between her parents and the old nun.

"…lost weight. She won't get out of bed. Doctor MacFarlane said she's got the blues and some meat and potatoes and exercise would do the trick but we can't get her out of that damned bed."

"She won't even let me change the sheets," she heard her mother complain. "She hasn't taken a bath in weeks."

"Trust in the Lord. Continue your prayers. I'll speak to young Genevieve. God has a plan and episodes like this are part of the plan. She'll be fine. I've witnessed dozens of girls go through this. It's natural. Perhaps you should leave the house for a few minutes while I speak to Genevieve?"

Gen could feel her father cringe at the mere hint of menstruation. She heard the chairs screech on the hardwood floor and her parents leave the house. She gently shut the door and crawled back into bed, her face smothered in the pillow. *If I don't breathe, maybe I'll die and that old bat won't talk to me.*

She could hear the Reverend Mother speaking but did not turn her head, one ear scrunched into the mattress, the other covered by blankets.

Gen was on the floor, cold and disoriented. Her face stung.

"Get up out of this bed, *now.* You were not given life by the Lord above to waste away on your filthy bed, day after day. You will obey your parents and you will return to school tomorrow."

She looked up to see the sardonic figure looming before her, a dark silhouette in a dark room. Gen knew it would do no good to argue. It was too hard to argue.

I can't believe she hauled me out of bed and hit me.

"Yes, Reverend Mother." A whisper more than a sentence. The pulsing redness of her face where the nun slapped her made the tears extra wet.

Reverend Mother Colford crouched down. "No time for weeping. Rise up and pull yourself together," the nun hissed. She grabbed a clump of Gen's hair and pulled her up from the floor. Gen screamed. Two more slaps, this time a backhand and forehand to each cheek. She pushed Gen to the floor.

"Up, I said!"

Gen wept but pushed her hands into the carpet. The agony of getting up exhausted her. Reverend Mother grabbed her as she was in a crouch and shoved her against the wall. Gen's bedside lamp fell and knocked over a bowl of decaying fruit.

"If you are not in class tomorrow when the bell rings, I'll be here shortly thereafter, child. Do you understand?"

Gen nodded her head absently. The nun went to the door, closing it softly. She slid down the wall, onto the floor and wept. She could hear further conversation now; her parents had reentered the house.

She took a deep breath, got up and went straight to the bathroom, turning only the hot water tap. She disrobed from her dirty nightgown as the water rushed into the bone-white claw foot tub. Gen went to the scale as the tub filled.

She had lost eleven pounds. She turned to the full-length mirror and regarded her figure. Gen could see her ribs and thought how comforting they felt against her fingertips.

A knock at the door. "Dear, are you alright? Reverend Mother said you had a good chat and you're going to school tomorrow."

Gen considered smashing the mirror. A big enough shard could slit her wrists. She looked around for scissors but there were none in the room.

"Gen?"

She turned away from the mirror and back to the tub.

"Yes, I'm fine."

"Supper will be ready when you're finished," her mother said through the door.

Gen did not answer. She heard her mother's footsteps grow distant down the hall. She turned the hot water tap off and watched the steam rise, inhaling the warm vapor.

She stuck her foot in first, which abruptly sent searing pain through the rest of her body. She shivered as thousands of goosebumps broke out atop her skin.

The rest of the leg now, more pain. She lowered herself into the water. Red-hot sensors fired in her brain. She sucked steamy air through clasped teeth. No screams, no cries. Only pain. *Yes, pain. Something.*

"The debate is over."

SHE SAT IN AN OLD OFFICE. Spotless walls made of hardwood, floors covered in cheap, brown linoleum but no dirt or grime to be seen.

The long summer passed. Gen sat across from Reverend Mother Colford in the nun's quarters at the beginning of the new school year. She sat with renewed confidence, the opposite of her last personal encounter with the old rancid bitch. Gen had spent much of the summer outside – swimming, hiking, gardening, playing pick-up games of field hockey with friends. She was healthier and mentally stronger than she had been four months ago.

Reverend Mother Colford's appeared larger, wearing her full habit and scribbling something in a black book.

Gen placed her well-written application on the desk of Reverend Mother. The old nun looked up from her notes and shifted her bifocals closer to her eyes.

"What's this?"

"I'd like to start a debate team at school."

Reverend Mother Colford set her glossy black-and-gold pen down and picked up Gen's essay, peering at it over her glasses. Disapproving lines presented on her forehead. She extended her gnarled hand and allowed the paper to float to the top of the wastepaper basket.

"The debate is over."

"Reverend Mother, you wanted me to get up and get out of my room, to live life. Isn't this what you suggested?"

Colford removed her bifocals and cleaned them with a soft white cotton kerchief, quietly massaging the lenses.

"Women, particularly young women, should not be involved in such matters."

"But I'd really like to do this. Five other girls in my grade have also said they'd like to do it too."

"And their names would be?" asked the Grand Inquisitor. Gen stared defiantly back at the nun, faintly narrowing her green eyes.

"Well, it was just a conversation, really," she deflected. She was not about to get anybody else in trouble. "But they were excited about the prospect."

Reverend Mother sighed, tsking and shaking her large head. She drew back the arms of her eyeglasses and laced them around her fleshy ears, normally hidden by the cowl.

"Genevieve, you should consider a career in religious vocations if you want to be a leader." Reverend Mother rose from her black leather wing-backed chair and crossed to lean on the front of her desk, blocking the faint sunlight as she approached Gen.

"You know, you remind me of myself at your age. Headstrong indeed but drive, perseverance, strength. The church needs young women like yourself to carry on God's message. The Good Lord only gives us what we can handle and he's given me a great deal." The old nun placed her hand on Gen's thigh with such deft that Gen was still looking at the old nun's face before she noticed.

"Marrying the Church is the ultimate sacrifice to God and His children. Service to those around us," said Reverend Mother Colford, her tone low and concerned. "You need someone to guide you, don't you think?"

Colford's shriveled hands lay on Gen's lap, casual and firm. She pressed down close to Gen's abdomen. Gen looked at the nun, scared and comforted, eyes darting up and down.

Pressure. Fear.

She could feel the nun's morning tea breath on her nose.

NO, she thought loudly, and then realized she had actually whispered aloud.

The nun did not stop. "Service to a higher power is all that we are put on Earth to do, Genevieve." Reverend Mother brought a crooked finger to Gen's ear.

Gen leapt from the chair, knocking Reverend Mother Colford aside.

The door crashed against the grand hallway. She ran, not looking back to see if the old nun was injured from the fall.

Smacking footsteps echoed on the ceramic tiles.

Curious eyes.

Head tilts.

Blurred faces of classmates and teachers.

Raised voices and whispers behind her. An alarmed nun checking on Reverend Mother.

What did Genevieve do now?

Gen smelled the harsh chemicals of bathroom cleaner. She sat on the toilet, feet pressed against the stall door.

"Gotta get out of here."

∞∞∞

Gen graduated high school as valedictorian. She decided on teacher's college. If she could help other young girls reach their dreams, she planned on doing it through public school and not be a negative influence like the nuns had been on her and so many others. There were good nuns, she knew that. Sister Irene had been particularly caring to Gen and her friends but she knew she had to teach in public school and definitely had no interest in becoming a nun.

She had dated little in high school. She took hardly any interest in boys and it became a concern for her mother, which only confused Gen more.

"They want you to marry a man but not too soon; but also, don't wait too long or don't be interested in a man from a different religion or from a different race," she complained to her friend Iris. The level of prejudice and racism was always there but never outright spoken; a pot of water simmering without boiling over into actual spoken words.

"They wanted you to be both available and unavailable at the same time," answered Iris. "My parents are the same way."

"We had to shoot it."

Genevieve was preparing for teacher's college in Fredericton as the summer wound down her senior year. She was walking along the battered King George Highway with Iris one evening in early August. Becoming a teacher was not her ideal job but she knew she needed a career before running for office. She understood people had to know you before they would consider voting for you. She had always read the newspapers and followed the media nightly on television. What was happening in Moncton with the wave of student protests, the events in Quebec with the sovereignty movement, a national healthcare system coming into place in recent years, oil development and resources railway in Alberta – it all interested her. Gen was keen to read everything and anything related to government and politics. Teaching, she reasoned, would be a good stepping-stone into public life.

It was 8:00 PM and the warm sun was low on the horizon. The angle of light hurt their eyes as Gen and Iris walked west along the road, chatting about music. Iris was wearing heeled shoes that she thought made her look more adult and stumbled on the crumbling sidewalk, rolling her ankle. She sat on the curb, groaning in pain. Gen had experienced injuries playing field hockey and put her light sweater underneath Iris's swollen ankle, elevating it, but did not know what else to do. They were quite a distance from their homes, with no pay phones in sight and were closer to the Newcastle hospital than home. Just as Gen was about to leave and go for help, a man approached them. He was a few years older, which she could tell simply by the way he walked. He had wonderful brown eyes and wore a green-and-black shirt, blue jeans and well-kept black shoes. His hair, she noted, was not quite a brush cut but not far off either. He already had crow's feet and the early stages of a furrowed brow.

"Is she all right?" the young man asked Gen. He was handsome but with a rugged quality about him.

"I think she's rolled her ankle pretty badly. It's sprained," said Gen.

"Happened to a mule we had once," the man said. "We had to shoot it."

Iris yelped and grabbed Gen's leg. The man grinned and Gen began laughing.

"I'm just kiddin'. Sorry, not the time to be making jokes. I've got a weird sense of humour. Let's get you on yer feet. I'll help take you to the hospital. My name's John O'Connor. Everyone calls me Jackie."

"I'm Genevieve. The mule is Iris."

"Ha. Ha. Very funny," said Iris. "Can I get some help down here, please?"

Jackie had a brief chuckle and they helped Iris to her feet.

"No wonder you sprained yer ankle. Them shoes are made for good streets. This is Newcastle. There isn't a stretch of level pavement in the whole town."

When they reached the hospital, Gen pulled a dime out of her purse and called Iris's parents and then her own house. The doctor on duty had said Iris would be fine but the ankle was badly sprained and she would need to be driven home. He wrapped her inflamed ankle, gave her Aspirin for pain and provided crutches that she should walk on for the next couple of weeks.

"What about you?" Gen asked Jackie. "How did you happen to be strolling by at that point? Were you on your way to your car?"

"Oh, I don't have a car," said Jackie dismissively. Gen got the impression he was oddly proud.

"You're from upriver."

"Oh? How's that now?"

"Your accent. Only people upriver speak like that."

"Well, there ya go. I've got an accent. Never knew I had one. Does it impress you?

"Not really. It would impress me if you had a car. How do you get around?"

"I get by. I canoe a lot. Or walk. Or skate."

"You canoed all the way to town?"

"Lord no! I got a ride in with my friend Donny. He's got a truck."

A man in his 20s from Miramichi that did not drive a car. It was like seeing a unicorn.

"I don't think I've ever heard of a man from around here without a car."

"Yeah, yeah. I hear that a lot. People got around for a thousands of years without cars. We'll be back to that again someday. Maybe when we finally get those flying cars in the year 2000, I'll get my license then. I'd like to fly a car."

Gen didn't know what to think of that and gave him a strange look. She had never met someone like Jackie O'Connor.

They stood there awkwardly for a few moments, the chill of 11:00 PM tickling their arms as they waited outside the hospital. Iris's parents pulled up to the emergency room doors. She made her way toward them on crutches looking completely and utterly bandaged, as if emerging from the trenches of Ypres.

"I guess that's our drive home. Thank you again for your help."

"Oh, no worries. Hey, would it be alright if I took you out for ice cream sometime?"

"Uhhh…how would you pick me up? You don't have a car."

"Oh, *you'll* have to come to me upriver. I promise you though that if you drive up, I'll show you the best damn ice cream in Northumberland County."

"You're full of shit. Everyone knows the best ice cream is Rose's Dairy Bar in Chatham."

Jackie's eyes popped out of his head. He started laughing so hard he doubled over. He could not recollect a woman cursing at him before.

"Well, I don't know about that but come up to Sunny Corner and I'll introduce you to Carl's Diner. I know it might seem odd for me to ask you to come to me but that's who I am. Don't get me wrong, I think you're pretty and everything. I just don't come to town very often. Although for you, it might be worthwhile getting a driver's license and a whole fleet of cars."

Gen was certain her mother would not approve of her driving the family car all the way to Sunny Corner to have ice cream with an older man she had only met a couple of hours ago.

She happily agreed.

"I think we'd better set a time and day right now. My parents won't like you calling. How old are you anyway?"

"I'm twenty-four."

"I'm only eighteen. I think you're a little old for me."

"I'm very immature. I assure you."

Gen laughed. "How about this Friday at seven?"

"In the morning or in the evening?"

"The evening, dough head."

"That, my lovely, sounds like a date."

Gen smiled and Iris gave her a nasty look as she catapulted herself forward on crutches.

"I'm fine. Really. Don't help. I'm good. Gen, we're leaving if you want a drive with us."

Gen turned to Jackie. "I'd better run. It'll take me an hour to walk home and it's already dark. How are you getting all the way upriver at this hour?"

"I'll make my way somehow. I'll see if my friend Donny is still down at the tavern, and if not, I'll just hitchhike or walk."

"But that's twenty miles!"

"Oh, I'll stop and sleep along the way if I have to. Wouldn't be the first time."

Gen shook her head, then leaned over, giving him a peck him on the cheek. Jackie blushed. She half skipped to the car, helping Iris with her crutches.

"Bye, Jackie"

"Bye, Genevieve. Now don't forget," he said with a wink.

"I won't. And you can call me Gen."

Iris's parents drove away. Gen looked out the rear window and Jackie waved at them. She gave a little wave back and was grinning like an idiot when she faced front.

"Who was that lad?" Iris's father asked.

"A good Samaritan."

"I'm so glad to be rid of him. He smelled like a pine tree mixed with pomade."

"He didn't do anything queer with you girls or anything, did he?"

Iris looked at Gen, who gave her a worried look. *Don't spoil this for me*, Gen said with her eyes.

"No, father. He was fine. Just some man from upriver somewhere. Blackville or Sunny Corner I think."

"Bunch of strange people upriver. Good that he was there to help but best to keep away from that lot."

Gen knew the last thing she would be able to do would be to stay away from *that lot*.

"I don't care if he's from big city Moncton!"

DESPITE THE ODD FACT that Jackie did not have a vehicle let alone a driver's license, Gen fell in love with him. She would lie to her parents and every Friday, driving to Boom Road where she would pick him up at the O'Connor homestead. Borrowing the family car, she told her mother and father she was going to a church youth engagement in Red Bank, which worked as an excuse until the time Father Matchett at the Red Bank Parish attended mass in Newcastle.

Gen's mother asked the priest how the youth engagement exercise from his church was going. Gen stood right beside her mother, her eyes pointed towards the ground. Christina, Gen's mother, bragged to Father Matchett about how much her daughter enjoyed driving upriver each Friday to attend. Father Matchett was completely unaware of such a group and when Gen's mother turned to ask her daughter, Gen was already outside and racing down the stairs. She had to come clean about the man from Boom Road. He was a perfect gentleman and no, they had not even so much as kissed.

The lie infuriated Christina. She now understood why Gen had taken a job at the local pharmacy, rather than going to teacher's college in Fredericton. The meager salary from the pharmacy did not provide much and Gen still lived with her parents. She must still abide by their rules. Her mother and father forbade her from seeing this older man from Sunny Corner.

"It's not Sunny Corner! It's Boom Road!" argued Gen. "And I'm a grown woman! You can't treat me like this."

"I don't care if he's from big city Moncton!" yelled her father. "You'll not see him anymore. You're not allowed to drive the car, you're coming straight home after work and if he comes around here, I'll cuff him in the ear!"

Furious, Gen left the room. She ran out of the house and stayed away all evening, until well past a suitable hour. It was getting cold by the time she returned, knowing she would have to sleep on the street if she did not go home. The relief on her mother's face as she came in the door was all Gen needed to see.

"Your father's been out for three hours looking for you!"

"Good."

"Don't act like such a spoiled child!"

Gen had decided to forego teacher's college and instead stay in the Miramichi area, eventually taking businesses courses at her former high school. She began to pick up the odd job, doing accounting work for some local businesses and soon falling into a job at her father's firm. She had never intended to stay in Miramichi forever. Jackie had a steady job at Sutherland's Sawmill, which he enjoyed. She knew that she was foregoing her future in many ways, but she loved Jackie. Perhaps they would pick up and move to Fredericton in a few years where she could attend teacher's college and Gen knew there were plenty of sawmills along the St. John River. She still had plans for public life in some way; at least she hoped that might happen. Fredericton would be an even better place for that than Newcastle.

By the time Jackie finally came for Sunday dinner, it was all but settled that they would be married. Gen was not sure if marriage was exactly what she wanted, but Jackie charmed her parents almost as easily as he charmed Gen.

"That lad should run for elected office!" Gen's father proclaimed, rubbing salt in the wound.

"He certainly has a knack for speaking," her mother said, nodding.

Gen felt strange. Happy her parents liked Jackie. Disappointed they never supported her in any meaningful way. She became trapped in something she wanted.

"Follow me!"

THEY WERE MARRIED ON JULY 1, Dominion Day, at St. Mary's Parish in Newcastle. It was a small ceremony, with only Gen's parents attending and her friend Iris as Maid of Honour. Jackie had his friend Boyd as best man, which embarrassed Iris, being paired up with a small man. It also soured Donny a little but Jackie knew he would get over it.

They drove to Jackie's homestead in Boom Road after the nuptials. For optics, the pictures taken that day show Jackie behind the wheel of the car and Gen in the passenger seat. It was unheard of that a man should be driven around by his wife, particularly on their wedding day. Gen's mother insisted that Jackie get behind the wheel for the photos. She was also agitated that Jackie would not shave his beard for the wedding.

"It still looks like he has a dirty face. It'll be in all the pictures for the rest of time!" she complained. Gen's parents quite liked Jackie but he was an odd man and did have some proclivities of which they did not approve.

Later, Gen drove so they could have dinner with Jackie's mother, Carol, who was referred to as an "invalid," a term that made Gen's stomach turn. Carol was still of sound mind though and had the ability to move about her own home to some degree. She did her best to cook the homemade roast beef dinner for her youngest son and her new daughter-in-law.

Gen loved that they got married on Dominion Day. It was her favourite holiday, and her favourite time of year, when the sun is strong and lingers in the sky until late, the stars and the sun floating in the twilight.

That evening after the dinner they took photos with Carol on the front porch before walking back into the field to take some more casual shots. Gen's mother insisted they get nice photos with foliage in the background. As they walked back to the field, the air was bursting with the aromas of mint, raspberries, spruce trees – all intermingled with the flavor of summer heat.

They did not count on June bugs still being around. When the sun finally ducked behind the trees, hundreds of the sticky insects appeared out of thick, hot July air and everyone got them caught in their hair. The group ran to the house, more than 200 yards away. The frenetic running stirred up mosquitoes, black-flies and no-see-ems. The little vampires feasted on the small congregation to the point where Gen became worried. Her nose, ears and eyes now filled with the insects and they all started choking, barely able to take in a full breath. Jackie dug out his lighter, emptied the kerosene lamp oil he had brought with him to lead their path back to the house. He tore off the sleeve of his good dress shirt, wrapped it around a branch he found on the ground, poured the lamp oil on and set the torch ablaze. Jackie began waving it around like a mad man, making desperate attempts to protect Gen and those around him. It set alight path for them and burned many of the insects in their way.

"Follow me!" Jackie shouted as he grabbed Gen's hand and rushed to the house and the mob fell in line behind Jackie and Gen.

The porch door slammed hard against the old wooden frame. The wedding party was now safely inside; sweaty, hot and bitten. They all started to itch and soon stripped down to their undergarments, clothes covered in smashed bugs, caked with mud and smeared with grass stains. Even Gen's parents stripped down, aided by Jackie's mother Carol, who was putting together some home remedies to soothe the bites. By the end of the whole saga, they were all sitting around the glassed-in front porch, sipping some water and panting, trying to cool down by the oscillating fan Jackie had recently purchased for his mother. Donny and Claire had shown up by this point, bringing celebratory beers for the newlyweds and were quite startled to find the whole lot of them (save for Carol) in their underwear, covered in calamine lotion, oatmeal and honey. The sight frightened Donny.

"Jesus Christ!" said Donny as he fell back through the door and down the steps.

"Close the door, for God's sake!"

The bug-bitten wedding party laughed. Everyone began enjoying a cold beverage and talking loudly. Donny brought his guitar and started playing George Jones, then Marty Robbins, followed by Johnny Cash. By the time he got to "Dreams of the

Everyday Housewife" by Glen Campbell, many of the attendees were dancing.

Gen could not help feel a little melancholy about everything. It was not how she imagined her wedding day. It occurred to her she had never really imagined having one in the first place.

After goodbyes, Gen and Jackie drove 25 minutes to Greystone Lodge on the Renous River, where Jackie had rented a cabin for a few days. He had gone up the day before and stocked the lodge with all the provisions they would need. When they arrived, she saw that Jackie had adorned every room with tulips, her favourite. The pretty flowers were *everywhere* – still on the stem or petals strewn across the cabin. They were on the dining table, on the couch, on the bed, in the bathtub. Jackie had paid Donny to drive him all over Northumberland County, buying every tulip he could find.

ooooo

HER LIFE WAS NOT HOW SHE IMAGINED. Twelve years had passed since they were married, and Gen still loved her husband. But she was unfulfilled. She never got to teacher's college and never set foot into politics. She did not even have children, though that was her choice and Jackie only ever asked the question once, after they were recently wed. He never asked again.

Jackie often quipped that he had no idea why she was with him. She loved him and knew that he loved her. She was still young at 35. She felt she had time and planned to go back to school to take further business and accounting courses. She did not want to spend any more precious years working under the table and doing people's taxes every year. She planned on finally going to college and obtaining her accounting designation. Gen was going to start her own firm, employing only women. She did not care about what double standard it might invoke. Women needed help and they especially needed it in rural New Brunswick.

Gen buckled her seat belt and turned the key, starting the

engine. She swung out onto Pleasant Street, pulling a U-turn to pick up Aunt Abigail at the drug store. Her '71 Plymouth Valiant always had a blind spot along the driver's side where the rail from the front window descends to the hood of the car.

A few streets away, Abigail waited impatiently, stomping her feet on the sidewalk.

He took his foot off the gas and the truck
began to slow, losing inertia.

AT 11:50 AM, Mrs. Sutherland came rushing out to the mill yard. Nobody had seen her move so fast before.

"Jackie, it's the police. You've got to come quick. They say it's an emergency!"

Jackie was brushing some sawdust off a piece of cedar with his hands. He dropped the board and knew it had to do with Gen. He ran as fast as he could to the office and picked up the phone.

"Mr. O'Connor?"

"Yes. What is it?"

"Mr. O'Connor, I'm Constable Rose with the RCMP. Your wife was involved in a serious accident in Newcastle and has been rushed to the Chatham hospital. Sir, her injuries are quite severe."

Jackie dropped the receiver, not bothering to hang up. He ran out to the yard and grabbed the first person he saw, Donny.

"Give me your keys."

"Wha?"

"I need your keys."

"But you don't drive, Jackie."

"Give me the fuckin' keys."

Donny fished in his pocket, handing the keys over to Jackie. He snatched them and ran to Donny's truck. He tore out of the mill yard, creating brown clouds and spitting rocks in his wake. He almost went into the ditch as he made a sharp turn on to Rural Route #1 but regained control and tramped on the gas pedal so hard he thought his boot might go through the floor of Donny's old truck.

ooooo

When he got as far as the Morrissey Bridge, he did not slow for the narrow steel truss passageway and continued through at a high speed, nearly colliding with other vehicles. He reached the infirmary, parked the truck at the emergency doors, turned the ignition off and ran into the hospital. Sweating and frantic, he rushed the desk, taking the secretary by surprise.

"Genevieve O'Connor. Where is she?"

"Sir? Just calm down."

"Don't tell me to calm down. My wife was in a car accident. Where is she?"

A nurse approached Jackie from behind, frightening him. He turned around with a hand cocked, ready to deliver a fierce punch.

"Mr. O'Connor. Please!"

"Where is she?"

"I'm sorry sir but we couldn't wait. She sustained serious trauma and just left in an ambulance for Moncton. We couldn't treat her injuries here. They're on their way to Moncton now."

"Rogersville or Trans Canada?"

"Rogersville Road. It's faster."

Jackie hurried back to the truck and took off for Highway #126. He left the four-way flashers on, peeling the tires as he ripped out of the parking lot. He sped along the rural highway, paying no attention to limits. He did not have a license anyway, and if a cop tried to pull him over he could do so after Jackie got to Moncton.

Thirty-five minutes later, he saw the backside of the white ambulance before it reached the village of Collette. He raced to catch up, wondering why he was gaining on it so quickly.

He could hear no siren. There were no flashing lights. He

took his foot off the gas and the truck began to slow, losing inertia. Jackie applied his foot to the brake and pulled over to the shoulder of the road. He put the truck into park, turning off the engine off as he watched the distance grow between himself and the ambulance.

"Ah true but the soul is the same."

Jackie arrived in Moncton, the sleeves of his shirt wet from tears as he walked through the doors of the hospital. He knew they would require a positive ID from a family member. He wished it were her mother or someone else, as terrible as that sounded. He did not care, though. He would have given anything for it to be someone besides him that had to identify the body. The thought of it made his knees buckle.

Jackie was only Jackie now, not Jackie and Gen. The feeling scared him. He sat down on a folding chair in the lobby and wept until he felt a light touch on the shoulder.

"Excuse me," someone said.

Jackie looked up and saw a large man standing there in blue scrubs with a box of tissue in his hand.

"Do you need these?" the man said in a large voice. He wore a nametag but Jackie could not read it. The man had a strange accent, something Jackie had never heard before. He was a giant. Jackie thought he would need a ladder to read the tag. He had to be nearly seven feet tall.

"Uh…thank you but I've got a handkerchief here." Jackie dug into his pocket and pulled out a blue handkerchief with white dots. He wiped his eyes and then blew his nose and stuffed it back into his pocket.

"Well, I'll leave these here in case you need them. Can I help you with anything?" His voice was rich and deep.

"I…I don't know. My wife is dead."

The large man crouched down. He put his hand on Jackie's shoulder but said nothing. Normally, Jackie would have thought this big guy with the funny accent was coming on to him but honestly, it felt so nice to have another human being touch him, he erupted in tears again. The man held out the tissue box and Jackie withdrew a handful. He wiped his eyes, his mouth and nose.

"Thank you."

"I am very sorry. I am a nurse here with the hospital. My name is Will."

"Nurse?" Jackie said with surprise. "A lad who's a nurse?"

Will gave a small smile.

"Well, that's just about the strangest thing I've ever heard. Didn't think there were male nurses."

Will nodded in agreement. "It is not that common but there are some."

"I thought you were a wrestler. How big are you?"

"Six feet and ten inches."

Jackie whistled.

"I thought so. I figured close to seven feet. I work with lumber so I've got a knack for measuring things by sight."

"What is your name?"

"Jackie O'Connor."

"Have you spoken with any of the doctors here about your wife, Jackie? Normally after someone has passed away, we do not leave family sitting in the lobby."

"I just got here a few minutes ago. I haven't talked to no one."

Will cocked his head and gave him a strange look.

"Then how can you be certain she is dead?"

"She's gone. I know it. The same way as if someone took my heart, my lungs and my eyes. I know she's dead." He barely got the last part of the sentence through his lips before crying again. He clutched the tissues in his hand and patted his eyes.

Will gave a few short, understanding nods. He grabbed a tissue himself and dabbed his eyes as well before grabbing a chair and sitting down next to Jackie.

"How come you're cryin'? You didn't know her?"

"We are all human, yes? I have seen a great many people die, both in my country and in my work. It is always sad, whether we knew them or not."

"I kinda figured you weren't from around here. Not too many black lads around these parts, 'specially with that accent."

Will chuckled. "You are right. It is not that common and even less common to be a nurse as well. I was not looked upon well in Ethiopia for choosing a profession that is normally performed by women. Men have too much pride. I have seen too many people die. I wanted to help. I cared for my grandmother when she was very ill and when the locusts came and the food all died and the crops were lost, I lost my family."

"Mister, I'm not sure I can listen to this right now."

Will paused and bowed his head lightly.

"Yes. Of course. Forgive me. I am so sorry for your loss, Jackie."

Jackie nodded slowly, dabbing his eyes with tissue paper.

"I appreciate the talking, it's just…I've been through lots of death. Father, mother, friends. The combination of them won't add up to losing her, though."

The din of the hospital emergency room surrounded them – announcements over speakers, people walking by in conversations, the clattering of a stretcher as paramedics whisked by them. They sat in silence. Jackie was unsure for how long, lost in his thoughts.

"Actually, could you go on talking a little more? Kinda relaxing listening to you. Need to fill the void, right now."

Will inhaled deeply.

"In my country when someone dies, it is quite intense. The women will scream and wail and call out the person's name. They will even scratch their faces."

"Jesus."

"And the men will sing songs and tell great stories about the dead."

"Sounds like the men have it easier."

"The process can take many days and sometimes a

thousand people may show up."

"That's way too many people. I don't even have steps to my front door because I don't want people to come visit me."

"By the time the funeral takes place, it can be almost a week."

"What religion do ya's practice there?"

"Orthodox Christian."

"Christians? Really? I had no idea."

Jackie had a strong urge to tell Gen about this man, this strange and interesting giant and couldn't wait to get home to talk to her. The hopelessness set in again. He began to cry.

"It is quite a spectacle and a very sad, drawn-out affair."

Jackie blew his nose hard.

"Sounds more depressing than what Catholics do. And it sounds like you've seen a lot of dead people."

"I have but that does not make it easier when you learn a friend has lost his wife."

"Me? Friend? Look bud, I just met you."

"We are friends, Jackie. Are we not all the same?"

"Mister, have you *looked* at me? We couldn't be more different."

"Ah true but the soul is the same. We all have a soul and when your soul is hurting, my soul is hurting, too."

Will patted Jackie on the knee.

"In my country, they say grief is the bill of happiness come due."

Jackie offered small, soft nods.

"Come. We go and see your wife."

"You drink whisky?"

JACKIE WALKED BEHIND WILL as they entered a waiting room for a meeting with a doctor. A kind-looking man in his late 50s, the doctor wore a white coat over his cream dress shirt, navy-blue tie with bright red stripes. Jackie heard him but did not really listen; it was as if the doctor was speaking from the top of a well and Jackie was at the bottom.

"Did you hear me, Mr. O'Connor?"

"I heard ya. Massive trauma and the medics did all they could to save her. Can I see her?"

The doctor cleared his throat but looked him directly in the eye.

"Mr. O'Connor…"

"Jesus, just call me Jackie."

"Okay, Jackie. You're a straight shooter. I can tell by talking to you. I'm going to be straight with you: your wife is banged up back there. Are you certain you want to see her right now? Because I've been doing this a very long time and I can tell you, I've seen the toughest men and women come in here thinking they can handle what they see because they want to see their loved one, one last time. All of them – *and I mean all of them* – wish they hadn't done it." The doctor pointed at the door to their left.

Jackie sat silently.

Will looked on with concern. Jackie choked back tears.

"I've got to see her before they paint her up and put her into a jeezless coffin and parade her about for the world to see. I've got to see her. You need a positive ID anyways, don't ya?"

"Yes, but there are other ways, too. We could always call another relative but you are next of kin, of course."

"Nothing can prepare me doctor, so we may as well do it now."

Will patted him on the back.

"Will, can you come with us please? Might be good to have you there."

"Of course, doctor."

"This way then."

The doctor led them down the bright hallway. The high sun shone through the windows, the afternoon light strong on the hospital floors. The sun's beams penetrated the windows and made the hallway fiercely warm. Jackie felt cold.

ooooo

The harsh chemical smell of the morgue overwhelmed his senses. Formaldehyde filled the air but there was also the undeniable scent of disinfectant. It was as if the hospital was trying to make you forget what the room truly was: a place for the dead.

They stood beside the gurney. The physician drew the white sheet with care down to her shoulders. The doctor was correct: Jackie was not prepared for the cold, lifeless face of his wife. That is what struck him the hardest. This is what he knew would stay with him until his own dying breath. Not the fact there were bandages around her head or that the left side of her face was bruised badly. Through the light sheet the bruising continued far below her shoulders and along her ribcage.

Her eyes were closed. Her mouth drawn down. *So unlike Gen.* She was the light in every room she entered. He used to say that hugging her was like hugging a blanket that had just come piping hot out of the dryer. She lay there, and all he could think was how his life was now over. He had to hold onto the bed rail. Will lightly put his hand on Jackie's shoulder.

"Can I touch her?"

"Of course," answered the doctor.

He gently reached over with his hand, steady as always. He touched the right side of her face; the side that was not so badly bruised. He quietly brushed the tips of his knuckles against her cheek.

This was someone else. This is happening to someone else, too. This isn't Gen. This isn't me. This is a bad dream. I'll wake up and she'll still be asleep beside me.

Anguish paralyzed him, cutting off his air.

Her skin did not feel like her skin. *After a person dies, that person is truly gone and the body is something else. A husk. Just a container.*

Jackie did not believe in God or religion or anything like a soul but what he did know now, looking at the body, looking at this *thing* – it was not Genevieve.

He had expected to weep and wail and gnash his teeth, to fall upon her, the way that Will had described how people in his village react when someone close to them dies. Jackie felt the opposite. What happened to *her*, he wondered. The part that truly made Gen. The consciousness, the laughter, the joy, the feeling. *Where did that go?* The sight of her only made him want to run.

"Okay. That's her. That's my wife, Genevieve O'Connor. Can I go now?"

The doctor nodded. "Of course. You can go whenever you please and we'll be in touch about transporting her back to you in Miramichi."

"Good. Fine. Thank you."

He walked around the bed and shook hands with the doctor. Will met him as he turned around to leave and guided him out of the room.

"Jackie, let us go and sit down and get something to drink."

"You drink whisky?"

"No but you can and I'll drink coffee."

"Yeah, I'll be needing something a little stronger than coffee."

"But won't you have to drive home later?"

"Yeah, but I don't even have a license, so I don't really give a shit."

"It was a good game though."

IN THE WEEKS THAT FOLLOWED, Jackie did little but work. He would toil 10 hours a day at the mill, staying longer than necessary. After six days of this, Mr. Sutherland told him to go home at a normal hour. To contrast that, Jackie would show up before the mill's regular start time of 7:00 AM to clean up and do work prior to the rest of the men arriving. It mattered little what time he left to go home, since he would work another 4 or 5 hours each evening – fixing the back step, clearing brush, sweeping the chimney – anything to busy his mind. He stayed outside with Ruby until dark each night; so late he could only hear her panting.

He lost weight.

He found some solace in retreating to the woods near his homestead. His mother having died a few years earlier, the property sat vacant. Jackie would walk for hours in the evening, or sit and drink by Little Brook.

Jackie used a refrigerator to smoke fish; an art taught to him when he was a teenager by his father. Close to where he grew up and just by Little Brook, Jackie, Boyd and Donny had transported his mother's old white fridge to the edge of the water – the appliance now flecked with rust and the paint withdrawn at the edges, the black handle loose at the fittings. They struggled to carry it from the road into a small clearing by the brook, then removed the door but kept the racks and shelves in place. It was the perfect mechanism to smoke shad, salmon, and grill all manners of delights.

The three men had spent a good many hours here with Claire. It was the brook they had grown up playing by when they were children. As grown men, they tended to sit by the old appliance in the woods, just out of sight from the road and anyone who may pass by. They were not doing anything illegal, as the brook passed through land owned by Jackie's family and most times the fish had been caught legally.

The clearing was only 70 yards from the road, but the foliage was so thick, no one bothered him. He often came just to listen to the sound of the water flowing over green, mossy rocks. He'd sit on an overturned blue milk crate, smoking a ciga-rette, drinking a beer and taking in the sounds and smells of the Acadian Forest. Jackie loved working at the sawmill but he appreciated the trees, the pines and birches and maples, their trunks rising high as if their tops brushed the blue sky. In some parts of the forest, the vegetation was so impenetrable, one could not see the sky on a clear day.

Jackie knew all too well from growing up in and around the woods that while beautiful on the edges, there are few places on earth as forbidding as the forest when darkness falls. The ghost stories of his youth haunted him here, his father's stories of ghosts behind the trees.

ooooo

Several broken gin bottles were found in Gen's car. The vehicle reeked as though rubbing alcohol had been poured all over the automobile, soaking the fabric. The driver of the truck was not charged, since it was Gen who had made the illegal U-turn.

Car collisions such as Gen's were not common in downtown Newcastle and as such, it made the front page of *The Miramichi Leader* days later. The shock of seeing the wreckage caused Jackie to drop the paper on the floor of the convenience store after he'd purchased it. It looked like a distant accident from a bygone era. Presented there in black-and-white sat Gen's car, smashed badly on the driver's side with the pick-up truck's front tires on top of her car. It was an older model that someone modified, the axles raised to give it more height. The photo had a tow truck in the background, as well as members of the volunteer fire department, police and several onlookers. The Canada Post sign loomed large in the background. Even in black and white, it was easy to see it was a sunny day. Jackie avoided this part of town now when he traveled in.

He did not want to have a full Roman Catholic ceremony but society, Gen's mother Victoria and Aunt Abigail dictated so.

Wakes were the worst. Jackie stood awkwardly by the body of what once was his best friend; Victoria, Abigail, and Gen's sisters stood to his left-hand side.

He hated every moment of it.

Jackie *did* appreciate that so many people came to pay their respects. For Jackie though, they were not paying their respects to Gen or Jackie or her mother or even Abigail. A good deal of people attended the services so that they could be *seen* by the rest of the community, making sure to write their names clearly in the ledger. None of these people, well-meaning or not, would be going to a hollowed-out home afterward, a home Gen and Jackie had shared for close to ten years. Jackie could not have cared less for the whole pageantry. Handshakes, bad tea, worse coffee, terrible breath, coughing fits, honking and sneezing into tissues and handkerchiefs, gooey sandwiches, formally dressed community members.

He was nauseous at every service.

All that waited for him at home was loss. He could not bear it. The day she died, he returned from the Moncton hospital, greeted by an excited Ruby, who had been left alone all day. She did not mess inside the house; she was so well behaved. He let her outside and then promptly collapsed at the table. He raised his head after several minutes and noticed a huge coffee stain on the curtain. He looked at the curved stain with confusion, scrunching his eyes together. He got up to ask Gen what had happened and was nearly in their bedroom before he realized she was not there.

Donny and Claire drove him to town for the services. After each of the three wakes he would walk aimlessly around Newcastle, returning only at the top of the hour when the service began and stood in line for hours, pretending to be appreciative, when all he wanted to do was sleep or drink; or drink then sleep. He detested standing there while the corpse of his wife lay on display, a ghoulish ornament, decorated and paraded. He could not look in the direction of the casket, though he was closest; within the contents lay something he could not identify.

He had taken to frequently leaving his post for the restroom. Leaving the line-up meant he did not have to speak to people for a few minutes, a bonus in an otherwise dreadful and gloomy affair. He took to sitting in a stall on the toilet lid, a moment to not have to pretend. He could sip on his flask, unencumbered by the community.

Why don't they give people chairs, for crying out loud? They've got chairs for every goddamn person in the place except for the people who need them most. He was quite sure Gen would want them all to be comfortable, particularly her grieving mother.

On one bathroom stall reprieve, Jackie realized he'd gained a new title.

He overheard two men talking. He did not recognize their voices. They were talking about baseball and Jackie almost leapt out of the stall to discuss something normal, something real that he enjoyed, if only for a few moments. He listened to feel like a human being again, not some poor bastard. He called them Dummy and Mr. La Femme.

"It was a good game though," said Dummy.

"Yup, right up until Newhauser blew it. Don't know why they brought him in," said Mr. La Femme.

"Catch that Expos' game the other night? Don't think they're ever going to make it."

Then it became hard for Jackie to hear what they were saying. They'd turned the taps on to wash their hands. He could only hear snippets now amidst the running water and paper towel drying.

"…stupid Mauch pulling…the sixth inning. Anyway, let's get…there…check on…"

"For sure…don't want to be that lad. Don't know how… being a *widower* and all."

The door opened and closed. Jackie could hear scraps of discussions for a few seconds, then stillness; alone again with the pulsating florescent lights.

Widower. It was a term he did not think applied to him and he had not considered it ever would. How could he be a widower? *Wasn't the man supposed to go first?* He put his head in his hands and rubbed his face. Even in death, Gen did not follow the proper order of things and that made him smile. His wife was singular that way: she followed her own path and would not let anyone tell her what to do or what to say.

Better get back out there.

He took a deep breath and then gagged, remembering he was in a bathroom stall at a funeral home. It now proved to be a good thing he had not eaten in days.

She crept upstairs.

JACKIE GREW FURTHER DEPRESSED. It was months before Claire used the term and he still did not believe it. Men do not get depressed.

"You don't look too good. Donny says the same."

"Thanks for your compliments."

"It's not like that Jackie and you know it. We're just concerned, is all. You're not the only one who lost Gen."

"You didn't lose your spouse though, did ya? Hope you never know what that feels like."

Claire opened up a jar of mustard pickles, pouring some out into a dish. She'd made tea and put out a small lunch in the hopes that Jackie would stay and eat.

"Well, me neither but we're just worried about you. You don't come for dinner when we ask. You don't even come over for tea or coffee or beer. You're not eating."

"I'm alright. Need time to myself."

Food had no flavor. The liquor gave him fleeting moments of relief but not happiness. It only served to numb his feelings. He hated how dreamlike it all felt. Jackie prided himself on having his feet firmly planted on the ground but this felt like he was falling. Even the cawing of crows and chitters of squirrels became distant, underwater noises. The river lapped against the canoe in a bizarre manner. Everything had changed, nothing made sense and Jackie felt listless. He was on a ship that was forever sinking.

Ruby whined at night in the bedroom. She went from room to room, looking for Gen. It made Jackie's heart break even harder. He could not change the bed sheets. He could still smell her on the pillowcase. Going through her closet and mementos felt like an invasion of privacy. He felt at any moment she might come into the bedroom and see him going through her things. The stillness of the clothing unsettled him; the wardrobe became creepy and unnerving to him. *Why are they still here?* Items he found in her drawers would never have an explanation now: a brittle chunk of driftwood, a piece of rose quartz glittering in the sunlight, a light grey guitar pick. Souvenirs from her past he picked up and placed on his nightstand.

Not even Ruby's company could make him feel less alone. She would crawl up next to him, looking for companionship. One day he was so angry and exasperated, he became cross at Ruby and pushed her away. She crept upstairs. Scared. Later, he grabbed a lump of ham from the fridge, climbed the stairs, fed her the treat and fell asleep beside her.

Lots of friends and family invited him over for dinner or a beer to watch his beloved Expos. Boyd stopped by repeatedly but was turned away. Mike Emery had Kenny Somers drive him to Jackie's house with a few bottles of whisky. Mike rarely left his house. Jackie turned them all down, including Victoria, Gen's mother, indefinitely red-eyed from crying. He wanted to be alone and feared that if he was in the company of others, they would ask him how he was doing or would inevitably bring up Gen, thinking it offered empathy. He needed to avoid all of it. He did not wish to be ungrateful; he could not fathom talking about her in the past tense.

Occasionally, he would come across the smallest of details. While picking up some basics at the convenience store – smokes, coffee, bread, canned ham, mayonnaise – a box of instant beef noodles caught his eye. He welled up and immediately left everything on the counter for the clerk to handle. He left the store in tears and nearly ran over Mrs. Sutherland as he exited, without saying excuse me.

When they first started living together, Gen would buy box after box of instant noodles beef mix and throw it in with a pound of hamburger, making meals for Jackie to take as leftovers. He balked at it, not liking the taste, until Gen told him he could cook for himself if he liked. He was silent on such things the remainder of their time together. The smell, the taste, it all came rushing back to him and he could not think of anything he wanted more at that moment than to walk into his house and find his wife preparing a cheap box of instant beef noodles.

Jackie was not prepared for any of this and spent nearly every dollar he had, including some he had to borrow from Mike, to pay for her funeral. Several times a week, a letter was delivered from the Government of New Brunswick, Publisher's Clearing House or Sears, addressed to Genevieve.

"Don't these fuckin' people know she's dead?" he asked, angry at the whole world for not stopping what they were doing and acknowledging that the world had lost one of its best. He had to write "Return to sender" on more envelopes than he cared to.

By the time their anniversary arrived at the beginning of July, Jackie entered his deepest depression. The day was cruel perfection. He did not know how to go on. He briefly considered giving himself up to the river.

He went to sleep early that evening and had his first nightmare about the woman.

II

"The very best."

T HE SUMMER OF 1982 lazily crawled from July to August. The dog days had set in. The sweet smell of goldenrod grew shoulder high and filled the air. The river became murkier. Speculation around a provincial election grew from non-stop media conjecture to near certainty. Most elections were held in the spring or fall and Jackie figured that since they were well past spring, ol' Richard Hatfield was gearing up for another run.

He was in the breakroom, reading the paper. The radio was blaring a song about a magic spell. Boyd came in to have lunch and found Jackie.

"'Lo Jackie," said Boyd.

"How she goin', Boyd?"

"The very best. Nice day, eh?"

"For sure. Listen: what does it say about a lad if he tells ya he's a conservative but all he does is gallivant around the country doing drugs? He's more like one of the Central American *El Presidentes* than a conservative."

"Yup. Yup," Boyd nodded in agreement. "They're gonna find that lad with dope on him someday."

"You know it. That lad's more doped to the eyeballs than Paddy asleep over in the corner there. Look at 'im!"

Paddy was resting his eyes in the corner of the breakroom. Renovations from the funding provided by Donny had not yet begun. Mr. Sutherland said he could not spare the man-hours over the summer to have the breakroom reconstructed and half the mill shut down. He pleaded with the men, conceding and said they could begin at the end of September when the majority of wood was cut and delivered from the summer.

"Yup. Yup. Young Paddy does like that dope."

"Now, I don't care what a lad like Paddy does but he ain't runnin' the province now, is he?"

"Nope."

"That's right. I think it was the drugs that clouded that lad's brain when he gave over millions to make that crazy car down in Saint John."

Boyd twisted the cap from his blue thermos and poured coffee into the top, taking measured sips.

"Yup. That ridiculous lookin' car. Why couldn't he try to bring a normal car company here? I got nothin' against him trying to create jobs but bring something normal."

Jackie folded the paper neatly and rested it on the table, picking up his own cup of coffee.

"Don't look like a car you could drive around these roads. Looks like a car Hatfield would want to drive, though."

"For sure. And the only thing Hatfield was manufacturing was one of them joints Paddy's so fond of."

Boyd could only nod in agreement. He finally got a chance to take a bite of his ham, cheese and tomato sandwich.

"And Doug Young, don't get me started on him. I mean, he's a nice enough guy but right now that Liberal party here is completely discombobulated."

Boyd continued to nod affirmatively while chewing. Paddy had stirred and approached the table.

"What about the NDP?" asked a lethargic Paddy.

"Oh yeah. Here we go! Ol' sleepyhead himself here, talkin' up the CCF! I'll be voting Parti Acadien before I vote for George Little and his band of commie-hippies."

"I just think they offer a few new ideas, is all," said Paddy as he opened his lunch can and took out his thermos of water.

"Don't let Mr. Sutherland hear you talkin' CCF," cautioned Boyd. "He's likely to fire you on the spot."

"But what about Medicare? We wouldn't have it if it weren't for the NDP helpin' out the federal Liberals and what's-his-name? Mike Parsons?"

"Pearson. Mike Pearson," said Boyd. "Or whatever his real name was."

"Here we go again!" exclaimed Jackie. He was standing up now, throwing his hands in the air, flailing about like a snake healer at the pulpit. Boyd grinned, adjusted his chair and settled in for the show.

"Listen here, Cheech: every time someone mentions Medicare or Lester Pearson, they gotta tack on the CCF to the discussion! Look Paddy, Medicare is a good thing but the Liberals woulda had the votes up in Ottawa no matter what the CCF did. Social Credit and whatever that Réal Couette party called themselves up in Quebec were gonna vote for it, too."

"I didn't know you were such a Liberal defender, Jackie," Boyd said, winking at Paddy.

"I'm not a Liberal defender. I'm just a defender of history. Am I right?"

"Yes, you're right about that, Jackie. Social Credit was gonna vote for Medicare, regardless. It's great the CCF or NDP or whatever made it happen in Saskatchewan first but it wasn't just them that gave us national friggin' medicare."

"I just think the NDP bring something new to the table," said Paddy.

"Well, I guess we know how Paddy's voting this fall."

Paddy removed a rollie from his cigarette pack and lit it. He blew a puff of smoke straight up in the air.

"Not necessarily though, Mr. Boyd. I'm just all for hearin' people out."

"Someone should punch that Hatfield in the nose. That lad has put more people out of work than dysentery," Jackie expressed to no one in particular.

"Maybe I'll vote different than the NDP," said Paddy. "How about you, Jackie?"

"It's a secret ballot, Paddy, but don't worry, I'll cast my vote on Election Day."

"Yeah, but who ya votin' for?" said Boyd.

Jackie rose from his chair, stretching his arms to the ceiling.

"Oh, probably Doug Young. Can't stand Hatfield anymore."

Jackie disliked the Progressive Conservative leader with a passion. He had the premier's picture up in his woodshed, but in classic Jackie fashion, framed by an old toilet seat. It had a few darts, a couple of nails and other projectiles sticking into the face or littered around the old photo of New Brunswick's premier. It was a proud tradition he'd carried from his father's shed who had a similar design for previous Premiers of New Brunswick: P'tit Louis, Hugh John Flemming and more.

Paddy finished his cigarette and pulled out another. Jackie was already on his second post-lunch smoke. There were only 10 minutes left before they had to get back to work. The sun beat down and as its beam crossed the yard, it would crawl into the break room by the time they went back to work.

The men turned as the sound of the office door opened and closed. Mrs. Sutherland left the office and was walking to her husband's truck. Once again, she looked over at Boyd and had a small grin on her face. Jackie caught the twinkle in Boyd's eye. He realized Jackie was watching him. Boyd promptly looked away and began to drink his coffee. Jackie raised an eyebrow at Boyd, now blushing.

"Jackie, I'm heading to Fredericton next weekend if you want to go punch him," said Paddy.

"Punch who?"

"The Premier. Whatshisface. Hatfield."

Jackie shook his head in disbelief.

"Hold 'er! Hold 'er! I don't really want to punch the premier in the face, Paddy. Just cool yer jets. Anyway, when are you going over?"

"Leaving Saturday morning and probably coming back the same day."

"Hmm. I do need a new paddle. Mine has seen better days. Maybe I'll get that new canoe I've been thinking about."

"Speaking of shiny new things, that's a nice new truck you got there, Paddy," said Boyd. "Where did you get it?"

Paddy's truck had been a point of discussion amongst the mill workers for the last couple of months. He pulled up in a blue half-ton Chevrolet one morning and parked it in the yard next to the other vehicles. Everyone watched him as he got out of the truck and walked to the mill. He never bragged about it to anyone, did not speak of it. The lack of bragging about a new vehicle caught everyone off guard.

"Oh, it's my sister's. She's not using it these days and said I could."

"Which sister is that?"

"Camille."

"Ah, okay," replied Jackie. Boyd nodded slowly.

Jackie was suspicious, since most folks knew Camille had been training to become a doctor. She recently finished her studies at Dalhousie University in Halifax and moved home after completing her course work. She was doing her practicum in Chatham. How she would have an extra, practically brand-new truck lying around to loan her brother was another thing, though.

Paddy changed the subject. "Anyway, I'm heading over on the weekend."

"Well, might take a drive over with ya," said Jackie.

"Sure Jackie, take a drive over with Paddy with all yer newfound riches," quipped Boyd.

"That's enough, Boyd. I don't even want that money. Still tryin' to figure out how to give most of it away."

It had become widely known that Donny had won the lottery and died tragically days later. It was all people talked about in the community for a number of weeks. *The Miramichi Weekend* even did a story on it, though it did not appear in *The Miramichi Leader* until the following Tuesday.

Nobody bothered a grieving widow about the large sum of cash her husband left her, but many people had approached Jackie. He gave a fair amount of it away and eventually had to withdraw the whole amount. He bought a safe on the advice of the bank manager and had it firmly stored at home, where he believed no one would ever find it. He did not mind giving the money to those in need or he felt deserved it. Jackie knew some folks though were only looking for money to go towards a new whirlpool bathtub with the fancy jets or something else they really did not need. He was actually more inclined to give folks twenty dollars when they asked for it, even if it were for a bottle of rum. Life is hard. Sometimes, people need a drink.

Jackie quickly alienated and irritated people. His front window was broken out in mid-July. Gossip spread through the community, and a good many people were saying nasty things about him – he sat in his house like some king, handing out money to whomever he deemed worthy. Jackie did not care what people said about him but also felt that it was his money and he would damn well give it to whomever he damned well pleased.

"You can give *me* some," said Boyd.

"How much do ya need?"

"How's about five hundred?"

"You know something Boyd? Why not? Donny'd prob- ably want me to give ya five hundred. Come on by tonight and I'll give it to you."

"Really? Shit. I should have asked for a thousand."

"I think I can manage that, Boyd."

"Right on, Jackie!" Boyd leapt from his chair, patting Jackie on the shoulder. "I'll swing by around eight. Expos are playing Philly tonight, aren't they?"

"Yes, they are."

"Well, I'll pick up a case and let's watch the game."

"Sounds good."

"How about me?" asked Paddy.

"You? With your big, new fancy truck? What do you need money for?"

"Anything's a help, Mr. O'Connor. Just because I got my sister's truck doesn't mean I'm living high on the hog or anything."

"Well, let me think on it, Paddy."

Paddy responded with a bow of his head but glint of distaste crossed his mouth. Jackie did not care for the way Paddy looked up at him.

The men packed up the remains of their lunches and headed back to work in the early afternoon sun.

Jackie hazarded a blink.

THE SUN WAS LOW IN THE SKY but the temperature elevated for an early autumn evening. The deciduous trees continued to show life with bright green leaves, still devoted to their branches, though some were threatening to turn the many colours of fall. Autumn in the Miramichi Valley is brief yet beautiful, Jackie thought while idly paddling his canoe.

A blue jay screeched. A salmon leapt from the water, devouring a fly. Jackie's late evening canoe voyage involved making a liquor run to the other side of the river in South Esk. He glided along with Ruby sitting bow. She occasionally dipped her snout in the cool river when she spotted a fish. Jackie paddled idly, allowing the light southwest breeze to do its work and carry him down river. It was not a long trip and he saw no reason to rush it. This evening was one of the exceptional times when he was alone on the water. No loud motorboats, no pontoons, nobody else canoeing or swimming.

He let his mind drift to Gen. Sometimes he would not permit her image to flood his brain. It was too painful. He often had to suppress the urge to think about her and live in his memories. The respite was wonderful but short-lived and always left him feeling melancholy. This evening though, he allowed his mind to think about her. He smiled.

He crossed the river to the south side and approached Shillelagh Hill. Ruby began a low growl, revealing her teeth, and Jackie pulled his paddle out of the water. The vessel slid quietly; small waves brushed against the canoe. He scanned the shore 60 yards away to see if there was a bear or some other animal that might put Ruby on high alert. Jackie could see nothing. He listened and then became aware of something alarming: there was no sound. Nothing at all. He could not even hear the water lapping against his canoe anymore. No robins peeping, no more jays shrieking, no fish jumping, no click clack of grasshoppers. All sounds of the natural world ceased.

No.

Jackie felt a sledgehammer of fear hit him, so hard his breath was taken; a form of panic that told him to paddle away from this place *now.* Ruby started whimpering. She looked at him.

"RUN," Ruby said. Jackie heard her speak clearly. "WE NEED TO GO." Her mouth didn't move but he heard her.

Something wicked lay in the woods, underneath the low hanging branches and brush, where the earth is cold and the heat of the sun does not penetrate. Jackie saw visions of the slick, unfriendly underside of a rock with grubs, beetles and worms crawling in the foul dirt.

He had been kneeling to canoe properly but stood up. He could not help it. He had to get a better view as the canoe slowly but gradually coasted to shore.

Ruby pawed his legs. Jackie felt the temperature drop. He looked closely, squinting in the disappearing sunlight and could see his breath. He knew the evening sun could play tricks on the eyes. Mirages often appeared at dusk.

They moved closer to shore. Ruby was now under the front seat of the canoe, cowering. Jackie could not recall his 60-pound Irish Setter ever reacting this way to anything. Not to thunder, not to fireworks, not even to the black bear that came on his land from time to time to eat crab apples.

A presence was waiting for them out of sight, in the woods. Jackie did not have his .30-30 with him for he saw no reason to carry it on this short trip. He reached down into the bag and hauled out one of the rum bottles he was delivering, unscrewed the cap and took a long pull. He carefully put the cap back on, set the bottle on the floor of the canoe and unfastened the button on the leather sheath of his hunting knife. He pulled the long, steel blade from the deer-leather sheath, the edge sharp and unkind.

They were now only 10 yards from shore. The only sound Jackie could hear was Ruby whining quietly and the sound of her peeing.

Why isn't she talking anymore?

Ruby doesn't talk. What am I saying?

He could see his heart beating in his fingers. All was still except for his right hand, white knuckled around the smooth wooden handle of the knife, brandished in front of him. Jackie stood tall, his feet planted on the floor of the canoe.

The canoe gently came to shore. The noise it made in the silence sounded like thunder as the fiberglass scraped atop the rocks.

Ruby yelped. *"Jackie, get back to the other side of the river!"* Only this time it wasn't Ruby's voice. It was Gen's. He had forgotten the comforting sound of her voice.

Stepping over the dog, Jackie placed his feet on greasy rocks and hoisted the canoe from the water. He felt something behind him. He turned, the hunting knife thrusting from his hand but all he slashed was the still air.

He took a deep breath, the first one in minutes, and heard a noise to his left. Spinning, he turned and pointed the hunting knife downriver.

Thirty feet away stood something bipedal. Jackie could tell it was not human; at least not anymore. It had breasts he could plainly see. The old Victorian blouse with a high collar and cameo broach attached at the neck was torn open, shredded in sections. It had a grey and craggy face, strewn with muck and dark blonde hair. Both eye sockets were hollow yet Jackie knew it could see him. Its left arm was missing below the elbow, a spikey chipped bone jutting from the stub. The right arm draped at its side and was twice as long as it should be, with the fore knuckles of the fingers touching the cold, damp shore. The creature wore a dark grey, tattered, blood-spattered skirt.

He stood, gawking at the ghost, a soul from some other place and some other time. It started to make a low humming sound and its long, protracted right arm began to rise, two boney fingers pointing at Jackie. He opened his mouth wide to scream, to curse, but no sound came out. He shakily presented the knife in front of him in defense.

Jackie hazarded a blink. When he opened his eyes, the wraith was an inch from his face. The humming was deafening now, the sound of 10,000 hornets.

A ghost. The Ghost of Shillelagh Hill. His father had been right. All the stories were true.

The smell from the ghoul crippled him. It was neither obscene nor pleasant but seemed to take in all the air around it. It opened its mouth and Jackie could see all of its teeth were present and white but the tissue inside, normally soft and pink, was the shade of bone marrow. The stink of ruin was its breath. Somewhere on the outskirts of the humming, he could hear Ruby howling.

The ghost looked toward the water. Jackie followed its path and turned his head to the left. The stillness of the evening river created a perfect reflection. Jackie could see himself and he looked much the same as he did when he awoke that morning. The phantom, however, appeared as she would have when she was alive: hair the colour of flax, fair skin with blue eyes, a beauty mark on the right side of her mouth. A woman in her early thirties but from a different era.

The woman from his nightmares.

He made no register of the words the reflection spoke. He could not hear above the droning. Her mouth moved in the reflection but Jackie only understood there was fear in her words. The eyes of the reflection showed terror. She had something to tell him and she was in danger, pleading with her hands.

When the reflection realized he could not understand her, the woman in the water raised her face to the sky, her mouth contorting in a scream. The reflection turned into what lay in front of him: a cursed soul, unsettled in death.

He blinked away tears and the ghost was 10 feet away from him. He blinked again and it was more than 100 feet away, the humming getting softer with each blink. His eyes flashed once more and she was gone, vanishing into the easy evening light. The humming and odor were replaced with the familiar smell of the river.

He was sitting on the ground with the eel grass towering above his eyes, the hunting knife lying on the shore to his right. He could hear Ruby whimpering.

Jackie took deep, rapid breaths, reached for the knife and pressed the tip into his left arm to see if he were alive. Red escaped his skin and he wept. He scampered into the canoe and lay on the floor while unscrewing the bottle of rum. He drank nearly one-quarter of it in a gulp. He pushed himself and Ruby from shore back onto the darkening water, scared to look in the river once they reached the channel, for fear the specter might come thrashing out of the depths and take him under. Daylight fading, he floated upriver with the incoming tide.

∞∞∞∞

WHEN JACKIE WASHED ASHORE, Ruby hopped out of the canoe. He realized the tide had carried him further upriver than where he lived but it mattered little. He was closer to Donny and Claire's house.

Or just Claire's house, I guess.

He dragged the boat up into the woods and tied it tightly with some rope he had in the canoe. He put another length of rope around Ruby's neck and collar. Then he remembered that she *spoke* to him earlier. He remembered her speaking to him.

He leaned down to look her in the eye. She was unable to speak, that much he could tell. Jackie patted her on the head.

He cut a path through the woods, making certain to stay clear of Claire's house. The last thing Jackie could do right now was talk to someone. He was frightened and drunk. No one would believe him with his breath reeking of rum. When he reached the chipseal, it was full dark and Jackie half-ran down the road.

When he got inside his house, he immediately poured himself another stiff drink of whisky, then drained it. He put some water in Ruby's dish but when he turned around, she was already asleep, as if nothing had happened.

Did she really speak to me? What the fuck just happened? I heard Gen's voice.

And the ghost. The woman. She's real.

Jackie drunkenly climbed his stairs and went into his bathroom. He needed to turn the light on but was scared to do so, fearing the ghost may have followed him home and would be waiting for him in the mirror. He took a deep breath, flicked the switch with his right index finger but kept his eyes closed.

He carefully opened his left eye. The image reflected was his own. Jackie had never looked worse, even when Genevieve died. He stripped his clothes off one by one and turned on the shower. He got in and twisted the knob to the right as far as it would go. He stood in steam of the water, trying to heat his bones. He stayed in the welcoming heat until the water began to cool. He turned the nozzle off and dried himself with a rough towel and scampered to his room. In bed, he reached over and snapped off his bedside lamp.

What was the woman trying to tell me? he wondered before falling down an elevator shaft and into a deep, dreamless sleep.

"You want the Half Lune-Moon or the Jos Louis?"

JACKIE WAS NOT CONVINCED he didn't have a stroke or perhaps imagined the whole episode the night before.

Jesus Christ, the dog was talking to me. I must have been dreaming or I'm losing my mind.

He was amazed he slept so deeply. After a cigarette and a cup of coffee, Jackie was up and ready. He always relished his ability to not get hungover, even now in middle age. He metabolized alcohol well. He stood on his back porch and checked his watch. 6:30 AM. A crow cawed incessantly and he turned to watch Ruby nose around the backyard. He took in a deep breath of morning air, already cool compared to a few weeks ago.

Something had tracked through the property last night. He figured it must have been a rabbit or maybe a couple of deer, though there had been a bear around as of late. He walked over to Ruby, who was still nosing around in the grass.

The grass had been tamped down in several places, he saw. It was hard to tell but Jackie spent a lot of time in the woods and knew that only humans make tracks like these. Big footprints. Someone as large, maybe even heavier than himself.

Somebody's been snooping around my house. With all that money in his safe, he knew exactly why. The question was who. *Were they looking for an open window?*

He checked his watch again. 6:38 AM. Paddy was late to pick him up. Jackie sat on his step while he waited for his drive to Fredericton and thought about possible thieves.

It could be anyone.

Maybe a few teenagers.

He thought about security and knew the house was locked up solidly but perhaps a security camera was needed. He would look into that after returning from Fredericton. *If Paddy ever decides to show up.*

He had spent little of the inherited money on himself and was happy at the prospect of getting a new canoe. Maybe a few other items at Jamieson's hunting store. Summer was already starting to wain and he'd had a difficult enough spring.

It's been a tough five years, be honest with yourself. Since Gen died, nothing's been easy. A little retail therapy never hurt nobody.

Paddy.

Where is that tit? Probably up late smoking marijuana and hanging with friends. That's the trouble with young lads; all they want to do is play.

Jackie never had that inkling. It was not that he wanted to

work all of his life. It was simply that in order to play, you had to work. It was a matter of life.

Relax, he told himself. *Be easy on the young lad. He's giving you a drive to Fredericton and back, after all.*

Jackie had hoped to be at Jamieson's for 8:30 sharp so he could get what he needed and store his purchases in Paddy's truck. He planned to spend the remainder of the day walking around the city, perhaps grabbing a couple beer at The Lunar Rogue on King Street while he waited for Paddy and whatever in hell he was going to buy in Fredericton. Too many times Jackie had been a little hard on Paddy, and while he was an airhead and a dope smoker, he was a good enough young lad. Jackie figured he owed the boy a couple beers and a bite to eat for offering to drive him over to "Freddy Beach" as Paddy kept calling it. When Jackie asked Paddy where the beach was, Paddy chuckled and said, "Oh I don't know, Mr. O'Connor. That's just what people call Fredericton sometimes." It sounded stupid to Jackie. He did not care what people called the capital city. What he knew about Fredericton was that it is precisely 95 miles from where he was currently sitting on his back step, it took approximately two hours to drive there and he was already behind schedule because Paddy was late.

He was stroking Ruby's head, a cigarette in the crook of his mouth when he heard the crunch of tires on his driveway. He turned his head and saw Paddy round the corner in his sister's truck. Jackie still didn't believe it. *Where did he get enough money for a new truck?*

ooooo

"Mornin', Mr. O'Connor."

A loud motorbike ripped by his driveway, a malfunctioning machine gun sound echoing through the misty morning air.

"Yer late." Jackie peered through the truck window, rolled halfway down. He put out his cigarette as he opened the door and threw his smokes on the seat.

"Yessir. Sorry 'bout that. Had to fill up the truck at the gas station in Sunny Corner. Ran inside to get some smokes and grab you and me a cup of coffee. Picked up a few of them Vachon Cakes. You want the Half-Lune Moon or the Jos Louis?"

"It's just 'Half-Moon'. Not Half-Lune Moon. That's the French part."

Paddy stared blankly at Jackie.

"Just give me the Half-Moon but hold on a minute while I get Ruby some more food and water for the day. We're still coming back tonight, eh?"

"Yessir. That's the plan."

"It better be. And along the way, how 'bout you tell me where you got this new truck. And don't tell me it's your sister's. No one – not me, nor Boyd nor anyone else believes that one bit."

Paddy shifted in his seat. "We'd better get going," he said nervously. "We're already late. I'll tell you about the truck when we hit the road, Mr. O'Connor."

"Good enough. One minute."

Jackie poured enough food into Ruby's dish to feed three dogs her size and filled the other with hose water.

After removing his money from the bank and putting the funds in the safe, Jackie had purchased a lock for the back door.

He did not worry about the front door. After Donny's incident earlier in the year, he sealed the door up with insulation and nailed it shut from the inside. Jackie turned the little button on the doorknob, sliding the large gold dead bolt. He then pulled and pushed the door several times until he was satisfied no one could break in.

He caught Paddy looking at him from the truck then quickly looking down.

Jackie grabbed his duffle bag, walked over and hopped in the truck. He put the bag on the back and got in the passenger side.

"Let's get going. Need to get some air flowin' through the

truck. It's already showin' sixty-six degrees on the thermometer."

"You bet, Mr. O'Connor. Let's hit the road."

Paddy pulled out onto R.R. #1, turning right to Sunny Corner. He made his way to R.R. #2 before navigating the turn to Warwick Settlement. From here on out, it was nearly a straight drive all the way to Fredericton.

Jackie thought it was generous of Paddy to get him the coffee. He opened the flap to take a drink and spit it out the window.

"Jesus Christ. What did you put in this? It tastes like baby formula."

"Three milk and two sugars. Same as me."

"That's disgusting." Jackie flung the coffee out the window, cup and all.

"Yer not supposed to litter, Mr. O'Connor. It's bad for the Ricosystem."

"It's *eco-system*, ya dope. Just drive. The day is half gone."

It was going to be a long drive to Freddy Beach, thought Jackie.

*"Well life is bleak, Paddy. Why should
the afterlife be any different?"*

FORTY MINUTES AFTER DEPARTING, Jackie and Paddy found themselves sweltering on the hot pavement of Route #8. A plane flew overhead, the sound of its engine penetrating the air. The waterbomber was flying low, looking for wildfires. The summer of 1982 was a dry season, baking the woodlands. Jackie remembered hearing on the radio this morning there were fifteen active forest fires in New Brunswick.

They were in the community of Astle, which Jackie knew to be nothing but trees and wildlife; even less so of the former with all the clearcutting that had been happening the last number of years. Nevertheless, there they were – right in the middle of a long line of automobiles. Jackie stuck his head out the window, stretching to look forward and backward at the string of cars and judged there were approximately thirty vehicles. This was the Government of New Brunswick's favourite summer activity, Jackie thought: highway construction.

"See, this is why we needed to leave by 6:30," complained Jackie. "We could have avoided all this if you'd just been on time. Now, we're stuck here, waiting for the jeezless sign turners to let us through. What a waste of time."

"I think we're gonna get through soon."

"You don't know nothin'. We're at the mercy of these lads and who knows how long we'll be stuck here. And there's a blind hill up there, so we can't even see what's happening. They could be paving or chip sealing or tearing up the road."

Paddy sat, loudly sipping his coffee.

"And that's another thing, I don't even have a coffee to drink while we wait."

"I bought you one though, Mr. O'Connor."

"That weren't no coffee. That was a hot milkshake."

Paddy stared straight ahead. He leaned over and turned the radio on.

"You're not going to get much here. We're too low and there's a lot of hills."

Jackie was correct. Paddy turned the dial slowly. Static and bits of sentences popped through the radio. He briefly picked up what sounded like a biblical story on an AM station but it only crackled and spit out the odd word of scripture.

"Christ, if that's all we got to listen to, I'm happy for the static. Or the beeping from the graders."

"You're not a God-fearing man, Mr. O'Connor?"

"Nope."

"How come?"

"Who's got time for that?" The large airtanker passed overhead again, filling the still air for a moment.

"Yeah but, you know, heaven and hell and all that." Paddy sipped his coffee, now nearly empty.

"Gibberish. Stories they told people in a time long ago

who didn't know what makes thunder and lightning. That's all it is."

"So, when we die, what happens to us?"

"We go into the ground or we get cremated. That's it."

"Sounds kinda bleak."

"Well life is bleak, Paddy. Why should the afterlife be any different?"

"That's kinda sad though, ain't it? I mean, what do you think happened to yer wife after she died?"

Jackie took a long pull from his cigarette and looked over at Paddy.

"She died. That's what happened to her. We cremated her remains and spread them in the river and that's that. She ain't in no heaven and she certainly ain't in no hell. The lad who smashed into her didn't get nothing. He had one of those stupid trucks with the raised axles. Sure, it was ruled Gen's fault, but if that truck wasn't so high up it wouldn't have rolled up on top of the car and smashed her face in."

They sat in silence. The long line of cars did not move. A dragonfly landed on windshield for the briefest of moments before taking off to hunt for midges, mosquitoes and flies.

"Sorry, Paddy. I don't talk to many people about Gen. Never really have after…"

"No, no. Didn't mean to bring it up."

Paddy threw the truck into park and shut it off.

"Mayzell save some gas while we wait."

"Now that's the smartest thing you've done all day. It's only 7:30 in the morning, so there's time yet to redeem yerself."

"The cooler in the back has some cold beers in it. Not sure if you want one so early."

"There's hope for you yet, young Brewster."

Jackie slid the rear window across and reached into the cooler in the bed of the truck. He pulled out two cold beers and used his lighter to pop the caps and handed one to Paddy. Paddy took a long drink.

"Keep that down, now. That car behind us is full of

Go-Preachers by the looks of 'em. They're likely to walk up here and start telling us what a sin we're commitin' by drinking so early. Or drinkin' and drivin'. Or drinking at all, for that matter."

Paddy took a look in his rear-view mirror. The men in the car were dressed formally for an early Saturday morning.

"What's a Go-Preacher?"

"A form of Christianity. They believe in the same as the rest of 'em, basically. Just a little different. There ain't much difference in any of it, far as I can tell."

"Don't you think there's something to what all the religions say though? There's always religion popping up everywhere. I mean, don't matter where you are: India, China, Italy, Canada, British Columbia."

"British Columbia is part of Canada."

"What? Why's it called British Columbia then?"

"Fucked if I know. Probably because the Queen and all her inbred cousins ruled the country until we had the Charter of Rights and Freedoms put into place back in April. And still, she's officially the head of the country. So, it didn't really change much."

"The Queen of England is the head of Canada?"

Jackie looked at Paddy and then fished in his back pocket. He withdrew his worn, leather brown wallet and smoothed out a well-used dollar bill on his thigh before turning it towards Paddy.

"See that? That's the Queen of England. Queen Elizabeth II. Ever wonder why she's on our money?"

"*That's* the Queen of England? I thought that was Harriet Irving."

"Well, around here we may as well put her on our money too."

"But you don't really believe in no religion?"

"The only one I ever saw or read about worth anything was Buddhism."

"What's that?"

"Comes from China. Or India. India, I think. Or one of

them places over there. More of a philosophy, really. You give up your attachments in life and that frees ya from sufferin'. In a nutshell."

"Wha? How's getting rid of my new truck gonna make my life better?"

"Because if you don't get attached to it, you won't miss it when it's gone."

"I just bought it though. Why's it gonna break?"

"It's not, ya dummy. But it will. Eventually. Take a look around you. The things we can touch don't have permanence. What I'm saying is, if you lose attachment to things you won't miss them. When you die, you don't take anything with you."

A chipmunk ran along the shoulder of the road, stopped and looked at Jackie. It darted back into the brambles to find cooler earth.

Paddy blew out a long sigh. "That's fucking deep. Kinda depressin'."

"Welcome to life, Paddy. An awful lot of it can be depressing."

"I like the idea of an afterlife a lot more. Seems a little happier."

"See there's the problem though. You like the idea because that's all it is: an *idea*. You don't like the thought of rotting in the ground and that you're no different than the worms that'll eat ya. I read an article a few years ago, mostly because Gen was a lot more worldly than me and she used to buy them National Geographics. One of them had an section about Tibet and the Buddhists there. When they die, they have a funeral or what they call a funeral in Tibet and whatnot. Then when they're all done the song and dance, they just take the body out to the side of the mountain and leave it there for the animals to eat."

"Jesus."

"Just the opposite, really."

"Why would they do somethin' like that? It's indecent."

"All depends on what you think is decent. We wrap people up in coffins that cost thousands of dollars and take decades to decompose. Over there, they take the body out and it feeds the birds and animals and they believe that's more natural and giving back to nature and such. Seems to me like it's a far more logical option."

"Mr. O'Connor, you're not gonna make us throw you on the side of the river for the coyotes to eat, are ya?"

Jackie chuckled, choking on his cigarette smoke.

"Well, I'm not exactly planning to go anytime soon, Paddy, but no, when my time comes, I'll be cremated. Don't like the idea of sittin' in the ground, rotting away like an old turnip. Fire me up and then the ashes go to the river. Maybe some of my ashes will find Gen's ashes along the way. Best I can hope for."

It grew still in the cab of the warm truck. The line had started to move along but still showed no signs of advancing quickly.

"I was awful sorry to hear when Mrs. O'Connor passed."

Jackie took a drag off his cigarette and sighed the smoke out of his mouth. He looked absently out the window. "I know."

"I know it was a few years ago now, but when I was really young, she was always good to me. You know she once gave me twenty bucks because we had no money at home and I needed new shoes? I went to town with Uncle Gene and I picked up a brand-new pair of Nighthawks. I only got rid of them a couple years ago. That was the nicest thing anyone ever did for me. And that weren't the only time. She used to give me a few dollars here and there when she saw me."

Jackie stoically nodded. After a moment he said, "Well, that was Gen. She cared about everyone around her, didn't matter if you were family or not."

The flag turner about 20 yards from the truck suddenly grabbed his walkie-talkie as an indecipherable noise squawked from the speaker. He brought it to his mouth. He turned the sign from STOP/ARRET to SLOW/LENTEMENT. He began waving his arm dramatically and vehicles began rolling forward.

"Finally. Thought we'd be here 'til noon."

They passed by the flag turner.

"Look at him. So much power," said Jackie. "Yer doin' the Lord's work out here!" he shouted as he went by the flag turner. The highway worker gave him a dirty look.

He stuck his torso out the window, leaning against the window frame.

"Yeah! Go ahead. Give us them looks! Lad makes fifteen dollars an hour to flip a sign. Unreal."

Henry sat contrite. He relit his pipe
and puffed away.

JACKIE AND PADDY ARRIVED on the north side of Fredericton at 9:48. Jackie had been checking his new watch every three minutes since they made it through road construction, his feet dancing in the passenger seat. It was one hour and forty-eight minutes later than Jackie had expected to arrive at Jamieson's.

By midmorning the strong sun they had felt in Miramichi had deteriorated, the yellow star cloaked in ominous clouds. The sun was a perfect circle as it fought to shine light through the greying veil.

Last night's vision sat in his mind, unwilling to budge no matter what he tried to think about to change his thoughts. He had done his best to push the feelings deep down with conversation or looking at the scenery as Paddy's truck whipped by the passel of villages en route to Fredericton. Every time they passed a township, the forest emerged again and his thoughts returned to dread and fear. The experience lurked, somewhere under his toes; an incessant, dreadful meditation. *Was it real? Did I have a stroke? Why did I see the same ghost from my dreams? How did she come to life out of my goddamn nightmares?*

Jackie had never spoken of the Victorian era woman from his nightmares, nor did he plan to speak to anyone about his possible paranormal encounter, either. No one would believe him; at least, nobody he knew. He was also drinking and could not go and tell someone he had seen a ghost.

Jackie recalled his father's ghost story, told around a winter's fire one dark night when he was a boy.

Jackie's uncle Francis, his wife, and Claire had come to spend the night at Jackie's house. The electricity went out with the heavy snowfall. Fifteen inches of sleet and snow fell during a powerful nor'easter that turned its rage into a full-blown face-searing blizzard on a dark February day.

While Jackie and Claire sat close to the woodstove, playing Claire's new board game Scrabble, the adults sat and chatted, drinks, cigarettes and pipes in hand.

"Oh my, it's howlin' like a banshee out there now," said Jackie's mother.

"Careful, Carol," said Henry. "You don't want to wake up that spirit across the river."

Francis began to chuckle.

"What's so funny?" Jackie looked up from the game. He was losing badly to Claire and by this point had lost interest in the game.

"Oh nothing, Jackie. Just yer old dad here has always been wary of ghosts and goblins."

"You never seen what I seen over there!" answered an agitated Henry. He stood from the table, swaying on drunken feet to stoke the coals in the wood stove.

"Look, I believe ya. Just thought you'd have forgotten about it by now."

"Are there really ghosts?" asked Jackie. Claire was lost in her game.

"No, son," said Carol. "Your father just has a wild imagination, that's all."

Henry sat contrite. He relit his pipe and puffed away.

Strange, all of this flooding back to him. He had never remembered the conversation until now but did recollect ghost stories and that his father had seen one. He now believed he had seen the same ghost. The Banshee of Shillelagh Hill. When his father saw her, his grandmother passed a short time later. That's what banshees were: an omen of bad news.

Jackie pondered what dark event lay before him.

Paddy ground to a stop, jerking Jackie from his memories. He hopped out of the truck, directly in front of Jamieson's Outfitters, situated close to the Westmoreland Street Bridge on Union Street.

"How long are ya gonna be, Mr. O'Connor?"

"Well, I kinda figured I'd be done by ten-thirty if you hadn't been so late and we didn't get stuck in all that construction. Now me whole day is thrown off. Better give me until noon or so. That work for you?"

"Sure thing. I've got to see someone over at St. Thomas University and then another friend at UNB, so I've got lots of time."

"They never shoulda taken that school outta Miramichi, ya know. Goddamn shame they did that. Kids could be coming there to go to college rather than travelling a whole two hours over here. Friggin' shame. Now what do we have but the mill and the base? Christ. Next thing you know, they'll be takin' them on us, too."

Paddy nodded his head in agreement.

"Maybe when I double back to get ya, we'll grab somethin' to eat somewhere."

"Sounds good." He was excited to get inside Jamieson's and review what they had to offer. It had been at least three years since he had breached its entrance, even though he still received their monthly catalogue.

Jackie slammed the door. He forgot to ask Paddy about the glossy new vehicle. No matter. It wasn't Jackie's business and he didn't intend to make it his concern.

Paddy pulled a U-turn and drove back towards the Westmoreland Street Bridge. Jackie turned and walked into Jamieson's, grinning as he opened the glass door and the bell chimed as if holy angels had flown in to herald his arrival. For the first time in his life, there would be no limit on what he could buy at his favourite store.

He took a deep breath.

BEING INSIDE JAMIESON's gave Jackie a feeling of euphoria. He looked around. Guns. Ammo. Mesh for a blind. A mounted salmon, silver, and celebrated on the wall. Reversible coats and vests, orange on one side, green on the other. A mounted deer's head. Hats and caps of all hunting colours – brown, green, orange, black – both fitted to one's head size and the modifiable kind. Gen used to chide him that he needed the adjustable sort of cap because Jackie's head often got too big when he was bragging about himself. The memory produced a grin.

Jamieson's was one large open warehouse. The family-owned outfitters had made major renovations in the years that had passed since Jackie last visited. They used to have a separate warehouse where canoes and kayaks were housed, along with a few boats that could be fitted for outboard motors. Today, they had canoes inside the main building, hanging from the rafters, as well as kayaks. Jackie did not know a single person that used a kayak and frankly, he felt they were for hippies. Maybe he should buy one for Paddy so he would never borrow Jackie's canoe again. He certainly would not be loaning out his new one to *anybody*.

There were new countertops with glass so one could properly observe knives and compasses. In the past, Jackie always had to ask for the jackknives and blades to be brought out from behind the counter. The guns were in a separate room altogether but it was still easy to see them and Jackie started to get overwhelmed. Jamieson's had turned into a big business. More and more people came to New Brunswick for fishing, hunting, canoeing and other outdoor activities. When he first started coming here in the early 1960s, the company was a moderate outfit.

He took a deep breath. The smells brought back wonderful memories of coming here with Gen on occasional trips to

Fredericton, when she would go hunting for records on Regent Street and leaving him to hunt in Jamieson's. He loved the smell of all the fresh gear, the worms for sale behind the counter, the chewing and pipe tobacco behind the cash, the brassy tang of bullets sitting row by row openly in boxes, and the oils for keeping and storing guns. He took in another long, unrestrained breath again. For the first time in months, he felt relaxed. He was home.

ooooo

Jackie was thoroughly engrossed in a compound bow. He did not hear Paddy rush to the back of the store to find him. It was now well past noon.

"And for sure this'll kill a buck?" said Jackie, turning the bow around in the light with his left hand while simultaneously crushing out a cigarette in a heavy, green ashtray with his right.

"Sir, that there's a bow with a fifty-pound draw-weight. A forty-pound one would take down a deer. What you've got will take down an elk, moose or bear," answered the clerk.

"Right on. Can't wait to get out in the woods back home when autumn comes"

"Where are you coming from today?" asked the clerk.

"Miramichi."

"Yessir. Lots of good hunting and fishing there. I hear Ted Williams has a spot up that way to fish salmon."

Jackie nodded his head in agreement. "Yeah, they say that, but I never caught sight of him."

"Hearing much about the election up your way?" said the clerk as he replaced some hunting knives Jackie was looking at back within the glass case.

"All kinds of chatter, for sure."

"You know we had one of them lads come in here a few weeks ago and did an announcement from the store? It had to do with conservation or something like that."

"Can't get away from it, can ya?" complained Jackie as

he turned the bow over to look at the other end. "Pick up the paper: there's Doug Young. Turn on the radio: there's Richard Hatfield."

"Now what about that bow?"

Jackie was stunned at the resemblance of the bow to his father's. This one was modernized and had a few extra bells and whistles but the colour, the shape, the size – it was almost exactly the same. It had gone missing after Henry died. Neither Jackie, his brother or mother ever discovered who had stolen the bow. He'd wanted one like it ever since.

"That your young lad, there?"

Jackie turned. Paddy had been taking in the whole conversation, standing back. He looked as jumpy as a jackrabbit.

"Him? Naw just a lad from home givin' me a hand." Jackie focused his attention on him. "Alright, Paddy?"

"For sure, Mr. O'Connor. Just didn't want to interrupt. Figured you'd be ugly at me for being late."

Paddy smoked feverishly.

"Yer late?" Jackie quickly looked at his watch. "Huh. How 'bout that? Never even noticed."

"Well, let's get you fixed up here at the cash and you can be on yer way. I figure we've taken enough of your money for today. But don't be a stranger, you hear," the clerk joked.

"Yup I think that's good enough for today. Paddy, be a good lad and bring the truck right to the front door. This guy here is as slick as they come. If I don't get out of here soon, I'll buy half the damn store. Gonna need to tie down the new canoe he sold me, amongst other items." Jackie held the black bow up and regarded it as if it were a newborn child.

"I'll go grab the truck."

Paddy darted off. Jackie shook his head.

"Seems like a good young lad," said the clerk.

"He's alright. Gets into a little bit of trouble now and then. A little soft in the head but the lad hasn't had the easiest go, if you know what I mean. Father's a real prick."

The clerk nodded, understanding the situation without knowing the details.

"So many of them smokin' dope and partying these days. No goddamn manners at all. Just craziness. You know I saw a girl over by UNB the other day with about five earrings in her head and another in her nose? I was lookin' fer a place to hang my keys!"

Jackie snorted. "She's a crazy world out there, for sure. I blame Hatfield. And Ottawa."

Customers milled about the outfit store, checking price tags on mackinaws and testing duck calls. The store was as alive as the forest; the outdoors inside.

The clerk wrapped up the items and Jackie waited patiently at the counter as he rang everything in: a new Old Town Discovery model canoe, a new paddle made of cherry, the prized compound bow and a heavy flashlight. The clerk had asked another attendant to get all the arrows for the bow. It was accompanied by some free trinkets, given all the cash Jackie had spent that day: a key chain, a coffee mug and a new cap, all stenciled in gold with Jamieson's.

"Okay sir, if you're good to go, here's the damage." The clerk leaned back hesitantly and turned the screen from the cash register around to show Jackie.

Jackie regarded the screen, pursed his lips and nodded. "Right on. Today, money isn't an option."

"Well, good enough then!"

Jackie had never been able to say that before. He never thought he would ever be in good financial standing to ever utter that phrase. It sounded foreign coming from his lips. He thought of his old friend Donny and smiled. Then he thought of Gen and wished she were here on this beautiful fall day, the sun strong and hot radiating through the large plate-glass windows.

"Where's the Cokes?"

After they loaded the gear and safely secured the canoe with frayed rope, Paddy pulled out of the parking lot. They proceeded to drive back on Route #8 to Miramichi. It was now almost two in the afternoon and a ravenous hunger suddenly gripped Jackie.

"Jeez, I forgot we were supposed to cross back over to the south side and grab a bite to eat somewhere. Need to get a big feed in me soon."

Paddy lit up a cigarette, his hand slightly trembling.

"You alright over there?"

"Yup," answered Paddy. "Just the rough road making my hand tremor a bit. I'm glad you said that. I know a little diner in Penniac, if you'd like to stop there, Mr. O'Connor."

"You must be hungry, too."

"Yeah, sure. I guess so."

Jackie tilted his head, giving Paddy a look.

"They got anything there besides hotdogs and fries? Like anything for adults?"

"They got all kinds of food there. I had a hot turkey sandwich once and it was good."

"Step on it, then. I'm buying. I'd eat the south-bound end of a north-bound skunk at this point."

Paddy sped up the truck to 40 miles per hour. The hilly landscape whipped by them as they began the steep downslope into the valley.

Route #8 became dangerous snake. Sharp turns came at them rapidly. Jackie started to get motion sickness from the harsh maneuvers of the truck.

"Yer goin' too fast now, Paddy. Slow down or we'll end up in the Nashwaak."

Paddy increased his speed.

"You said you were hungry."

"Yup and I'd like to survive long enough to eat, so slow the fuck down."

"I know how to drive, Jackie." Paddy rarely spoke with an edge, particularly to Jackie. Jackie looked away from the road. The speed was making him nauseous and the danger was making him anxious. The many colours of fall went hurtling past his eyes.

Paddy continued lashing the truck around corners, dipping and climbing the hills. Jackie did his best but by the time they pulled into The Hen House Diner in Penniac, the motion sickness had gotten the better of him.

"Ya look green," said Paddy.

"What's the matter with you? I told ya to slow down! Now I'm so sick I don't feel like eatin' anything."

"Sorry about that but I like to drive fast through there. Makes me feel like I'm a race car driver."

"You ain't and this ain't no race car or track! We coulda flown off one of them cliffs!"

"Yeah, but you said you wanted to get here because you were hungry."

"Well, look at me now! Christ."

"Tell you what: they got takeout. I'll get you a hot turkey sandwich and me a bite to eat too and then if yer feelin' better, you can eat it on the way back."

"Fine. Get me something. I'm sure I'll be hungry eventually. Just don't drive so fast again."

"You want something to drink, too?"

"Get me a Coke. And ask for a cup of water. I'm dry as all hell out here."

Paddy disappeared inside and Jackie sat with the window open. There was little airflow through the valley, just the afternoon stillness of early autumn. He raised his cap, trying to get some cool air. The nausea began to subside.

Fifteen minutes later, Jackie was crushing out a cigarette in the dirt, still waiting for Paddy. The old diner was busy on Saturday afternoon; he could watch the crowded patrons inside eating and see the servers deftly moving about the throng with milkshakes and french fries. Two of the red picnic tables outside were occupied. One table had a family of six – two parents and four young children. The mother looked tired.

At the adjacent picnic table sat two young people, a boy about 18 and a girl the same age, maybe even a year older but Jackie could not tell. He could not hear what they were saying but he knew by the body language and smiles that they were enamoured with each other. It made him think of all the times he and Gen used to stop at diners like this on frequent trips throughout New Brunswick.

Paddy came out of the diner with a loud bang, the door jarring everyone; since his hands were full, he'd kicked the door open. In his left, he held two Styrofoam containers, and in his right, a dark green plastic bag. Jackie wondered what was in that, since he also did not see the drinks.

"Where's the Cokes?"

Paddy set the containers awkwardly down on the hood of the truck.

"I'm goin' back in for them. Gotta run back in and pay, too."

"I told you I'd pay for lunch so here's fifty for the two dinners, the drinks and gas money to come over and back with."

Paddy reached across the hood and retrieved the bill.

"Jeez this is fancy. I don't see too many of these kinds of bills."

"Do they not teach anything in schools today? That's MacKenzie King."

"He looks a little like Mr. Sutherland."

"What's in the bag?"

"Oh nothin'. Just picked up a souvenir t-shirt of this place for my girlfriend in Douglastown."

"That looks like more than one shirt."

"I got two. One for her little sister, too. Let me run in and grab those drinks and then we can hit the road."

Paddy did not leave the bag in the truck, Jackie noticed. He took it with him. When Paddy came back out, Jackie had already moved the containers off the hood into the middle seat of the truck.

"How's yer stomach? Feelin' any better?"

"No, not really. Wish you hadn't been drivin' like a friggin' idiot. I brought some Rolaids with me and just took a few. Should be alright in a bit."

"Good enough," said Paddy. He fired up the truck and turned back onto Route #8, heading northeast. Jackie looked at the sky. He could smell the thunderstorm before the clouds appeared on the horizon thirty minutes later.

"I'm expandable."

PADDY DROVE WITH ONE HAND, scarfing his hotdog and fries down as they whisked away from Penniac. Doaktown had passed by before Jackie's appetite returned. While they drove, and while they had reception, they listened to a rerun of "As It Happens" from earlier in the week. Jackie was fine with listening to Elizabeth Gray and Alan Maitland. They had discussed the upcoming New Brunswick election in depth, doing leader profiles on Richard Hatfield, Doug Young and George Little but when the new weekend program "Saturday Afternoon at the Opera" came on, he reached over and turned down the volume without asking. Paddy did not protest.

"So Mr. O'Connor, I was wonderin' if I could ask you for a favour?" Paddy finally said.

"What's that? Last time you asked me for a favour, you nearly wrecked my canoe."

"So, everyone knows you got a bunch of money after Mr. McGivney died…"

"Oh, *everyone* does, do they?"

"Well, it ain't like its no secret or nothin'. I'm just saying."

"Right. Is this what people talk about behind my back? What did people talk about before I inherited a bunch of money?"

"How you never talk about your wife dyin' to anyone."

Jackie sat sullen, staring straight ahead. Silence passed for more than a minute when he finally broke the stalemate.

"What's this favour. How much are you looking for?"

"Its not like I can't pay you back. I just…we don't have a lot and I was wonderin' if you'd help me out. I can pay you back.

Honestly. Priority number one in a couple weeks' time. I mean, you just up and offered Mr. Boyd a bunch of money the other day, so I thought there'd be no harm in asking."

Jackie took a drag off his cigarette, then exhaled the smoke through his nostrils. He caught a glimpse of himself in the passenger mirror and did not like the lines in his face. He removed his cap and crossly scratched his head.

"What do ya need it for?"

"Well…I was just sayin' we don't have much…"

"I know that but what do you *need* it for?"

"Okay, I'll be forthcoming with ya: I got into some trouble."

"So, this has nothing to do with your family being hard up. This has to do with you getting into some trouble. Trouble with who?"

"Mike Emery."

"Mike?" Jackie was taken aback. "What's goin' on? How'd you get in trouble with him?"

"He asked me awhile back…or rather kinda *told* me…to start dealin' some dope for him."

"Mike's dealin' dope? Is that what's in that goddamn bag in the back?"

"Honestly? Yes, sir."

"You got me ridin' in the truck with drugs?"

"I had to pick it up at the diner. That's why I had to come to Fredericton in the first place. I had to go to the universities to make some money pick-ups for him. That's why I drove so reckless and made you sick. Sorry. I didn't want you coming into the restaurant with me. I'm in deep with Mike and he's gonna send Kenny Somers after me if I don't pay him."

"Uh huh."

"I think I'm… *expandable.*"

"Expendable."

"Yeah, that."

"Well, holy fuck, Paddy. What the fuck are you doin'? How much dope are you sellin'?"

"Lots."

"Why don't you let me talk to Mike."

"I don't think that's gonna do much good at this point. He's pretty mad."

"Didja cheat him out of money?"

Paddy was silent.

"Is that how you bought this new truck?"

Paddy said nothing. Jackie rolled his window down further. The humidity did little to alleviate the lack of air he felt around him at the moment.

"You goddamn idiot. How much do you owe him? He's not a lad you want to be owing money to."

"Nine grand."

"Nine! Jesus, I'm in the wrong business. You cheated Mike Emery out of nine grand?"

Paddy stared straight ahead at the meandering highway.

"Christ Almighty, Paddy. You need to have yer head examined. You know I've seen Mike send Kenny Somers to beat the piss out of someone just for cheatin' him out of *twenty* dollars? I've seen Mike stab a guy over nothing. Yer lucky yer not dead."

"I'm kinda worried, Mr. O'Connor."

"Kinda worried?" Jackie yelled. He drew out a cigarette and lit it before continuing. "Kinda worried," he mumbled with the smoke in his mouth.

"Can you loan me the money?"

"Let me talk to him first, at least. Jesus Christ Almighty. You lookin' for an early grave?"

Paddy said nothing but Jackie could tell the boy was scared. He was gripping the steering wheel tightly, his white knuckles sticking out of rosy hands.

"I'll figure something out with him."

Paddy just nodded his head. Jackie could see tears below the lids in the young man's eyes. He was doing his best to keep them from overflowing.

"It's alright, boy. It's alright. I'm gonna talk to Mike tonight when we get back. Supposed to make a delivery for him in the morning, anyway. Take a deep breath. Jesus."

They continued north along Route #8. They sped by the gas station in Blackville, getting closer with each mile. The violet clouds Jackie had seen in Penniac had followed them north.

Dogs always know.

PADDY TURNED THE TRUCK into Jackie's dooryard at suppertime. The was sun noticeably lower on the horizon than it had been the week prior and the evening air cooler than it had been the day before. The chill of early autumn caressing necks and numbing the fingers.

Jackie hopped out of the truck and walked to his house. He could hear Ruby inside, eager to get out. He unlocked the door, patted her on the head and she ran to the truck to greet Paddy. Jackie looked at him playing with Ruby and knew he was a good young man. Everyone makes mistakes. Ruby would not go near anyone who was harsh or mean. *Dogs always know.* He unlocked the large deadbolt. The hinges creaked slightly as he pushed the door open. Jackie opened a drawer near the kitchen sink, searching through the clutter – elastic bands, batteries, refrigerator magnets – until he found what he was looking for: a portable tape recorder. He had no idea where it had come from but likely Gen picked it up somewhere. It lay dormant in the drawer until now. He plunked two batteries in along with the microcassette, tested the audio, replayed the recording. His own voice sounded foreign to him. Jackie did not know if he would need the recorder but better to be safe than sorry.

He gathered up the blue tarp beside his house, which had been weighted down with a large chunk of shale. He shook it out and walked to the truck, where Paddy followed to help him unload the canoe. The dark clouds approached quickly, twisting along the slate sky. Jackie wanted to get the canoe under the tarp to protect it before the wind and rain struck. He could feel the dark, cold storm on his skin.

Jackie lit a cigarette once he finished and motioned for Paddy to take one. Paddy lit the smoke with his lighter.

"When are we going to talk to Mr. Emery?"

"We? Since when are you coming? I figure you should let me handle this myself."

"I was thinkin' about that. You're always sayin' a person needs to be responsible for their actions, Mr. O'Connor."

"True. Think you should probably sit this one out, though."

"No, sir. I got myself into this mess. I appreciate your help and think I will need it honestly, but I'd like to be there, if it's all the same to you. If you're gonna speak to him on my behalf, the very least I can do is be there."

Jackie flicked the ash from his cigarette. It blew away in the rising wind.

"Good enough. Let's head there now. Maybe we can beat the rain and get inside before we drown." As he uttered the words, he felt the first pellets of rain sporadically pepper his skin and clothing.

Jackie admired the lad. On the drive home, he'd considered phoning Boyd and asking him to come along. Though Jackie and Mike had been friends most of their lives, everyone regarded Boyd Meeks as a mediator; a *slightly* more sober second thought. Jackie thought better than to involve anyone further, figuring he would be able to iron out the situation between Mike and Paddy.

"Don't you want to unload the rest of yer stuff?"

"Naw, not enough time if we have to go to Mike's. Just needed to get the canoe off since the weather might damage it sittin' on top of your truck. You've got the cap on the back, none of it will get wet. I need to pick up booze for tomorrow's delivery anyway. It'll be a help to have you drive me back with all the liquor."

"So…we're going now?"

"Yup. Mind if we take Ruby with us? She's been cooped up all day."

Paddy crouched down and stroked her mane.

"Not at all."

"I don't have to get around. People come to me."

MIKE'S HOUSE WAS NOT A LONG drive from Jackie's place. Paddy was cruising below the speed limit, Jackie noticed. Though it was only a short distance, the topography and neighbourhood made it feel like another world. Jackie looked out the window, thinking how the world looks different when you want to go somewhere versus when you *have* to go somewhere.

Mike lived close to the water. His movements had been limited due to his disease, so several upgrades were made to the house. Jackie had often suggested Mike move to a better location, but as Mike would intermittently remind Jackie, "I don't have to get around. People come to me."

One flank of the house was defended by the Miramichi River. No one would attempt to approach from that side. Over the years, Mike had had several men like Kenny Somers, Donny McGivney, Boyd Meeks and of course Jackie, help by putting dead heads and large rocks in the water. Jackie used to joke that it was "Mikey's Moat," a quip only he or Kenny Somers could get away with.

The remainder of the house appeared unprotected from the outside, but Mike Emery was a paranoid man. He installed reinforced glass in all windows and nailed them shut. Mike barely left his home and it made the air inside stale and tired.

The house was equipped with a security camera at the front door. Mike could view anyone coming to the door from a small, black monitor situated on his kitchen table. He had paid a premium for the system.

Jackie was not sure if he was dumb or simply did not want to know about Mike's undertakings. Maybe there had just been too much going on in his life the last number of years to take notice. He thought about what Paddy confessed on their drive back from Fredericton. He always told himself to mind his own business; that what other people did was their affair, so long as it did not interfere with him. He questioned that manner of thinking one million times after Gen's accident, saying to himself that if he had only interfered, he might have changed the course of her life and she would never have been killed. As they turned into Mike's driveway, he wondered if he should have been paying closer attention to what the people around him were doing.

Was that the warning from the ghost?

Mike might be disabled, but Jackie knew he was quick with the sidearm holstered on his cracked and eccentric belt. Most people joked the gun at his hip was empty, that it was all for show.

Jackie knew better.

He had seen Mike unholster the Browning 9mm as fast as any man *and* fire accurately at short range. Jackie wondered how quick Mike would be if he was not afflicted with multiple sclerosis.

He knew other weapons were within Mike's reach: a Mossberg 500 shotgun was affixed to the underside of the table and a Colt Cobra .38 Special in an ankle holster. No doubt like everyone else, Mike carried a knife on him somewhere, too. These were the weapons Jackie was aware of; he could only guess what else was in the house and what Kenny Somers carried. He had seen Kenny Somers use his fists or, occasionally, a black and silver Rawlings softball bat. A nasty look was all Kenny Somers needed in most instances.

But Jackie didn't doubt he was armed.

As he approached the dilapidated steps to the decrepit house, Jackie knew they were being watched.

Jackie crushed out his cigarette on the dampening dirt before climbing the shoddy steps. Paddy followed him.

He knocked.

A sheepish Paddy stood behind. Jackie could smell the boy's fear. Death might very well await Paddy on the other side of the old splintery door, painted black. Jackie had known Mike his entire life, and for the first time he felt real anxiety as he entered his old friend's home.

"Come on in!" Mike called jovially from the other side.

Jackie uneasily gripped the brass doorknob, turning it with a squeak.

"What happens if I say no?"

"WHO'S THAT BEHIND YA? A shy pup?"

"Ha! Worse than that," shouted Jackie, overcompensating for his nerves and thinking how Mike could be a cheeky bastard when he wanted to be. The entryway was filled with old shoes, and a window that had not been cleaned in a decade. Above them, a dirty bulb with no fixture cast dim light, giving the entryway a dark shade of yellow.

Mike's house smelled like a whisky bottle with cigarette butts doused in rusty water. The walls were mired in smoke and old booze, and the tiled floor was broken and chipped in many places. It had been so long since anyone had cleaned it, not even Mike could say what the original wall colour may have been. Currently, it was greyish brown. A few windows had deep orange curtains and were the only brightly coloured feature in the entire house. They were always closed. Windows that did not have curtains had dark bed sheets or bath towels shabbily nailed to shut out anyone who dared peer in. The window next to Mike's chair was painted black, slits of light fighting through where it chipped. The room felt heavy, airless, and Jackie struggled to breathe in the old shack.

"What's on the go, Jackie? What are you doin' here with a bad apple like Paddy Brewster?" Mike sounded like he was teasing, but everyone knew behind every jape there lay a loaded question and, potentially, a loaded gun. Kenny Somers sat across the table from Mike, stoic as always. He wore a white polo shirt under light navy-blue jacket, tan pants and his battered Boston Bruins hat.

"We just come back from Fredericton. Went and got a new canoe today."

Mike adjusted his position and looked past Jackie. "You've got a lot of balls showing up here, Paddy Brewster. After what you did to me."

For Jackie, the light of the room dimmed even more. "Mike…"

"Hold on now, Jackie. Now, tell me about your big trip to Fredericton. How's the high life, anyway?" Mike's speech was slurred a bit and he looked sleepy. He yawned widely.

He sat with his arms crossed, his beige recliner awkwardly pulled up to the kitchen table, specked black with cigarette burns and gouged by beer caps. Numerous extension cords snaked through the house to the table, where he also had his television and endlessly oscillating fan - hairy with dust. The table also shouldered the telephone, answering machine, coffee maker, toaster oven, microwave and an old lamp, painted gold on the shaft with a cherub clinging to it. The lampshade was a deep crimson with dull gold trim.

"Oh, it was alright. This dough-head behind me cracked my other canoe last year. Been a strange few months. Every Tom, Dick and Harry has come lookin' for twenty bucks here and fifty there."

"No doubt. No doubt," said Mike. Kenny Somers lit one cigarette from the coal of another, remaining silent. He crushed the finished smoke on the kitchen floor. He sat in an old rocking chair that had been painted black, the floor squeaking with each forward motion.

From the television, the Expos' game prattled on. Mike sat silently in his chair.

"So anyways, the young lad says he done wrong by ya."

"He did, indeed. You must be warmin' for an early grave, boy."

Paddy hung his head low, pulling his cap down further.

"What's the matter? You think you can bring my old friend around to protect you from being a rotten, stealin' little prick?" Mike said through gritted teeth. Spittle covered his lips.

Kenny Somers stood.

"Hold'er now, Mike. It ain't like that."

"Oh, yer gonna tell me what is and what ain't, eh? Don't go usin' our friendship to help this lad out. He better have my money for me at this very moment or he's about to find himself on the wrong end of this fuckin' shotgun."

Mike withdrew the Mossberg from beneath the table. Kenny Somers unbuckled the sheath on his hunting knife.

"Okay. That's enough, Mike. No need to scare the lad to death. I'm payin' his debt for him, if yer gonna be so cantankerous. Jesus."

Mike looked at Jackie through clouded eyes, and Jackie knew he had judged the situation poorly. And then it hit him:

Paddy had never intended to pay back the money; he did not have to. He just delivered the biggest cash cow to Mike on a silver platter.

He had been duped. A surge of alarm rolled through his stomach. He felt his bowels start to relax.

How could I have been so fucking blind?

"That will make it easier on all of us, Jackie. Especially you and the young lad."

"Christ, Mike. We've been friends all our lives. There's no need for this. I'll just give you the money."

Mike quizzically looked at Jackie; a blaze of hurt behind his cloudy eyes.

"Okay then, Jackie. Fine. But how come you never offered before?"

"Didn't think I had to. Figured with all the liquor you were running, you were making enough cash. Now I understand yer runnin' weed, so yer probably coining it these days."

Kenny Somers turned his head to Mike. There was a brief pause before they burst into laughter.

"Someone want to explain to me what's so goddamn funny?"

Mike wiped the corner of his eyes with the sleeve of his dirty maroon coat, the cuff rolled back to the middle of his forearm to show a nasty scar where an ex-girlfriend, Rayline, once tried to rob him while he slept, stabbing him with a vegetable peeler in the process. Jackie could also see a lot of little needle marks on his forearm. Something he had never noticed before.

"I'm not running dope, Jackie. Well, not the kind yer thinkin' of anyway."

Jackie looked over at Paddy who could not meet his eye.

"You told me it was marijuana!"

"I said dope, Mr. O'Connor."

"It's heroin. Lots of money in that junk, Jackie. *Lots.*"

"People around here do that sort of shit?"

"You'd be surprised."

Jackie *was* surprised.

Mike's face had the complexion of a dead eel, his eyes glassy and sleepy.

"That's what I've always loved about you, Jackie. You're a little wet behind the ears. Yer old school."

Jackie felt like such a fool. He shoved his hands in his pockets.

"Now, if we can get back to business, I believe you was gonna give me the money Donny gave to you."

"Well, I mean, I spent some of it."

"How much you got left?"

Jackie was not about to tell Mike how much money he had. "About eighty thousand."

"That'll do."

Jackie immediately regretted saying he had even that much money remaining. Mike was too quick to accept eighty thousand. He clearly would have taken any number Jackie gave him.

"Mike, what's all this about? You can just ask me for money, ya know. None of this is called for."

"Afraid it is, Jackie. Afraid, it is. Paddy's not the only one who has debts." Mike had laid the Mossberg on the table, inadvertently knocking over a tin ashtray. He made no motion to clean it up. Kenny Somers was still standing, shuffling his feet.

Jackie shook his head. "Mike, you never made mention of this all summer when you knew I had the money."

"Things have changed these last few weeks," said Mike through a yawn. "And young fucking idiot here beside you made matters worse with the people I owe. So, I need the money you have, Jackie. Sorry my friend. That's the way it's gotta be."

Jackie looked at Mike's face, trying to find reason behind the glassy eyes.

"You're the one that's always said a man's gotta be held responsible for his actions. I'm responsible for quite an outfit and I owe a debt to some bad fuckers."

Jackie wondered just what kind of people Mike thought were *bad fuckers*, considering how his old friend was rotten to the core.

"What're ya in to?"

Mike, agitated, shifted in his chair.

"Fuck all this. Confession time's over. Let's get this movin' so we can keep goin' on with our lives. Kenny Somers here is going to go to yer place and get the money. I know you have it stashed in a new safe. I don't blame ya. People will just walk into your house these days and steal from you," said Mike.

The storm that had followed Jackie all the way from Fredericton was now in full force. Heavy globs of rain smacked the windows while thunder rolled.

Kenny Somers started buttoning his coat.

"Now? You want us to go now? Christ, we'll get struck by lightning."

"Now. I've got to get my situation taken care of before Monday. He'll ride with you lads over to your place and bring the cash back here."

"Ruby's in the truck. There ain't room for all of us. 'Specially with that stick shift."

"Well, Ruby can stay here with me," Mike said. "You know how much I love dogs."

When they were kids, Jackie brought his childhood dog over to play and Mike spent the whole time trying to hit him with rocks. Jackie got so angry with Mike he did not speak to him for months. He had no intention of leaving Ruby there.

"Paddy, be a good lad and drive Kenny Somers and Jackie over to his place. Come back directly now," Mike said. His head wobbled and it looked like he might fall asleep mid-sentence. "You and I have things to discuss."

Paddy remained silent in the back but removed his cap and lit a smoke.

Jackie was not fearful any longer. He was furious.

"Mike, I'm gonna give you this money because I don't want it anyway. But I'm tellin' you this: I'm done workin' for you. I don't want nothin' to do with you and yer businesses any longer. Take the money. Let me and Paddy go our way."

Mike patted the shotgun on the table.

"That won't be happenin' either, Jackie. I've got too many commitments now. You'll still be helping me out. I know about yer system on the booms and nobody suspects someone like you. A good man. A lottery inheritance. A widower. I'm gonna need yer help. And Paddy ain't goin' nowhere either. I mayzell tell ya's now that our business dealings are gonna have to continue."

"Or what?"

"What? What was that?"

"What happens if I say no?"

Mike's expression didn't change but his eyes grew dark. Paddy rubbed his arms anxiously. Kenny Somers stepped forward, a little too close for Jackie's liking.

Jackie had his right hand in his coat pocket, the blade of Donny's jackknife already flicked out, deftly maneuvered with his thumb and forefinger. He knew it was not big enough to kill Kenny Somers but he could do some serious damage with it.

His whole arm felt numb. His heart raced.

Mike looked quizzically at Jackie, idly picking up the shotgun.

"Seems like yer trying to get me to talk an awful lot, Jackie. What say I get the big lad here to frisk you?"

"Touch me, Kenny Somers, and you're dead."

Mike hefted the shotgun in Jackie's direction. "Jackie, don't be such a spoiled sport. Ya always got yer back up, don't ya? Now, just let Kenny Somers pat ya down."

Jackie neatly folded the knife back inside his pocket without anyone knowing and nodded his head.

Paddy backed up and Kenny Somers moved towards Jackie.

"What am I supposed to do? Put my fuckin' hands up like I'm under arrest or something?"

"Shut up and don't move," said Kenny Somers, speaking for the first time.

"Put yer arms out wide."

Jackie stood there, feeling like an idiot. He also knew his little ruse was about to be uncovered once Kenny Somers got to his left coat pocket.

Kenny pulled the jackknife out of the pocket and Jackie's hunting knife out of the sheath on his belt. When he got to the left side, he froze.

"What's this?" Kenny Somers pulled out the handheld tape recorder, the wheels turning and the red button pushed down on top. He turned around and showed it to Mike.

Mike lifted his head with wide eyes. Jackie could see hurt in his eyes. "Well, well. Seems as though yer not as green as I thought, Jackie. Smart thinkin' getting me to confess. I was wonderin' why you was asking all the questions. You always mind yer business and keep yer nose out of others, even when it's nasty business. Ya gave yerself away."

Jackie glanced over at Paddy, a scared cat backed in the corner of the entryway, hoping for escape.

"Jackie ol' boy. Not good. We got an issue, now."

Kenny Somers pulled a hateful looking cudgel from behind his back.

"Where were you stickin' that, Kenny?" Jackie chided.

Kenny Somers' mouth turned into a big smile, distracting Jackie. Kenny smacked him hard on the ribs and then the back of the head. Jackie went down quickly, stars in his eyes and for a couple seconds, lost consciousness.

"Fuck!" said Paddy.

"Another word out of you and I'll bury you at the bottom of the fuckin' river," Mike snarled. Paddy retreated into the corner. "Gimme that thing, Kenny."

Jackie heard the discussion as though he were under water.

Kenny Somers tossed the tape recorder to Mike. He removed the microcassette, tearing the tape out and mashing the recorder with the butt of his fist. Shards of plastic popped and spit.

"There. Now that's taken care of. Paddy, pick up Jackie and help him to yer new truck. You know, the one you paid for with money stolen from me? And get on over to Jackie's house and get that money. I know you got it hidden over there somewhere."

Paddy moved to help Jackie. He could feel the lump on his head forming as he fumbled with his hat and put it back on. His skull pounded, his ribs ached.

"And what happens to me afterwards?" asked Jackie, stumbling to his feet.

"Get the money. Then we'll talk about that. I didn't realize you were such a fuckin' rat."

Jackie knew he would not live to see another sunrise.

Kenny Somers grabbed the Mossberg off the table. Jackie and Paddy started out the door in the crashing rain, the big man in tow, a gun haunting their backs.

"To Hell with him."

THE THREE MEN LEFT Mike's house, the rain bitterly slashing their faces. Jackie was barely able to see Paddy's truck, though it was only a short distance away. Thunder roared. He wished lightning would strike him. *It would put an end to all this trouble.* All three men were soaked before reaching the truck.

Ruby had been patiently waiting. Jackie never understood why some dogs were terrified of thunder and others were not. Ruby was most certainly the latter.

Paddy was already on the driver's side of the truck, waiting for instructions from Kenny Somers, who whipped the passenger door open and grabbed the scruff of Ruby's neck. Jackie overflowed with rage as she struggled against the big man's grip.

"Don't touch that dog!" He balled his hands into fists.

"If Mike says she stays with him, the fucking mutt stays with him," Kenny Somers yelled over the rain.

Jackie knew there was no getting around it. He unclenched his hands and started for the tailgate of the truck.

How did I get to this place? What am I doing here?

"Where are you goin'?" asked Kenny.

"Getting' her leash. It's in the back. She might take off with all this thunder and lightning."

"Hurry the fuck up!"

Jackie turned the plastic handle for the cab door. Paddy came back to help him with the tailgate, ears tucked under his collar.

"What are you doin'? We didn't bring no leash," said Paddy, the door of the cab now raised above them, providing brief respite from the pounding rain.

"You run away from here, Paddy. You hear me. You get away from here *now*."

Paddy looked at Jackie. "What do ya mean?"

"We're gettin' out of here alive tonight." Jackie picked up the compound bow from the bed of the truck, followed by two arrows with vicious broadheads. Paddy stared.

"No. Don't do it. He's got a gun."

"To hell with him."

"What in fuck are you doin' back there? Hurry up or I'll shoot this fucking dog!" shouted Kenny Somers.

Jackie peeked around the back of the truck.

"We're coming!" he hollered as he notched an arrow.

Kenny Somers cursed and hauled Ruby violently out of the truck. He wrestled with her, trying to hold on the mane of the heavy dog. She howled and shook, fighting his grip.

His back against the tailgate, sheltered by the flap of the

truck cap, Jackie took in a deep breath, the damp air cold and misty. The driveway was a river of mud. Ruby yelped over the roar of the rain.

Jackie was not proficient with a bow. The guidance and practice he received as a child from his father was minimal. Everything was slippery. His hands trembling, Jackie leveled the bow.

He darted an eye around the corner of the truck. A hunched-over Kenny Somers had his foot lodged on Ruby's neck. Jackie breathed deeply through his nose, remembering what his father taught him, then spun around.

He slipped in the mud, almost falling to the ground. Kenny Somers' eyes grew and he released Ruby, trying to raise his shotgun. The driving rain made it greasy in his hands and it fell into the muck.

Jackie was still sliding around, cursing as he did but regained his footing enough to draw the string of the bow and loose the arrow. It sang through the raindrops, piercing Kenny Somers through the cheek, going through his face and skewering him to the door of the truck. On his knees in the mud, he spit and gagged and uttered garbles of shock and pain. The dropped shotgun lay at his side.

"Jesus fucking Christ!" yelled Paddy. He ran to Kenny Somers – now a ghastly, bloody mess. He was still gagging and spitting, trying to say something. He hung there, clutching and slipping on the muddy earth, trying to stabilize his body. Paddy turned, heaved and vomited his late lunch.

Jackie had meant to hit Kenny Somers in the chest. It was mere luck he hit him at all in the conditions. He shook his head. Ruby ran to his side, thankful and cowering. He patted her head and put her in the back of the truck. He picked up the Mossberg, wiped the mud off the barrel and handed the bow and extra arrows to Paddy, not bothering to look at Kenny. He started back toward the house, feet slopping through brown puddles of cold autumn rain.

"Where ya goin?" shouted Paddy.

"Shut up, Paddy. I'm being responsible for my actions."

"Miserable excuse for a friend."

JACKIE WENT TO THE WINDOW on the side of the house. It was painted black from the inside, but he could squint through a spot where the paint had peeled away. He watched Mike, doubled over, putting a needle into his arm. It made Jackie queasy; his old friend had become a drug addict and he'd never known.

He watched Mike untie the elastic band around his arm and slip into a daze, his head rolling back and forth. A satisfied smile crossed his lips, and he reached for a beer from the table. Jackie pulled his head back from the window and crept over to the door, opening it quietly.

Inside the doorway, he heard the sound of a beer can popping open, followed by Mike taking a long slurp.

Jackie stood in the entryway, barely breathing. He didn't know what his next move would be. He didn't know what he was doing. All he was certain of was he wanted to make sure he and Paddy were out of this situation with Mike.

He whipped around the corner, cocking the shotgun and pointed it straight at Mike.

"Don't move, Mike."

"Jesus H. Christ!" The beer can flew out of Mike's hand. He reached for the gun at his hip but his normal quick reflexes were sluggish. Jackie fired a shotgun round into the ceiling, spitting dust and drywall across the room. He cocked the gun again, filling the chamber with a shell and pointed the barrel at Mike. Loud chatter from the baseball announcers filled the room. The television volume was almost deafening.

"Fuck!"

"I said don't. Fucking. Move."

"Where in fuck am I supposed to go? I'm crippled!"

"You know what I mean. Take that gun out of your holster and the thirty-eight at yer ankle. I know they're there."

Mike's face twisted in confusion, his narrow eyes staring

at Jackie. Jackie was afraid to blink.

Mike unflappably put his hands to his side, open and welcoming. "C'mon now, Jackie. No need for this."

"Fuck you."

The house was busy with sound – the storm outside and Dave Van Horne and Duke Snider commentating on the game in the background. Mike reached for the 9mm at his side to withdraw the gun.

"Slowly," said Jackie.

"How fucking fast d'you think I can go? I barely move these days."

"I've seen how fast you can draw. Don't play stupid."

Mike pulled out the gun and laid it on the table.

"Now the ankle."

Mike slowly reached down to take out the Colt Cobra Special. Rain began trickling in from where Jackie had shot a hole in the ceiling.

"I'm dockin' yer next ten deliveries for puttin' that hole in my fuckin' roof! How am I supposed to fix that tonight? Fucking place is gonna get soaked!"

Jackie kept the Mossberg pointed at Mike. At this distance, he would cut him in half if he pulled the trigger.

Mike softly laid the .38 on the table.

"Jackie, me and Kenny Somers were just fuckin' around. I *do* need the money but there was no way I was gonna hurt you. C'mon now. As far back as we go? You think I'd really do that?"

Jackie paused to wipe rainwater away from his face, keeping the shotgun directed at Mike. His clothing was soaked and he felt the chill of the wet clothes on his skin.

"I know you would."

"Started dealing the heroin to make some cash, then started taking it for the pain. The MS has been getting' worse."

Jackie felt a pang of pity but brushed it away.

"That ain't my problem anymore."

Paddy rushed into the house, the bow in hand. He was shivering. Ruby followed behind him, dripping water on the floor. Mike narrowed his eyes.

"Where's Kenny at?" said Mike.

Jackie and Paddy remained silent.

"You killed him?"

Jackie continued to hold the gun level, never taking his eye off Mike. His hands didn't shake anymore.

"He's dead," confirmed Jackie.

"Holy fuck!" Mike furiously shuffled in his chair, attempting to get to his feet. "No! Yer both dead now," Mike shouted. "Yer fuckin' dead!"

"Paddy, get over there and tie this son of a bitch up."

"With what?"

"With yer fuckin' shoelaces. How should I know? Find something."

"I ain't dyin' with my hands tied," said Mike. You can shoot me right now, Jackie O'Connor. Miserable excuse for a friend. Didn't even offer me any of yer newfound riches. I had to come and take it from you. *Me.* Yer friend for more than thirty years."

"Eat shit."

Paddy was scouring the kitchen counter, frantically hauling open cabinets and drawers, pans and dishes clanging, throwing items about the countertop. He found some twine in the cabinet below the sink.

"No need for that, Paddy. Shoot me dead now, Jackie, 'cause if you come over here to tie me up, I'll grab that gun off the table and shoot myself in the head."

"I said don't move."

Ruby started barking wildly outside, startling Jackie. He heard a noise and looked to his right.

Kenny Somers was on top of him before he knew it.

Not dead.

The arrow still pierced his face, though it was broken in half. His face was a mess of blood and ragged lumps of flapping skin. Blood slicked down his body, soaked from the rain.

Hunting knife in hand, Kenny Somers slashed at Jackie. The blade connected with Jackie's arm as he sprang out of the way. The pain seared through his bicep. Kenny was right up against him. Rough, croaky sounds emitting from what used to be his mouth. Kenny reached for the shotgun, but Jackie pulled the trigger. Blood and guts flew everywhere, splashing across Jackie's face. He choked and fell to the floor with Kenny on top of him.

Jackie struggled. The dead man's huge mass prevented him from moving. He heard a shot go off, followed by Paddy screaming. He grunted and rolled Kenny's body off and heard two more gunshots, muffled by Kenny Somers' back. Jackie squirmed on the floor.

"Stay still you fucker!" yelled Mike. His eyes were alert and wild now.

Jackie pushed and rolled away from Kenny Somers' body. Another round from Mike's revolver fired into the floor, spitting pieces of linoleum and wood around. Jackie propped himself up on his knees, cocking the shotgun. He looked over at Paddy, groaning in the corner, holding his leg.

Mike pulled the trigger but only clicking noises followed. He dropped the .38 on the ground and held his hands in the air.

"Now Ja…"

Jackie fired the gun.

Mike's face was covered in his own blood and spit. There were a few ragged gasps and panic in his gaze. He flopped in his chair and fell against the table, his head clunking against the security camera monitor.

Jackie took a deep breath, setting the shotgun on the tiles, breathless. All about him was carnage. He could taste metal in the room from the bloodletting. He was covered in someone else's tissue, and his heart drummed so powerfully he worried he was having a heart attack.

You're alive. Don't die.

He heard the cacophony from the TV of the dismayed crowd in Pittsburgh. Tim Raines had crushed a homer off Rick Rhoden, deep in right field.

The Expos had tied the game in the sixth.

"Boom Road? Is that a real place?"

Constable Woods and Constable Bower responded to the dispatch. The call came through while they were getting a late evening dinner at Jennie's Canteen in Newcastle.

Bower picked up the radio, putting his cheese dog on the hood of the cruiser and wiping his mouth.

"This is Constable Bower. Go ahead, dispatch."

"Constable, we received a call at 9:33 PM from a man who would not give his name. He stated there were multiple individuals with injuries in Boom Road. Do you know where that is?"

"Boom Road?" piped in Constable Woods. "Is that a real place?" He had finished his cheeseburger, stashing the refuse in the garbage bin and overheard as he was walking back on the graveled parking lot. Woods was relatively new to the force and had only graduated from depot 18 months ago.

Bower covered the receiver. "Yes, it's real," answered Bower. "Dispatch, I know where Boom Road is. It's upriver on the north side. Rural Route #1, a few minutes east of Sunny Corner."

"You'd better take the address and get up there. It sounds like a shootout from the old west went down."

"Great," replied Constable Woods. "Bower, you better drive. You know this place –"

Constable Bower was already behind the wheel, turning on the lights and siren.

"Get in. Let's go."

Constable Woods slammed the door, belting up as Constable Bower ripped out of the tiny canteen parking lot, red and blue lights flashing along with tires spraying gravel.

Woods motioned, formulating an explosion with his hands. "Boom like *'boom*?"

ᐧᐧᐧᐧᐧ

Paddy sat on the step, smoking a cigarette. Jackie cinched his belt above the bullet wound in Paddy's leg, tightening it around the thigh to slow the blood loss. His own arm bled from Kenny Somers' knife but not profusely. He'd already ripped his sleeve from his shirt and bandaged it as best he could. Moths and blackflies hovered around the outdoor light. The air crackled and snapped when any got too close.

It stopped raining, the night now cool and fresh. Jackie could not get enough of the cold air. Steam seeped from his brow and shoulders. In the truck, Ruby was whining, prancing back and forth on the back. He did his best to ignore her. If she was outside, she would be interfering with a crime scene.

He'd pondered setting the house on fire, throwing Paddy in the truck, taking him to the hospital and fleeing the scene, leaving the police and neighbours to piece together what happened; that was not his style, though. If he showed up at the hospital with Paddy shot in the leg and a knife wound of his own, it was bound to trigger the police regardless.

He was not a criminal. Not a real one anyway. Not like Mike had become; at least, that is what he told himself while he sat outside waiting for the cops to arrive. His fingerprints were all over everything and given how small the community was, it was inevitable the cops would come to speak to him at some point. Part of him wished he had died. So much had happened this year. He did not understand the world anymore.

ᐧᐧᐧᐧᐧ

Jackie, covered in blood, watched the cruiser pull into the door-yard just after 10 PM. He watched a Mountie spring from the passenger side of the cruiser before the vehicle came to a full stop; a large flashlight turned on, and his hand was on the butt of his service revolver.

"Jesus Christ," the officer gasped.

"Hands! In the air! Now!" demanded a second officer, out and shielded by the door of the police car. He drew his sidearm and pointed it at Jackie. Ruby howled in the truck, barking and pawing the windows. The truck cap's rear window wheezed open.

Jackie threw his smoke to the ground without extinguishing it, the wet earth swallowing the coal. He stood up to show the officers he had no weapons on him. The cop got out of the driver's side, withdrawing his sidearm and standing behind the door, as well.

"I said hands in the air! Both of you!"

Jackie grew irritated. "Hold your horses! We ain't dangerous."

"Hands!"

"I heard ya! I'm puttin' them up!" Jackie put his hands in the air. Ruby's incessant wailing made the wind seem calm. She jumped and prowled the back of the truck.

Jackie raised his hands and his jacket rose up as well. In the gleam of light, the second constable must've thought he saw a weapon on Jackie's belt. He pointed his gun in the air, firing a warning shot.

Jackie ducked his head down.

"Holy fuck! What're ya doin?"

"Cease fire!" said the other cop.

Ruby escaped through the window, baring her teeth at the officers.

"Sir! Call your dog!"

"Ruby! Settle! Sit girl!"

Ruby barked madly and continued to bare her teeth. Paddy was attempting to stand up but was weak from blood loss. He slid onto the cold mud and passed out.

"Here! Now, girl! Come here! Don't shoot her. Please." Jackie held a calming hand up to the officers.

She barked angrily again, frothing at the mouth.

Jackie darted over to her, spooking the second constable. He fired a shot at the sudden movement, the bullet catching Jackie in the thigh.

"Holster that side arm, Woods!"

Jackie grabbed his leg.

"You stupid fucking idiot!"

Ruby stood in front of him, growling.

"Don't shoot her, ya dummy. She's only protecting me!"

Constable Woods holstered his gun.

"Holy shit! Holy shit!"

The other cop got on his radio and called for backup.

"Dispatch! Dispatch! This is Bower!" the constable shouted into the police radio mic. "I need medical assistance, ASAP. Officer's gun discharged. Two civilians wounded. Both in the leg."

"Backup requested. What is your location?" the dispatcher squawked.

Jackie grabbed onto Ruby's collar. He held her there and it all came crashing down. He began to sob. He tried to stay awake but his lids fluttered in the night, the darkness flashed with red, blue and white lights. He heard the Mountie shouting instructions into the radio before slipping into blackness.

There was nothing.

JACKIE SAT STERN in his new canoe, the water in the river veiled with ice. He blew on it, shattering the ice with a puff of air. He knew he should be cold, only wearing his ball cap, a light, long-sleeved shirt and pants to match, along with his normal steel-toed work boots; however, he did not feel cold at all. He did not feel warmth. No chill or iciness touched his skin, nor did any heat or uncomfortable sweat. The sky far above him was bruised blue, branches of white clouds swimming throughout. A faint, tender snowfall sprinkled his face. He had no paddle. The light snow had collected on shore mixed with mud, producing a translucent slush, like wet brown sugar stirred in a mixing bowl for cookies. The kind his mother used to make for him as a boy.

Looks good enough to eat with some butter and some brown

bread. That would go nice with a cup of coffee.

He realized he was famished, ravenous. His midsection lurched. A form of hunger he had never known gripped his insides.

Jackie looked toward the bow where Gen would always sit. Instead of her, it was the banshee from his nightmare, once again, in human form, and not the terrible, contorted geist that appeared before him on the riverbank. She sat facing him, dressed in a white blouse and long dark skirt, the cameo prominent at the collar. She looked elegant. Content.

"Who are you?" he asked.

The banshee stared at him without expression. There was a sadness in her eyes that caused him to cry. The tears crawled down his cheek. She turned her head toward the sky.

Jackie looked up, squinting to see if there were anything above him. Only the dark blue sky hung above his head.

He blinked, bringing his head down to look at the ghost again but she was gone. He was alone. He looked down into the water and saw her below the thin sheet of ice, her arms wrapped around Gen. He pounded the ice with his hands, cutting them as he thrashed. The ice was as frail as a tulip petal but he could not break it. He yelled and yelled but they faded into the depths of the river, sinking like pebbles until he could no longer see them.

The canoe began to take on water. He looked for a cup, a bowl – something to bail water out of the canoe with but there was nothing. He started using his hands, dipping into the water, scooping and freezing his fingers to the bone, attempting to throw it over the side. The water was pouring in from somewhere and as hard as he tried, the canoe continued to sink. He felt the chilled, iciness of the sky. Even though he was only a few feet from shore, he could not get out. He prepared to descend into the water, forever lost to the deep channel of the river.

"I'm in heaven."

JACKIE OPENED HIS EYES. Squinting, he tried to assess his location. White surrounded him. It was painful to lift his eyelids.

Where am I?

Maybe I kicked the bucket after all.

Can I still think if I'm dead? "Well, I'll be damned..." he breathed shallowly. "I'm in heaven."

"That's a funny way to say you're in heaven," a woman's voice answered in the distance.

"Wha?"

"You're awake. That's a start."

Jackie tried to move but a sharp pain bolted through his leg. He reached down and felt bandages wrapped firmly around his thigh. He tried again to move, this time his leg, but twinges of discomfort reverberated throughout. His arm was attached to cords and machines.

Fuck, they made me into a computer. I am in the distant future. Maybe I've been in a coma and it's the year 2000.

"Who's that? Can't see."

"It's Claire."

"Oh, hi."

"Oh, hi? That's all you've got to say, right now?"

"Oh, hi...Claire?"

"You're lucky yer not dead."

"Am I in the Chatham or the Newcastle hospital?"

"Chatham."

"Thank goodness. How long have I been out for?"

"About a day."

"Jesus. Mr. Sutherland's going to dock my pay."

"I think that's the least of your worries right now, Jackie."

"What d'ya mean?" He could see her now – the painful light had diminished and his eyes had finally adjusted. Claire sat in a wooden chair adorned with pale blue cushions. She looked like she had not slept, but her attire was all business: a red suit with a navy-blue blouse and gold brooch above her heart. He could not make out what it was but could tell it was very nice. Maybe a bird, perhaps a flower. He liked that his cousin was doing well with her new supplement business. He had not seen Claire in months, so he was surprised to find her sitting across the room.

"What do I *mean*? Jesus Jackie! The police are outside the hospital door! They haven't left since they brought you in. Boyd has been calling me night and day, worried sick." She began to whisper. "There's all kinds of crazy stories that you went there and killed everyone and that you're some kinda…kinda gangster. What the hell happened up there?"

Jackie stopped, attempting to take a breath that just wouldn't go deep enough. Too much had happened in the last 24 hours. Claire bowed her head. He took a gulp of air.

"Best not to say. Don't know the law. I feel like I was actin' in self-defense and fearin' for my life but it's probably best if you call that big lawyer fella we dealt with for Donny's will."

"He ain't a defense lawyer, Jackie. He deals with wills and estates."

Jackie attempted to adjust his body. Shifting in the hospital bed caused a great deal of pain.

"God almighty! That hurts. Well, call that lawyer to find me a defense lawyer, then. I know I did nothin' wrong, but I might need someone."

Claire nodded and said she would.

"Paddy. Where's Paddy? He alright?"

"Yes, he's going to be fine. He lost a lot of blood but thankfully the first responders got there quickly. Having that fire hall in Sunny Corner likely saved his life. Guess the volunteers got on scene pretty quick."

Jackie rested his head back on the pillow, relief washed over his face.

Claire leaned in again, even though the officers were outside and the door was closed.

"Jackie, what happened up there?"

Jackie pursed his lips and drew in a sharp breath.
"Bad things."

"Just helpin' out a friend."

THE POLICE WERE NOTIFIED by the nurse that Jackie was conscious and an officer, Inspector Carl LeGresley, was sent to question him. He was a small man with a bald pate and large beard. Crow's feet and bags surrounded his eyes. Jackie thought he wore the absolute plainest clothes he had ever seen on a man. Brown pants with a beige turtleneck that only accentuated the man's lack of physique, a light brown leather coat with a belt that was semi-tied, hanging loosely around his waist.

This man is a baked potato.

His appearance aside, LeGresley was a veteran of the Royal Canadian Mounted Police, currently in his 24th year with the force. Jackie's case was assigned to the major crimes unit and with no ranking officer in the Miramichi area, Insp. LeGresley was tasked with the interrogation.

"Okay, Mr. Jackie. Shall we begin?" asked LeGresley.

Jackie looked over at Claire. She motioned for him to speak.

"Are ya gonna charge those fuckin' idiot cops for shooting me in the leg?"

"Jackie…"

"Mr. O'Connor, I'm sure it's already been explained to you: the officers acted in self-defense. I've spoken to them at length. We have a process when such incidents occur. I assure you a full investigation will be made into the actions taken by the two officers."

"Fine. Good. They should get what's coming to them. That was a fucking flashlight on my belt."

"Sir, it was a volatile matter. Police officers must take into account everything that is happening and the situation was fluid with…"

"They shot me. I had a flashlight on me. That's it."

"Okay, that's enough, Jackie," said Claire. Jackie clamped his mouth shut and crossed his arms. *Christ, sitting in this johnny shirt is embarrassing. Everything smells like piss here.*

"Monsieur O'Connor, we need to discuss the other matters first and then I promise you we can talk about that portion of the night of October second."

"Good enough, then."

"So, take me through what happened."

Jackie went into detail about what led he and Paddy to Mike's house. He knew the inspector would need in-depth knowledge of what happened and Jackie was pleased to provide it: how Mike had been peddling heroin, how Kenny Somers was his enforcer and how they planned to continue using Paddy as a drug mule and force Jackie into their racket; that Mike Emery was planning to rob Jackie of the money he inherited after Donny passed. He went through every aspect that he could recall from that night. It happened so quickly that it was hard to keep the order of events straight, but he did his best.

"My understanding from conducting interviews is that you knew the deceased quite well. Is that factual?"

"Yup. Unfortunately."

"How long have you known Patrick Brewster?"

"Pretty much all his life."

"You transported alcohol illegally for Mr. Emery, isn't that so?"

Jackie looked directly at Inspector LeGresley.

"Yes, I transported booze for Mike but it had been legally purchased."

"So, you helped him bootleg."

"Who told you that? I don't know nothin' about that. I never saw any money exchanged and nobody paid me. I just thought they were all gifts Mike was sending to people and I was helping out an old, crippled friend."

"*That's* your position? You delivered alcohol as gifts to hundreds of people each year?"

"Yup. I never saw no money. Just helpin' out a friend."

Jackie made the deliveries but was never paid in person. Mike kept tabs on everyone that he sold contraband to in a battered blue cookbook. It had the perfect spacing for writing all the information down – who bought what products and when. The ledger was always at Mike's side and he knew for certain the cops had already found it. When the booze was delivered by Jackie or someone else, Mike would send Kenny around the next day to collect. It kept everyone from being directly involved in any form of transaction.

"Mr. O'Connor…"

"That's all I got to say without a lawyer present."

"And may I ask, why don't you have a lawyer present at this time? It's certainly within your right."

"I got nothing to hide. I didn't do anything wrong. Them lads, Mike and Kenny Somers, were rotten to the core. I didn't know it until it was too late. Or almost too late, I guess. If this goes any further, I'll speak to a lawyer, but I felt I should tell you everything and let the chips fall where they may."

Inspector LeGresley jotted some notes, then flipped the cover onto the notepad and placed it in an inside pocket of his trench coat.

"Very good. We'll see what the judge thinks about your recollection, Mr. O'Connor."

"I take responsibility for my actions. I make no bones about it: I shot Kenny Somers with an arrow and later had to shoot him with the shotgun, which I also used to kill Mike. They were going to kill me and Paddy. My only regret was I didn't act sooner or we wouldn't have gotten into any of this mess. I also regret calling your idiot cop friends because they fucking shot me in my goddamn leg."

"I think that's enough for today, Inspector," Claire said softly.

"Very good, then. Rest up for your appearance in court, monsieur."

Jackie said nothing. Inspector LeGresley left the room.

Jackie watched him turn to the left, then pass by again when he realized he was going the wrong way. Claire stayed behind and moved over towards his bed.

"The bedding is the all the same in hospitals, eh?" she said, lightly touching the white flannel sheet with blue trim.

He sighed and nodded his head in agreement. Jackie clicked the button to alert the nurse.

Christ, my leg hurts.

"Who's been looking after Ruby?"

"Boyd's staying at your house. She's fine."

Jackie took in a deep breath. He was suddenly very tired.

"You've had a lot happen this year."

"I know, I know."

"I'm leavin' so you can get some rest."

Jackie turned his head to his cousin. She looked exhausted but a twinkle lay beyond the lines beneath her eyes. He could see she was in a good place. He smiled and grabbed her hand while she rested on the rail of the bed.

"Sounds good. Hey, I've been pressing this damn button but can you ask the nurse out there to come in? I also want to see if I can get the TV hooked up? Want to know what's goin' on with the election in few days and see if they're airing the ball game."

"You don't sound very concerned about the fact you may be charged with two murders, Jackie."

"I tell the truth. I'm telling the truth now. What more can I do?"

*"Ya gotta hand it to the lad. He knows
how to campaign, don't he?"*

A WEEK LATER, RICHARD HATFIELD won a majority government, taking 39 of 58 seats in the general election. Few New Brunswickers were shocked by the result, given Hatfield's popularity and his ability to elect a number of francophone members.

Conversely, the Liberals were a disjointed mess, having elected four different leaders since the previous campaign in 1978. The NDP finally managed to crack the legislature, with Bob Hall winning a seat in Tantramar. Times were changing.

Jackie watched the results at home with Boyd. They played numerous games of crib while occasionally commenting on the results from around the province. Ruby lay under the coffee table, feet turned up in the air and snoring.

His new television was broadcasting the results and the two men drank beers as they witnessed schoolteacher Paul Dawson defeat their own MLA, John McKay, by 500 votes. Across the river on the south side, Morris Green easily held on to no one's surprise. In Chatham, the young lawyer who had successfully defended boxing champion Yvon Durelle in his murder case, scraped by and won his seat. Young McKenna was an outsider, having moved to Chatham from the southern part of the province to practice law some years ago. Jackie took note it was the same firm he hired his lawyer from. The other seats, Bay du Vin and Miramichi Bay, went to the Tories, albeit not convincingly.

"Well, there ya have it. Another Hatfield government," said Boyd. He pulled an end table around from the side of the chair and kicked his feet up. He had a pile of beer cans underneath him.

"Yup. Couldn't expect anything else, what with the Liberals scrambling."

Boyd nodded. "Ya gotta hand it to the lad. He knows how to campaign, don't he?"

"That and luck and timing. All about the timing in politics." Jackie extinguished his cigarette in his emptied beer bottle, set it on the ground and immediately cracked another.

"How's that leg?"

Jackie looked at his left leg, propped up on some pillows at the end of the couch.

"Alright; still sore and having a time getting around. Doctor told me I should take a month off work, so I should be back next week sometime."

Boyd nodded. He looked around the living room, taking in a deep breath. "I was talking to Paddy yesterday. He's doing okay, he says. I think the medication they have him on dulls the pain in his leg."

"Yeah, he calls me about once a day now that we're both laid up for a while yet. Lad is higher than an airplane. I guess that's alright."

Boyd took a long drink from his beer.

"And what's on the go with yer case?"

"Well, my lawyer, she works with that lad who just won tonight in Chatham, says the investigation is still ongoing. I paid my own bail at the hearing, so I just have to stick around Miramichi until we get to the discovery stage, whatever that is. Fine with me. I mean, where in fuck am I going?" Jackie pointed to his leg.

Boyd chuckled. "Yup."

They sat silently as they watched the results continue to pour in, the panelists and pundits commenting – who won, who lost, where the upsets were, what went right for the Progressive Conservatives, what went wrong for the Liberals, the huge breakthrough of the NDP seat in the southeastern part of the province.

"The funeral for Mike was well attended, despite what happened," said Boyd, unsolicited. "Mr. Sutherland, the Mayor of Blackville, even the oldest Abraham boy was there. The one that runs his father's Royal Bank branch in Chatham. Couldn't fucking believe the crowd."

Jackie took a drink of beer. He said nothing, keeping his focus on the television.

"Big turnout."

"A *massive* Christian burial, eh?" joked Jackie. Boyd chuckled and nodded.

Jackie looked at the talking heads on television.

"And you ain't sore at Paddy for everything?"

Jackie took a swig of beer and coughed.

"Naw. Pretty hard to be too angry with the lad," Jackie answered with a shrug. "It ain't his fault, as I see it. He was strong-armed into most of this by Mike."

Boyd paused and shifted in his seat.

"Craziest fuckin' racket I've ever heard of, that's for sure."

The commentators on the television continued. Results were coming in from polls that were late reporting. They watched for a few more minutes until Jackie finally said "Change the channel would ya. Game One of the Cardinals and Brewers is on."

"Oh, right on."

Boyd jumped up and grabbed the giant remote for the huge satellite Jackie had installed a few months ago. He found the new American station, Entertainment and Sports Programing Network. It was all sports, all the time. Boyd spent most of his evenings at Jackie's watching every sport imaginable, now. They both pretended it was because of the satellite dish.

…which were the more serious offenses.

THE INVESTIGATION BY THE RCMP into the deaths of Michael Daniel Emery and Kenneth Beauregard Somers on the night of October 2, 1982, concluded, and the results were similar to what Jackie had already explained to police. The conclusion was easy to ascertain once Inspector LeGresley and the investigative team extrapolated the security footage, equipped with audio. Even still, the result of the investigation still took months to complete and it was late spring of 1983 before Jackie was cleared of all charges related to the bloodbath. Jackie had to go into extensive detail about what happened outside by the truck. There was no security footage of that portion of the incident; the angle of the camera only surveyed as far as the decrepit steps; however, it was apparent he and Paddy were being extorted.

Jackie was only cleared on the charges related to the killings, which were the more serious offenses. He was charged and convicted for the illegal manufacture, distribution, or sale of goods; in this case, alcohol. Inspector LeGresley had gathered enough evidence and in-person accounts of Jackie transporting booze by canoe that he felt charges were warranted. He was ordered to pay a financial penalty of $2,000. Jackie was irate about it, but when he consulted with his lawyer and discovered that he could easily face larger fines or jail time if he took it to court, he relented and paid the fine.

The matter of Jackie's injury by the RCMP was ruled justifiable. Constable Woods testified that he felt threatened. He was an officer of the law and along with Constable Bower, he was responding to a serious incident. They were relieved of any punishment. Jackie wanted to pursue charges but the last year had taken such a toll on him, he dropped the whole thing. He wanted to move on and put the past behind him.

Paddy Brewster was convicted of drug trafficking in the summer of 1983. The police had found sufficient evidence and witnesses to back up the charges laid. Due to the extortion by Mike and no prior offenses, Paddy was only given a light sentence: three years in prison with possibility of parole in 18 months.

ooooo

Between the months of the incident at Mike's in October 1982 and the dropping of charges in the spring of 1983, Jackie recovered from his injuries and worked at the sawmill. He, Boyd Meeks and several other men renovated the break room – Donny's wishes finally coming true.

Much to the malign of Mr. Sutherland, the room became a proper place for the men to eat lunch, take a smoke break and even had a proper washroom. Boyd took it upon himself to fashion a beautiful sign made of rock maple. The engraving on the sign read "McGivney's Lunch". Jackie thought it was a fine place and the men all agreed that Donny would be happy with the outcome. In late November when the renovations were complete, Claire came by to see the result. She loved it. She brought her new Polaroid camera and took pictures of the men standing in front of the sign and the new lunchroom. The pictures were tacked onto the wall above the coffee maker after they were passed hand to hand so everyone could see. Mr. Sutherland refused to be in any photos.

"Here, I brought you something," Claire said once the crowd had cleared. She handed Jackie a bag with a number of plastic jars, varying in size. Some had powder in them and others had gel capsules.

"What's all this?" asked Jackie, holding one of the jars up to the light.

"These are the supplements I sell. I want you to try some. It'll help you feel better."

"I feel fine. I don't need these, Claire. I'm happy yer doin' well at sellin' this stuff but I don't think it's for me."

"It's all free, even though I know yer a rich man," she joked. "Just give it a try for a few weeks, follow the instructions I wrote down for you and see how you're feelin' by the new year. If you don't think it's done anything for ya, then toss them out. I'm willing to bet you'll be feelin' better though."

Jackie shook one of the jars with capsules.

"How much you wanna bet?" Jackie cocked an eyebrow.

"A hundred bucks?"

"Oh, okay then, yer royal highness. Yer on."

Jackie began taking the supplements each day as Claire instructed. The gel capsules were easy; he could simply down them with water or his morning coffee. The powdered protein was rough, though. The instructions said to mix with water or milk. Jackie hated milk, so he tried with water and threw it all back up in the kitchen sink. He thought it tasted like a mixture of old, musty wood chips and chalk dust. He took to mixing it with chocolate pudding, which improved the taste greatly.

Claire was right. He *did* feel better and noticed he had more energy. He was not completely convinced it was the supplements or the fact he was no longer bootlegging; all those added pressures now gone from his mind made it easier for him to sleep. He could not deny though that physically, he felt able to do the work of a man twenty years his junior. He found that through the winter when he skated to work, he could do so without feeling quite so tired and his muscles always healed a little faster. He figured that Claire would become a rich woman if this was how supplements help people.

∞∞∞∞

Later that year, Mrs. Sutherland abruptly died from heart failure. She collapsed at the office on a cold October afternoon. Boyd was inconsolable. In the immediate weeks that followed, Boyd missed a number of days of work (the mill had only shut down for the afternoon wake and the day of the funeral). He said he was sick and could not come in. Jackie and the other men at the sawmill covered for him. Mr. Sutherland had said if it were any other man, he'd have fired them long ago but could not afford to lose Boyd. Mr. Sutherland barely noticed his wife had died, except for the cost of the funeral and loss of money when the mill was shut down.

The biggest bouquet at the funeral was unlabeled. Boyd moved in with Jackie after she was placed in the vault for the winter months. By now the ground was frozen too hard to dig a grave. Boyd moving in with Jackie was only a formality by this point. He'd been spending so much time at Jackie's house, either helping his friend after the shooting or watching sports, he may as well have lived there. Boyd had never enjoyed living in his parents' home. They neglected him as a child and the house was the only thing bequeathed to him after they passed. He left it and the hurtful memories contained within its walls without a second thought.

"How she goin'?"

A LITTLE OVER A YEAR AFTER the incident at Mike's house, Jackie finished a hard day's work at the mill. The October sun shone stronger than expected. It was the sort of beautiful fall day Jackie enjoyed: cool morning with warm afternoon and the promise of a fresh evening.

The men were sweeping up, tidying for the next morning's routine at the sawmill. A few cracked beers, including Boyd. Jackie waved him off and said he'd see him later that night. The Edmonton Oilers were playing the Montreal Canadiens and he wanted to get home well before the game. Boyd said he'd be down in time to watch. Most everybody watched any game when Edmonton played. The young phenom Wayne Gretzky was tearing up the league.

He walked along the path to the river, thinking about Paddy, only four months into his sentence at Dorchester Penitentiary. He and Boyd had taken the bus to Moncton to see him once a month and planned to continue doing so. It was difficult for them to visit their friend in jail but more so on Paddy. Jackie could easily see he'd lost weight in the brief time Paddy had been incarcerated. Mentally though, he seemed almost chipper the last time Jackie saw him.

ooooo

"How she goin'?" Jackie said as Paddy sat down on the steel chair. It screeched as he pulled it from the table across from Jackie and Boyd.

"Pretty good. They're teachin' me in here. Sayin' I can get my Grade Twelve by the time I'm up for parole in about fourteen more months."

"That's good, Paddy," answered Boyd. "Friggin' Professor Brewster over here!" They all drank cans of Coke. Paddy slurped his generously. Conversations between families and visitors threatened

to envelope their chat. They had to lean in close to hear one another.

"And no one's messin' with you or anything in here, eh?" asked Jackie.

"No. Not so far, anyway. It's been hard, though. I miss just being able to go to the store. Having someone watch over me all the time is pretty weird. Kinda strange the things you miss the most when you don't have them."

"You look thin," said Boyd.

"Yeah well, the food ain't great, honestly. Not exactly Myrtle's Diner back home."

Jackie nodded in agreement.

"Well, keep your head down and just be good. You'll be out in no time."

Paddy agreed, swallowing the remainder of his cola.

"So, what's goin' on back home? What's all happening?"

∞∞∞∞

Jackie assured Paddy there would be a place for him to work once he was released. It would be a battle with Mr. Sutherland. He'd already stated he didn't run some work release program but too many of the men working there liked Paddy. Jackie would talk it through with Mr. Sutherland. The old man would relent after a series of brief tantrums.

He approached the shore where Ruby was nosing around the cold riverbank, overturning stones and clawing at deadwood. Soon, it would be too cold to canoe and he'd have to wait for the ice to freeze solid before skating to and from work each day. He would walk in the interim or hitch a ride with someone.

Jackie looked around him. Autumn was in full force, the Acadian Forest lining the shore of the river like a painter's palate. He looked across the river and thought of the ghost he'd seen there last year. He had not dreamt of her since the night at Mike's house.

"Alright Ruby, let's head on home."

Ruby rushed to the canoe, splashing in the water and

jumping in. Jackie shoved off and paddled down river. A flock of geese honked above them, a V pattern heading south. Though the days were getting cooler, the warm evening sun still peeked above the trees and massaged their backs. Lazily drifting down the river, Jackie looked up at the cobalt sky and took a deep breath.

Shawn Lawlor is not an award-winning author (yet) but has been writing his entire life. He's previously written screenplays, none of which were produced or filmed but wow, they were funny and certainly enjoyable to write. This is his first novel, which probably shows, but he's still quite proud of it. He's originally from Miramichi, New Brunswick. Closer to Sunny Corner really. Actually, more like Red Bank. Cassilis, if we're being honest.

Shawn lives in Halifax, Nova Scotia with his wonderful, incredible family.